# THE
# FIRST
# EMMA

# THE
# FIRST
# EMMA

## CAMILLE DI MAIO

*Wyatt-MacKenzie Publishing*
DEADWOOD, OREGON

# The First Emma
Camille Di Maio

ISBN: 978-1-948018-76-0
Library of Congress Control Number: 2020935066

Cover photo ©Serg Zastavkin.

Archive photos used with permission from The University of Texas at San Antonio Special Collections.

"Creative Commons Emma Koehler circa 1936" on page 308 from UTSA Special Collections, the Zintgraff Collection, ©Rio Perla Properties, LP., licensed under CC BY 4.0 (https://creativecommons.org/licenses/by-nd/4.0/)

"Creative Commons Pearl Brewery circa 1910" on page 309 from UTSA Archives Special Collections, the Zintgraff Collection, ©UTSA, licensed under CC BY 4.0 (https://creativecommons.org/licenses/by-nd/4.0/)

"Creative Commons Emma Koehler circa 1910" on page 313 from UTSA Special Collections, the Zintgraff Collection, ©Alamo Colleges Foundation, licensed under CC BY 4.0 (https://creativecommons.org/licenses/by-nd/4.0/)

Wyatt-MacKenzie Publishing
DEADWOOD, OREGON

Wyatt-MacKenzie Publishing, Inc.
Deadwood, Oregon
www.WyattMacKenzie.com

*To Rochelle Weinstein and Suzy Leopold—if nothing came from my book career except your friendships, it would all be worth it.*

*To Tonni Callan, Andrea Katz, Leila Meacham, Susan Peterson, Teri Wilson, Kathy Murphy, the Pulpwood Queens and all bookish friends from Texas, this is for you.*

*And to Kristy Barrett for being the loveliest Queen Bee ever.*

*Inspired by true events*

# PROLOGUE

*San Antonio, Texas*

November 12, 1914

EMMA HADN'T WOKEN with murder on her mind. Only a desperate wish that the terrible pain would go away. She'd been plagued with relentless migraines and had stayed in bed for the better part of a week. The lace curtains let in light that intensified the throbbing in her temples, so she'd darkened the room by tying her quilt to the corners of the window.

It was her mother's handiwork, stitched in the aptly named *crazy house* pattern, and reminded her of better days.

A sachet of lavender from the garden lay next to her pillow, its fresh buds plucked late in the summer, but its scent had faded along with its crumbling purple buds.

She listened as the *other* Emma stood in the kitchen brewing tea. The water being poured into the pot, the staccato click of the gas igniting the stove. Quick moves echoed across a house that was nearly void of furniture. These were the actions of a woman who was surely anxious to return home to the arms of her adoring, though lackluster, husband in New York. Mr. Daschiel had won over Miss Dumpke even though he could exhaust an army with his droning monologues. But eloping with him had untangled her from the women's unseemly arrangement.

To think it had all begun with such innocence.

Emma was under no illusion that the other Emma had returned for any other reason than guilt. Only scant words had passed between them these last few days. The necessary ones that allowed one to nurse the other. "How are you feeling today?" and "Here's a cocaine lozenge for your pain."

What else was there to say? A litany of apologies from each of them would not engender a return to what their friendship had been before it all unraveled.

By late afternoon, the few cicadas that remained for the remnants of the autumn season hummed their mating song in the distance. It was the only sound that didn't add to Emma's migraine—it was a lullaby of sorts. A love song nearing its end. Like the lavender at the end of its bloom.

How appropriate.

Closer in, the sound of a motor alerted Emma to Otto Koehler's impending arrival. It was easy to tell that it was him. Few people around Hunstock Avenue possessed such contraptions, though sharp-eyed investors believed that they would be all the rage in a few years. Five hundred dollars got you the Runabout model of Ford's latest achievement. Bottom of the line, though Otto could easily have afforded the more luxurious Town Car.

He could afford a thousand of them.

It was not the particular hum of the automobile that announced his approach, however. It was the way in which he drove it, straining it to the limits of its capabilities, to the point that Emma could sympathize with its plea for restraint.

Otto rode with such ferocity. Eager to get the job done, much like his lovemaking.

Yes, the women had spoken of it and made comparisons.

His footsteps fell upon the stairs with ungainly effort—especially as they landed on the rotted fourth step; the one he kept imploring the two Emmas to repair. But he hadn't hired them for their carpentry skills. They were trained nurses, brought in from the Hanover region of Germany to care for his invalid wife. So the step remained untouched and Otto shouted a curse every time he visited the home he'd purchased for his two mistresses.

It sat just blocks away from his beloved Hot Wells Hotel on South Presa. The storied resort he'd purchased after a fire bankrupted its first owner. Otto's vision for it drew celebrities and tycoons and politicians from around the country, augmenting his already legendary status as a world-class businessman. Guests indulged in its healing sulfur waters while peacocks and ostriches raced in organized spectacles.

He was a man beloved by the public, but increasingly reviled by the women in his life.

Emma pressed a down-filled pillow over her ears as the other Emma's voice, muffled through the cushion, mingled with Otto's more insistent one. They were arguing. She could easily guess why.

Darkness and quiet were the only remedies for headaches of this severity. Why did Otto have to choose today to make a visit?

As he neared the bedroom, his medium build cast a larger shadow, lit from the sun-drenched window in the front of the house. Emma opened her eyes as much as she could without a recurrence of the searing pain, and she noticed that he had not shaved his substantial mustache, despite her pleas. He'd dismissed her complaints that it scratched her skin when he pressed his lips against hers.

Mary Pickford had complimented him on it a few years ago and he hadn't been seen without it since.

Mary Pickford never had to kiss him.

Otto entered her room without knocking. It was his name on the deed, after all, and they were his employees. Well, Emma Burgemeister remained so. She was paid handsomely for her work and still received the usual funds even during this bedridden time. Fifty dollars every month for services as a nurse to his wife.

In addition, he'd dangled a promise to give her the deed to the tiny cottage and a gift of twenty thousand dollars.

It was more than most immigrant women could hope for and she didn't complain. Security came with strings and the notion of love was a luxury built on quicksand.

But so far, neither of the offerings had come to pass.

Emma's eyes adjusted to the light peeking in from the kitchen, and she could barely make out the wild look on Otto's face as he crumpled a paper in his hand. She didn't have to see the type print on the thin, yellow page it to recognize what it was. She'd known it would upset him and had anticipated this moment.

He tossed his bowler hat on a table and took a deep breath.

Emma clenched her fists under the blankets and felt the quickening of her pulse in her fingers.

"What do you mean by this?" he asked, throwing the receipt at her with surprising force. Otto Koehler was not a violent man. Just a headstrong one. But Emma Daschiel's recent marriage along with Emma Burgemeister's refusal of Otto's proposal had unhinged him of late.

"It is for the new wheelchair for Mrs. Koehler."

"The old one is perfectly good. She hasn't complained."

"Not to you, but I noticed that the turns around your house are difficult for her to maneuver and the thick rugs slow her down. This new model has smoother bearings and larger wheels. She's been quite excited for it to arrive."

He slumped into the cushioned chair across from Emma's bed and ran his fingers through thinning gray hair. There was something pitiful in his sigh that almost moved her to change her mind.

She knew he loved his wife. Had loved her ever since he came over from Germany so many years ago to start a new life in St. Louis. He'd met her when he was a young man and after they'd married, he convinced her to move to Texas with the wild idea of starting his own brewery. Until her car accident four years ago, she'd been quite spritely, Emma had been told, and her convalescence had been his undoing.

Yes, he loved his wife. To the degree, at least, that Otto could love someone beyond himself.

Emma softened her voice, not wanting to argue with him as he had with the other Emma. He didn't take well to being challenged by a woman and conciliation was a trait he prized.

"I should have asked you. But this wheelchair will be good for her, Otto. It's not as if you can't afford it."

In fact, Otto Koehler was one of the richest men in San Antonio—and in the country. With business and real estate holdings so vast that even his lawyers and accountants could barely keep up. But maybe his miserly ways had been the very thing that built his wealth. He didn't spend a penny that wasn't necessary or that wasn't an investment of some kind.

As proven by purchasing the one house for the two Emmas.

The less expensive automobile.

His harried breathing calmed as it always did after his quick rebukes. He stood up and walked to Emma's bed, rubbing his hand gently across her aching forehead.

"How are you feeling today, my love? Any better?"

Otto's fingers moved down her face in a familiar journey, brushing her cheek, her neck, her jawline. His rough skin had earned its abrasive texture from decades of sifting through the shipments of barley, crushing their pale brown pods between his fingers to release their scent and deem them worthy—or not—of being used in Pearl Beer.

He always had a faint smell of sweetness attached to his tweed jackets as well: the pure scent of fresh hops before boiling water and yeast and spices were added in the vast steel barrels. Not that she had ever been invited to see them in person. A recent newspaper article had lauded his magnificent building on Avenue A and showed many pictures of the operation. The black ink residue on her fingers was the closest she had ever come to that part of his life.

It was an article commissioned, no doubt, by Otto, who'd grown more and more anxious of late over dry activists who campaigned for the prohibition of his beloved industry. Of his Pearl Brewery.

Otto had always counted on his mistresses to distract him from such troubles. And now he was losing even that.

Emma bit her lower lip as his hand continued downward and rested against the side of her breast. For all his faults, Otto knew how to elicit a response that could make her forget the unusual nature of their relationship.

He was an excellent lover.

She curled her toes and tried to steel herself against the temptation to lose herself in his touch and escape, even briefly, from the damnable headaches.

But she had to put an end to this. What small affection she'd once had for him changed when he announced that he was going to leave his wife.

It was one thing to keep up this affair, almost an hour's ride from the opulent home he lived in with Mrs. Koehler in the Laurel Heights section of the city. To share the comforts of a warm bed with a man who'd been robbed of that particular pleasure when his wife was no longer able to be that kind of companion to him. But the thought of *replacing* her patient was repugnant. Mrs. Koehler was a formidable woman. Kind but firm. Smart as anyone Emma had ever met. An excellent employer who had given her no reason to pursue this betrayal to that extent.

Mrs. Koehler had given her husband enough slack in the reins to pursue the necessary manly endeavors. But leave her? She was not likely to be so pliable. She protected the reputation of Pearl with the ferocity of a mother to a child and the scandal would have made headlines across the country.

Emma had told him no. She would not consent to him divorcing his wife on her account. She would not marry him.

But he continued to beg.

Emma grabbed his wrist and threw it from her, satisfied with the slight *thud* as it fell against the corner of the nightstand.

"Darling," he whispered as he hovered over her ear. "Please reconsider. Marry me and you'll make me the happiest man alive."

"No," she insisted. The third such rejection in as many weeks. She propped herself up on her elbows.

"Emma," he pled. He put his knee on the mattress and spoke in a low, heavy moan that indicated how eager he was to return to her bed.

"No," she said again with all the force she could muster. "Otto, I'm not going to marry you. It's over. All of this is over."

She clutched his shirt in her hands and shoved him off the bed. He fell against the nightstand with all his weight this time, sending her silver hand mirror across its marble surface. It stopped just short of crashing to the ground. A precious memento of the life she'd once had on the other side of the world.

A reminder that she wished she had never left.

It was difficult to see his reaction in the dim room where he was nearly a silhouette. But he righted himself and moved forward again. A shot of fear rushed through Emma's body. Otto had never had so much taken away from him in so short a time: his wife's health, his first lover's marriage, his second lover's refusal. A desperate man might do anything.

As he drew nearer with wide steps, Emma slipped her finger under the pillow and felt around for the .32 revolver he'd bought for her to protect against coyotes. Its cool metal frame gave her some reassurance.

Just in case.

She felt his body fall upon the mattress, his hot breath landing on her neck in frenzied kisses. His hands trying all the things in all the places that had once excited her.

"Get off of me!"

"Don't leave. Don't leave me," he begged. His tone had turned to one of despair and each sob was more wretched than the last.

So much could be hers if she acquiesced. Wealth. Comfort. Affection. It was all very tempting.

But some things were worth more than that.

Emma threw the blankets toward the foot of the bed. "It's over!" she insisted.

She listened for sounds from the kitchen but couldn't hear the other Emma in the house anymore. Had she gone outside when Otto arrived? That had always been their arrangement before she left to marry Mr. Daschiel. Only one woman in the house when Otto came around to visit.

She slid her hand under the pillow again, this time clutching the revolver. The sweat on her hand fell on its leather grip. She pulled it out in a quick motion and placed the barrel against Otto's chest, pushing him away as she sat up.

He jumped back, sweat rippling down the wrinkles on his forehead. "You're crazy."

Otto waved a finger at her and turned toward the living room.

Emma lifted herself out of bed, arms weakened after convalescing. She walked across the wood floor in bare feet, avoiding the board that had worn and would splinter her skin. The light from the next room sent more pain to her head and her eyes winced as they took it in. But she could see Otto standing in front of her, just beyond the sofa, a case knife drawn from his pocket. His hand shook, but his eyes fixed a hard gaze on her.

Her heart beat quickly and a sense of terror seized her.

He'd called *her* crazy? She'd only meant to frighten him away. But there was a look about him that that held more than a threat.

He stepped toward her and the knife slashed her arm.

She fired the trigger in response. Three times.

Neck.

Face.

Heart.

Otto crumpled to the floor, clutching his chest. Heat raced to her cheeks and she dropped the revolver on the ground next to her. She collapsed next to his body and pulled away his vest, ripping the buttons from their threads.

*What had she done?*

Only then did she hear the other Emma, who ran in from the porch. A look of horror passed between the women.

Otto's thin-framed body writhed on the wool rug, a thick red pool forming on his white shirt. His blood mixing with hers. His eyes fluttered, looking between them.

"Emma," he whispered as he took his last breath.

But they didn't know which woman he called out for.

Emma, his first mistress.

Emma, his second mistress.

Or Emma, his wife.

## Wealthy brewer found
# BATHED IN BLOOD

Wealthy brewer found bathed
in blood, victim of girl's pistol.
'I shot him!', she cries hysteri-
cally. But won't tell why.

*The Winnipeg Tribune, Winnipeg,
Ontario Canada December 5, 1914*

# CHAPTER ONE

*Baltimore*

1942

SNOW HAD FALLEN on Baltimore, early for this time of year. The streets below the windows on the fourteenth floor of the office building were desolate, blanketed with the white dusting that usually appeared weeks later.

By the time Mabel could leave work, it might reach to her ankles and she hadn't brought the shoes to accommodate it.

She stepped away from her typewriter and looked down onto the park. The frost from the panes chilled her, but not as much as the letter sitting in her breast pocket.

She pulled a cigarette from its pack and put it to her lips. It shook as she trembled. In anger. In hurt. In disgust.

There were no matches to be found in her desk, though she was certain that she'd left them there. Mr. Oliver must have riffled through her drawers again. Her boss had a bad habit of snatching things from the secretaries' desks. His company, so his property. Not that he'd ever said so, but his actions certainly demonstrated that belief.

Mabel folded her arms and pulled the cigarette to and from her mouth, pretending, at least, that its rich tobacco scent was filling her lungs with the warmth that had faded since she'd read the letter.

Her red lipstick formed a dark ring around its edge. It reminded her of Artie. They'd met at the New Year's Eve party of a mutual friend. She was not at all *that kind of girl* but there had been something about the way he'd swaggered over to her on the dance floor, put his arms around her belted waist and kissed her right at midnight.

Her very *first* kiss.

She'd been overwhelmed by it, but not unpleasantly so. Quite the opposite. When he pulled away, she'd noticed the red stain left on his mouth. Embarrassed, she raised her thumb to wipe it away, but he held her hand back.

"Not like that," he said. "Let's rub it all off the old-fashioned way."

He'd kissed her again, harder, and she'd lost all sense of where they were or when they were or the fact that she didn't even know his name.

She learned, once he'd succeeded in removing all the color she'd so carefully applied, that he was called Artie Walker. He was shipping off to basic training in a few weeks and wanted a girl who would send perfumed letters to him when he left for the war.

Mabel looked at her unlit cigarette again and snuffed it into the ashtray out of habit. The end of it cracked, not having been softened first by the flame of a match. Just as well. It made everything smell and she couldn't afford them anyway. She returned to her desk and placed her fingers on the typewriter. The stack of correspondence to be written and mailed out was piling up and she shouldn't let one letter, the one that had changed the course of her life, deter her from the job at hand.

She knew she was lucky to have this position at all. Her diligence in typing school had paid off, earning a recommendation by her teacher to the owner of a moderately-sized textile company. Several of her friends were toiling in munitions factories. And each day posed a danger that an errant explosive would detonate and kill them all.

She turned a fresh piece of paper in the typewriter and began crafting a letter from Mr. Oliver's directions.

*November 13, 1942*
*Clipper City Fabrics*
*212 E. Fayette Street*
*Baltimore, MD*
*Dear Sire,*

Not *Dear Sire*, it should read *Dear Sir*. Though she had no doubt that most of the business owners she'd met would welcome the error. Kings of their own little kingdoms. Mr. Oliver and his ilk.

She pulled the paper from the roller and crumpled it. A crisp new white one went into its place, because mistakes were not acceptable. Bosses like Mr. Oliver expected a pristine correspondence, by whatever means it had to happen, even as he demanded impossible typing speeds.

It was a common plight among women. High heels, child-rearing, letter-writing. All must be done to perfection, pain and ugliness hidden from view. Pearls on the neck, hair in a wispless bun. Don't disgruntle the men who'd had such a trying day at the office by suggesting the women suffered, too.

She sighed. Would it always be this way?

Mabel's fingers hovered over the keys, but her heart wasn't in penning a missive about a faulty cotton shipment. It seemed so irrelevant when there were bigger issues in the world. Just once she'd like to write up something that mattered in a bigger way. But it was no use; newspapers weren't looking for female reporters and she had no experience other than typing up Mr. Oliver's complaints.

She set the cotton letter aside and unfolded the one from Artie.

She'd been so excited to hear from him. His correspondences had been all too few, surprising for one who'd professed his love for her in such a bold and public manner. But maybe that was the nature of fighting in a war: it took all your attention and she reasoned that he was doing a noble thing by being overseas.

Yet plenty of her friends had received tomes and tomes from their own sweethearts. Wouldn't an army cook have time to drop her a line once in awhile?

She intended to read it one more time, still in disbelief that it was even real.

Then she'd look for her matches on Mr. Oliver's desk and burn it.

*Dearest Mabel,*

*I can't tell you where I am, or they'll redact it, but it is England, as you know. Ugly time, but welcoming people. They're so relieved to have the U.S. troops here. Thank you for the socks you knitted. They are too small for me, though, so I've passed them on to a buddy of mine.*

*You have been a real sport, and being with you got me through the tough times leading up to training. I meant it when I said that I wanted to spend the rest of my life with you and that we would marry when I return. In the little church in Towson where my grandparents exchanged their own vows.*

*But war changes a man, and the thought of fighting makes him ponder all sorts of things he might not have otherwise. Though I've only been here for five months, it might as well be five years. Every day could be my last, and it is cause to reevaluate what is truly important.*

*And what is important to me is that I have fallen in love. An English girl named Ellie Tate. Her family owns a pub in the nearest town. I'd go to drown out the sounds of the battlefield whenever I could and as it happens, I also lost myself in her attentions. I've asked her to marry me and she's said yes. I want her to have my grandmother's wedding ring. The one I gave to you. You deserve something much bigger anyway and from someone who can love you more.*

*I regret that it is not me after all and I hope it doesn't cause you too many tears. You're swell and I think we could have made a good life together. But I've found something else—someone else—instead.*

*If you can put some extra postage on the package, it might get here a bit faster. I'll send you some money for it when I can.*

*Fondly,*

*Artie*

Naming her felt, somehow, like an additional injury. Provoking an image of the girl who would wear the ring that Mabel would undoubtedly send. Because as much as she would prefer to sell it and pay off some long overdue accounts, she would not let her anger toward Artie rob her of the principles that were dearest to her. He'd already taken too much.

Not *everything*, though. Thankfully. Mabel wasn't so unwise as to let his entreaties about how long he'd be away sway her firm belief that certain intimacies belonged to the proper time: after the vows were spoken.

Maybe Miss Tate had no such hesitations.

Her friends had warned her. Ginger most of all. They'd disliked Artie from the first moment at the dance. They'd cautioned her it was much too forward of him to have kissed her like he did, deaf to her protestations that it was romantic.

It had been a common disagreement as their courtship continued, Ginger always insisting that he didn't treat her as he ought. But her friend had admitted her wrong judgment of Artie when he gave Mabel his grandmother's wedding ring.

And now this.

It wasn't enough to rip it into shreds.

Mabel set the stack of letters aside and carried Artie's into Mr. Oliver's office.

Surely, the matches would be there.

"GOD WILL PUNISH YOU FOR WHAT YOU HAVE DONE."

Mrs. Daschiel asserted that she admitted Koehler at the house and he went to Miss Burgemeister's bedroom. A few minutes later she said she heard her friend exclaim "God will punish you for what you have done."

*The Houston Post, November 15, 1914*

# CHAPTER TWO

MR. OLIVER'S DESK was an impossible mess.

He demanded that his employees keep immaculate work areas. He wanted to see pens in cups, typewriters perfectly parallel to the edges, telephone cords untangled.

"We have an image to maintain," he'd say, insisting that the orderliness of the main room would be seen by current clients and prospective ones. He never invited them back to his office, though. He always met anyone important in a conference room. Void of clutter. Void of life.

Not that his office was a bastion of vibrancy. He kept his curtains nearly shut, letting in only a strand of sunlight from each of them, casting stripes that cut across the room. The lamps were dim, the couch made of dark brown leather. No wonder he wore thick glasses. Mabel was only nineteen years old, probably fifty years his junior, and even she had to strain her eyes to see anything.

Maybe he was some kind of owl. Or rat. Nocturnal.

She closed the door behind her and opened one set of curtains enough so that she could see.

The view was unremarkable and she had to hand it to him that there wasn't much to look at beyond the panes. The scenery was as stale as the air in the room. But the light was welcome. She picked up piles of papers and books scattered on the desk, as well as long strips of accounting receipts that could be wrapped around a Christmas tree if the Scrooge so chose.

She'd made her way through nearly all of it when she finally found the book of matches that he'd taken. She knew it was hers—it was red with a gold-embossed logo from her favorite bookstore on East Lombard—If the Book Fits. It was doubtful that her employer had ever visited a place as charming as that.

Mabel pulled Artie's letter from her pocket again and held it between her fingers as she slid the wooden stick against the striker. The flame burst to life before dwindling. It filled the space with the distinct smell of smoke that reminded her of the fireplace of her childhood, back when they had a little bungalow and before Pops took to drinking.

But that was so many years ago, its memory faded into mere scent. She could no longer recall the exact color of the bricks or the particular grains on the wood of the mantle. Only a photograph of her atop it along with those of her parents and brothers.

She heard a noise outside the door, a familiar shuffling that could only be her boss. She blew the match out and stuffed the letter back into her pocket. As Mr. Oliver turned the handle, she clutched the curtains and closed them to the exact width they'd been before.

"Girl!" he said as he entered the room. He'd never bothered to learn her name since she was as interchangeable to him as the last and the next. But he always called her Miss Sullivan when a client was around, though it was not anything like her own. Hers was Hartley.

"Mr. Oliver," she answered. He reminded her a bit of the pictures she'd seen of Winston Churchill. Balding, white hair, overweight, gruff.

"What are you doing there and why do I smell smoke?"

"I was looking for the Casey file, and I saw a cockroach scurry past the desk. So I lit a match in the hopes of shooing it away."

She set her jaw tight, hoping that such a ridiculous lie would hold up. It was not in her nature to tell a tale, but something about him always made her feel uncomfortable and she didn't feel like explaining further. He wouldn't want to hear about her personal life, nor did she care to share it.

"There are no cockroaches in this building other than the boys in the mailroom who never get my packages to me on time."

His eyes held hers and she knew she'd be stuck there until she told the truth.

"I—I was going to burn a letter."

"One of mine? Why would you do that?"

Mr. Oliver walked toward her and set his briefcase on his chair. His nose was beet red. From the cold? Or from drinking? Pops' was often a similar shade, with angry little capillaries winding around like a road map.

"No, it's not one of your letters. It's something of mine. I was in here looking for my matches."

He raised a fist and coughed into it. Phlegmy.

"Must be some letter if you want to get rid of it so thoroughly."

And then all she'd held in for days bubbled up. Here of all places. In front of crusty old Mr. Oliver. Mabel pursed her lips trying to hold back the tears that would not relent. But to her embarrassment, they took their own counsel and before she could run out of the room, they poured out. Her shoulders shook and she buried her face in her hands. She bent forward. Surely her cosmetics were running down her face, adding to her humiliation at giving in to such vulnerability here in his office.

"Dear, oh, dear," he said. His voice sounded softer than she would have expected. "What could be so bad as to bring on those kinds of tears?"

"My fiancé."

He sighed, slumping his shoulders. "Oh no, did you get the telegram? Has he been taken by this dreadful war?"

Not even the stodgiest old man could be unmoved by the tragedy overseas and he was no exception.

She shook her head, still not looking at him. "No. He has met another girl over in England and wants me to send my ring back."

He grunted.

"Is *that* all?"

"Is *that* all?" she repeated after him, appalled that he could consider it such a trifling thing. "He's broken my heart." Even as she said the words, they indeed sounded trivial. A failed romance was the least casualty among many. But that didn't mean her pain wasn't real or that her stakes weren't higher.

Marrying Artie would have given her a future when everything else had been taken away.

Loss had its own language, usually an unspoken one. And Mabel was fluent in it.

"There, there," he said. "You're right."

Mr. Oliver stepped forward and pulled Mabel into himself. Her arms fell to her side, unsure of what to do. What an odd position to find herself in. He suddenly seemed more tender than she'd ever known him to be and she thought that this might be what it was like to have a grandfather. The kind who would nurture her wounded feelings, reassure her that everything would be all right.

But she could not bring herself to embrace him back. This was still *Mr. Oliver*. The mailroom boy called him Olive-breath, and though it was not a fitting description, he hadn't earned any flattering ones to take its place. It was impossible to see him as anything but the curmudgeon everyone knew him to be.

She felt his wrinkled cheek next to hers. Her eyes looked around the room, still bewildered by the circumstance.

Then he pulled away a bit, turned his face and kissed her. On the lips. Only once, but he lingered there, and she was too stunned to move. Maybe he took that as some kind of silent agreement because he pressed a little harder. He didn't hurt her, didn't force her, but he stood there, his fat lips pressed against her quivering ones. It was like watching something at the cinema: as if it wasn't happening to her and she was merely an observer.

But when he put his arms back around her, it reminded her of how Artie had done the very same thing. She didn't know what she'd done to invite either situation, but all she could think to do now was to run.

Run like she should have when all her friends warned her about Artie.

Easier this time because everything, just everything about Mr. Oliver doing this was wrong.

She pulled away and hastened to the door, pausing to grab her purse and coat from her desk. Mercifully, she had no personal items to decorate her small space.

Hers did not have the photographs of family or the vases of silk flowers to beautify the otherwise dreary space.

Only her matchbook. Her silly little matchbook.

She ran to the elevator and looked back. Mr. Oliver had not followed her, but the crack where she hadn't closed the door all the way taunted her. Like he could step out any minute and call her back in.

Not that she would go. But she didn't want to see him and his old Winston Churchill face. Not now, not ever.

The elevator was too slow. She couldn't stand there and wait for it to rescue her like some mechanical knight.

She would rescue herself.

She raced down the hall and pushed open the door to the stairwell. It was fourteen stories down, but they seemed like nothing as she hurried to the bottom, two by two until she reached the lobby. People walked by as if nothing had just happened. As if the last shred of fabric in her already frayed world had not just unraveled. They'd had normal mornings where they'd poured their coffee and eaten their eggs and read stories in the newspaper about bad things happening to other people.

Mabel stepped outside and glanced at the streetcar sign. If she took the bus named Route 20, it would end seven blocks away from her tiny apartment, north of here. But many stopped here at this downtown location and she would take whichever came first. She saw a cloud of exhaust surround one as it approached. It was a Route 11. She had no idea where it went; it could go to Timbuktu for all she cared. She didn't want to stand on this sidewalk with these people who carried on with their days not knowing that hers had turned black. Again.

And she didn't want Mr. Oliver to come looking for her.

Mabel boarded the 11-line streetcar and found an empty bench in the third row. She rested her head against the window, barely noticing the dirt encrusted around its edges. As it pulled away toward the next street, she released a breath that she must have been holding all this time.

Safe.

She reached into her pocket for her cigarettes but felt only pieces of lint and the wrapper of a butterscotch candy. The desk. She'd left them on top. No matter, though. She was done with all that. The next girl could have them. The next Miss Sullivan.

She envied whoever that girl would be; it was a good job. Leaving would mean that Mabel might have to work in a munitions factory like her friends because she would never receive a recommendation letter after running out like this. It had all been too good to last. Maybe she wasn't meant for anything more and had dreamed of bigger things in vain.

She'd have to start looking elsewhere tomorrow.

She put her hands down and gripped the seat as the bus lurched forward. A newspaper brushed her hand. Mabel looked down and saw that it was open to the classifieds.

One word would change everything.

WANTED.

# I SHOT HIM

"I shot him to protect myself and friend," is the terse and only statement made by Miss Burgemeister as she lies, half hysterical, on a cot in a hospital. It is believed her defense will be the assertion that Koehler drew the pistol and threatened her and that she fired in self-defense. But the two women refuse to explain further and the engrossing mystery grows deeper.

*The Winnipeg Tribune, December 5, 1914*

# CHAPTER THREE

Wanted: *An aspiring female writer who is interested in recording the story that an old woman would like to tell. Must be willing to travel to Texas. All expenses paid as well as room and board and a modest stipend. Respond to the address below with a three hundred-word essay about yourself and why you would like this position. Please include a small photograph. Send to Mrs. Emma Koehler, 310 W. Ashby Place, San Antonio, Texas.*

MABEL HAD TO READ it three times through tears that had gathered in her eyes, distorting the newsprint like a magnifying glass. But she brushed them away before they could drop and dampen it. She looked to her side and behind her, wondering who might have left it there, but the immediate seats around her were empty. She picked it up and set it on her lap, flattening the creases out and taking a deep breath before her thoughts could run away with her.

Maybe this was one of her mother's gifts. Mabel had been only twelve when she'd died, the liver cancer overtaking her from the inside out. She'd instructed Mabel on all the ways to care for her father and brothers, and comforted her with the words *I'll send you little gifts to let you know I'm thinking of you.*

At first, Mabel had seen them everywhere. When Black-eyed Susans would bloom in the spring, little Mabel would think, *Mama's favorite! It must be a gift.* Only when she was older did she learn that it was the state flower of Maryland and they were more common than fleas on a stray dog when the humidity came around. And later, when a butterfly landed next to her on a park bench, she thought it was a visit from her mother. Only to find out that it was the beginning of their migration from points north to points south.

Over the years, she'd quickly dismissed the childish notions that her mother was sending messages to her because if she was honest, things had gone more wrong than right. And a mother who had the ability to reach out from the beyond wouldn't have allowed it all.

Not only what happened with Artie. But with her brothers. With her father. Mr. Oliver.

So Mabel cleared her throat and reminded herself that the ad in the newspaper was only what it appeared to be. Not a gift, not a sign. Ordinary black ink on flimsy gray paper, amounting to no more than a coincidence that someone left it there, open to this page.

Still, there was something about it that was an answer to a prayer she hadn't prayed.

A different job. A different place. A different life.

There was only one problem. She wasn't an aspiring writer. She wasn't any kind of writer, save for her work at the textile company. She'd gotten good enough marks in school in that subject, and she devoured books like other girls devoured candy. But those weren't qualifications for that kind of position.

It was best not to dwell on what couldn't be.

Mabel looked out the window. The streetcar had veered away from the path that her normal 20-line took, but only by a few blocks.

She shoved the newspaper into her bag and scooted to the edge of her seat.

"Next stop, please," she said to the operator.

"Yes, miss," he obliged. And he slowed several corners down.

It slid to a halt, as the tracks were already icing over.

The operator's cap canted to the side of his head and he looked out his window. He rolled it down, pulled his hand into his sleeve and pushed off the snow that had collected in a layer.

"You be careful out there, miss. It'll be icy now."

"I will be. Thank you."

She stepped off the streetcar, hopping over a puddle that was already crystalizing. Holding on to the side of the bus until she was safely on the sidewalk, she switched her bag to her other shoulder and walked in the direction of her apartment.

The detour hadn't added much distance, but in this weather, it seemed like double. The frost chilled her nose and cheeks to the point where she couldn't even feel them. Mabel tightened her collar around her neck, put her head down, and made it at last to her stoop.

Shaking, she turned the key on the fourth try, and shut the door behind her. The marble hallway and stairs to her third-story walk-up glistened with small pools of water left behind by other tenants who'd come in from the snow. It had never felt like home as much as the bungalow had, but it was the last place the family had all lived together.

She gripped the railing and stepped around the wet spot, but as she reached her floor, she slipped, falling two steps and banging her knee against the hard edge of the wrought iron railing. It throbbed in agony and she rubbed her hand along it, hoping that she hadn't ripped her last good pair of stockings. But she found a hole and the beginnings of a ladder-like run.

It was the last straw.

If Pops wasn't somewhere on the streets drinking. If Robert hadn't been killed in Europe. If Buck wasn't missing somewhere over the Pacific. If, if, if. One of them could have saved her like she'd saved them after Mama was gone. But they'd all left in one way or another.

This time, Mabel didn't stifle the painful tightening of the chest that preceded the second cry of the day. She'd had to be strong, so strong. And she didn't think she could be strong any longer. If the floor would only envelop her she'd happily disappear into it. Mr. Oliver had deepened the fissure, and the fall—that stupid, slippery step—finished her. Her sobs echoed in the cold, empty hallway, amplifying it until it sounded like three or four or five women crying.

War was hell? Yes. That was true. But not only for the troops. For the ones they'd left behind. The ones who had to bury them. Worry about them. Douse it all away with the oblivion of alcohol.

All this liberation women were supposed to be achieving as they filled the jobs that the soldiers vacated had not been awarded to Mabel or Ginger or any of her friends who arrived home after dark exhausted and spent, somehow having to muster the ability to do it all again the next day.

But as wrenching as the cry was, when she had poured it all out until the melted icicles and the tears were no longer discernable from one another, a new sensation took over her. The realization that she could wallow in the deep unfairness that had overtaken her life. Or she could leave it. Start over.

Recreate herself into whatever this person in Texas wanted her to be. *Aspiring writer?* Mabel would become a fire-eating acrobat if it meant the chance to escape from this cold confinement.

She pulled herself up, pain shooting through her leg as her knee swelled, but the frigid weather served only as encouragement to put this winter behind her and start afresh in a place that had probably never seen snow. The likelihood of getting the job was dismal. She knew that. There might be hundreds of girls applying. Way more qualified ones, every bit as eager to escape the danger of the factories or the roving hands of men too old to take up the fight. But the mere act of sending in an essay would encourage her to look for opportunities she might not have before, try for the things she wanted to do.

To figure out what those things were in the first place. Dreaming beyond the borders of Baltimore had never been a consideration.

But wherever it led, be it Texas or Timbuktu, she could not

forget that Pops might knock on the door and need her someday. Or that Buck might be found alive and come home. The Marines had sent a letter informing them that he was Missing in Action: a letter on light brown stationery that delivered equal doses of hope and despair to the receiving families.

Still, she'd spent too long waiting and waiting for hopes that were never fulfilled. She'd leave a forwarding address with her landlord and face those situations as they came.

If they came.

For now, she'd dig out stationery that had only ever been used—wasted—on Artie, and sent a letter to San Antonio.

Justice of the Peace R. Neil Campbell, who resided in the adjoining cottage, was the first to enter the house. Miss Burgemeister had a deep jagged cut on her right wrist. A case knife was found lying on the floor. Miss Burgemeister was arrested by Sheriff John W. Tobin. Prostrated, she hovered between life and death at the Baylor hospital for a number of days.

*Santa Cruz Evening News – Santa Cruz, California January 15, 1918*

# CHAPTER FOUR

*Koehler Mansion, San Antonio*

1942

EMMA KOEHLER SAT in the turreted parlor room and caught her breath. Her arms throbbed from the effort of rolling herself in the wheelchair across the house and her hands were raw with chafe.

She had only to ring the bell that was affixed to the handle of the chair and any number of nieces or nephews or cousins would come to her rescue. There were always several milling around, visiting for the day or staying for a duration in one of the countless bedrooms on the floors above. When they weren't bowling in the one-lane alley in the basement, they were compliant enough to join her for a round of *Skat* or *Doppelkopf*, even agreeing to use her German decks. Those had suits of acorns, leaves, hearts and bells rather than the more modern French ones of clubs, diamonds, hearts, spades. She knew that the younger family members snickered behind her back at her old-fashioned ways even as she provided them with money for their passage, sponsorship for their citizen applications, and a roof above their heads until they found work.

But Emma was growing increasingly weary of card games and conversation. Her mind couldn't keep up with their younger, sharper ones. And she wasn't sure she wanted it to.

She'd begun to feel every one of her eighty-three years.

Despite the constant presence of a rotation of family, Emma preferred the assistance of her employees. In fact, she would go so far as to say she *trusted* her employees more than her blood. They, at least, were transparent in their expectations: fair pay for honest work and nothing more. Family, on the other hand, could be shiftier. Were their kindnesses given out of genuine affection for an old woman? Or was theirs a hope that upon her death they would increase their share of the inheritance she was sure to leave?

Among the Koehlers and Bentzens who passed through her leaded glass doors, there were personalities of either kind. The trick was knowing which was which. Several were disturbingly transparent: Marcia and Ernestina no doubt went to sleep every night hoping for news that Emma had passed during the moonlight hours.

Had she ever borne a daughter—or a son for that matter—she imagined it would be different. A child of her own who had suckled at her breast might have shared a bond that extended far beyond a common surname.

But that had never come to pass, so Emma Koehler transferred these affections to the people she hired. She could choose them according to their skills and circumstances and character.

If only family came with references and résumés.

She lifted a feeble hand to the sheer white curtain that dimmed the light coming in through the windows of this polygonal room. It was thin like a bridal veil, softening the features that lay behind it. Lately, she preferred it this way.

Life, filtered.

The sun was nevertheless brilliant today, dashing children's hopes for a white Christmas. It was a rare thing in this part of Texas, but Irving Berlin's song had romanticized it. The crooning voice of Bing Crosby was all she heard when her nieces turned on the radio. Sleigh bells in the snow and all that nonsense.

Emma preferred the warmth, especially when they'd been deprived of it the past few days. Sometimes she opened the curtains and let the sunlight rest on her face, visiting like an old friend. It didn't care if the skin it rested on was baggy and wrinkled. It gave blindly.

She listened for the sound of Helga's footsteps on the gravel driveway, but all was silent. Her current nurse had walked to the post office to send some packages and promised to bring back the mail upon her return. But she must have gotten detained. Such long lines this time of year, she was told. Gifts sent to loved ones for the holidays, provisions sent to the boys in the war.

A voice spoke behind her. A niece who'd arrived from Mecklenburg a month ago. Emma had already forgotten her name. There had been so many through the years and her aging mind couldn't keep up. But she did recognize faces, and this girl possessed a gentle one.

"*Tante Emma, die zeitung.*"

She handed the newspaper to her aunt, but the old woman refused it.

"English," she insisted. It was part of the agreement. If Aunt Emma was to sponsor you to come into the United States, you were expected to speak the local tongue. Her generosity would extend only so far; you would make your own way, the sooner the better, and English was a requirement to do so. Even better if they could shed their accents.

This was all the more vital now that the government was arresting Germans *en masse* and sending them to internment camps. Enemy aliens. As if they hadn't lived here for decades and contributed to the robust fabric of the country.

These were dangerous times.

The girl's cheeks reddened and as the words played in her mind, Emma decided to at least join the effort and try to recall her name. She was a stout thing. Bountiful, her mother would have said. That's how she'd tried to remember them all: associate an image with the name. Ah—that was it. Leizel. A name that meant God's bounty. The Maker had certainly used a larger mold when casting this one, but the reference helped her.

"Paper," Leizel managed slowly.

"*Newspaper*," corrected Emma. But the attempt was an admirable one. "*Paper* could mean many things."

"Nees-pah-per," the girl tried and it was enough for Emma at the moment. She was still new and at least up for the challenge. Unlike some of the lazy ones.

"Set it there," she said, pointing to the table next to her. Leizel did as she was asked and disappeared back into the foyer.

Emma cared little for the headlines; she'd be gone soon enough and the news of today would mean nothing when she lay in the grave. But no doubt her family would be atwitter at dinner on Sunday with the interview she'd given to an untried reporter who'd come by asking her questions about the brewery. Emma expected there would be more in due time—they were approaching the sixtieth anniversary of Pearl Beer, and San Antonio was already preparing great fanfare for its native and beloved company. Even as there was a war going on across the ocean. But perhaps people were eager for some reason to have gaiety. The Fiesta City, it was called, and not for nothing.

Not surprisingly, the reporter had been more interested in the story of three decades ago. Otto's murder. The other Emmas.

Anything they wanted to know about that incident could be found in archives and they needn't bother her to rehash things that had been put in print long ago. Emma Koehler had no patience for unoriginal questions. If they wouldn't do their homework, she wouldn't give her time. She had too little of it left.

But sometimes, a well-meaning relative would answer the telephone and grant an appointment without asking her permission before knowing that she detested such things. They always brought back memories she preferred to forget and allowed the past to inhabit her thoughts for days after. Yesterday's young man had at least asked one interesting thing: What was her secret to living fifteen years beyond a woman's life expectancy?

"Pearl Lager," she'd replied.

She directed all things back to her beloved brewery. Her only child.

As for the rest, she would tell it her way. In her own good time.

Emma glanced at her wristwatch and wheeled herself to the parlor door. It sat to the right of the grand staircase and was the place she most liked to do the work of correspondences and bill paying. The house was not without a study. That one was across the hall, but it had been Otto's domain all those years ago and was never to Emma's taste. Dark blue walls and even darker paneling. Its best light came in from the octagonal alcove, but even that was so masculine in its design that Emma felt suffocated just being in there. So it remained unused, and depending on the attention of the most current maid, sat dusted or undusted.

The parlor, on the other hand, had once been a most lively gathering spot for philanthropic and social bigwigs alike. Hemming and hawing over Otto's latest business endeavor, or imploring the Koehlers for donations in support of the charity du jour.

It was in this room that Emma suggested to Otto that they incorporate ostrich racing at his Hot Wells Resort; a notion conjured during a dream after a particularly raucous night sampling some of the newest offerings from Pearl.

Emma had always had the best ideas.

On occasion, Otto would admit it.

The parlor was also the most cheery place in the house. Light pink walls, creamy brocade curtains from floor to ceiling around the curved bay of windows. And Emma's favorite: the iridescent green glass tiles that surrounded the fireplace.

Otto's only contribution had been the odd frieze of a woman's naked form with vines growing out of her reproductive organs.

Ridiculous enough on its own, but a perpetual mockery of the fact that she had never been able to give him children.

What were the odds that his two mistresses had never borne children, either? She'd long suspected that the fault had lain not with any of the women he'd bedded, but at Otto's own feet. All those decades ago, though, it was presumed that such a failure was distinctly female.

How many times had she said she'd redo this room and get rid of the silly art piece? Too many. But there were always more urgent tasks at hand.

She heard the front door open.

"Helga?" she called.

"Mrs. Koehler, I have the mail."

At last.

Helga's accent was perhaps the most pronounced of all the nurses Emma had employed ever since her automobile accident so many years ago. It reminded her of her dear stepmother's, bringing comfort in these uncomfortable days.

"Good, good. Any more letters?"

"None, ma'am. Not for the past three days. I think the advertisement has run its course. Have you made a decision?"

Emma removed three from the top drawer of her desk and handed them to Helga.

"These are the most intriguing out of the bunch. I wanted to see what you think."

Helga pulled up the hard-backed chair in the corner, careful to not let its wooden legs scrape the floor.

The nurse was of good German stock, as all of them had been.

Well, all had been German. Not all had been good. The two other Emmas, the affairs, Otto's death. No, not all had been good.

Helga took the letters from her and as she read, Emma fell into the light doze of the elderly that lasted about ten minutes, but refreshed like an ale on a summer day in Texas. Though she'd likely be dead and buried before the mercury shot up the thermometer. She should have had an Alpine love of the cold given her heritage, but she herself was one generation removed from the German homeland, having been born in St. Louis. And she'd lived in Texas long enough to consider it home.

"Is there anything to deliberate over, Mrs. Koehler? This one seems to be the most qualified."

Emma awoke and continued as if there had been no break in the conversation and appreciated that Helga never drew attention to the interruption.

The nurse held out the one with the Brooklyn postmark and handed it to her. "This young woman is eminently better than the others. A degree from Columbia in journalism. And a beauty. Look at her picture."

She turned the woman's photograph around so that Emma could see it. Indeed, she was a *looker*, elegant in the way that her niece, Ernestina was. But that was decidedly *not* what Emma was aiming for. This was not a beauty pageant. Emma had asked for photos because she wanted to see their eyes. Those proverbial windows to the soul that would tell her which girl would be the right one.

"*Nein*," Emma said. "Not this one."

"Then why did you save it if you've already decided against her?"

"Because I doubted myself. But as I look closer, I think no. There's something too ambitious about her."

Emma had not let Helga in on the entirety of her plan, so it was not fair to expect her to judge them with the same criteria.

"And this one?"

Helga showed her the next letter and photograph. A young lady from Michigan. But Emma could tell that she held a similar opinion to herself on this. The letter was perfect, as if the girl was trying too hard to make a good impression. And though that wasn't a sin by anyone's definition, it was a character flaw as far as Emma was concerned. Sincerity was a trait that was too undervalued, though Emma held it in the highest regard.

She shook her head, and Helga did the same, setting it aside.

"The last one." Helga set it in Emma's lap.

Yes. As Emma held the letter and the photo, she felt as right about it as the first time she'd opened the envelope. The girl from Baltimore. She was no Lana Turner, but that would keep her from being vain. Yet she was pretty enough to turn the heads of some young men. She looked something like Emma had in her own youth: the light brown coloring to the hair, the roundness of her face. And her eyes ... they had seen pain. They understood hard work. They had kindness even among the wounds. In spite of them, even.

And her words were honest.

*I am not a writer,* she'd started. And that was perhaps Emma's favorite line from the hundreds of responses she'd received. Girls falling over themselves to laud their accomplishments. That wouldn't do.

"Send her a ticket and wire her some money for incidentals," instructed Emma. "And invite her to come as soon as she's able."

She tapped the letter against the side of the desk.

"Mabel Hartley of Baltimore, Maryland. She's the one."

## CHARGES OF MURDER

Charges of murder were filed today against Miss Burgemeister and Miss Daschiel. The latter waived examination and was remanded without bond. Miss Burgemeister will be arraigned when the hospital authorities will permit. Miss Daschiel made a statement but the district attorney refused to make it public.

*The Reno Gazette-Journal – Reno, Nevada November 13, 1914*

# CHAPTER FIVE

*Koehler Mansion, San Antonio*

1943

MABEL'S SUITCASE ALMOST fell from her hand. The bus to the train station had been delayed when a water line burst on Greenmount Avenue, causing it to flood and slowing traffic to a near halt. She'd had half a mind to get out and walk, but they progressed enough that she didn't think she could do any better. Besides, she was carrying with her all she owned, and though it wasn't much, it was still enough to slow her down.

By the time they pulled up to Baltimore Penn, the last call for the southbound train was announced. The letters on the board fluttered with such rapidity that it was difficult to read them. Cities and times and tracks were a blur.

"Watch where you're going, doll!" In her hurry, she hadn't even realized that she'd bumped into a man selling newspapers.

"I'm so sorry. But please, can you tell me from which track the southbound train is departing?"

Her pulse was racing. Missing this train would be a disastrous beginning to this new life.

"Read the board."

He pointed overhead and she concentrated until she saw the listing for the one heading to Atlanta. Track three. She hurried over there, gripping the Samsonite handle, now clammy with perspiration.

The gateman was closing the door. He wore the weary look of one who had spent a lifetime in this work, boredom etched onto leathery skin.

"Please! Please. I have to get on this train."

"Doors are closed."

"But I have a ticket."

"Doesn't matter."

She gave it to him anyway and he looked it over.

He sighed. "Well, we can make an exception since it's first class."

First class? She hadn't seen that on the ticket that Mrs. Koehler had sent. Only an indication that she was in Car One.

He opened the door and she followed his long steps with her shorter ones. The smell of the diesel engine was overwhelming and the noise too clamorous to hear anything. But the gateman waved to the engineer and motioned that there was one more passenger.

"That door there, Miss. Good thing you didn't bring a trunk. There would be no time to get it on board. One more second and they would have left."

A door unfolded in three parts: a top, a middle, and a ramp on the bottom. The conductor stood several feet above her in a godlike stature as he reached out his hand for her bag.

If he was put off by her rumpled appearance, he said nothing.

Inside, she was met with a new worry. The train car was filled with men and women so spectacularly dressed that she almost gave into her spent nerves and left to find the more humble surroundings of coach. Here, the women wore hats with colorful plumage that extended high above the seatbacks. The men donned starched suits pressed to perfection, miraculously unwrinkled despite sitting. Shoes shone like mirrors and not a wisp of hair was out of place. In contrast, she knew she was a sight. Her dress wrinkled from the bus ride, her hair in disarray after hurrying through the station.

The conductor showed her to the front of the car. A woman was applying her lipstick while looking at small mirror affixed in its case. She did not look up when Mabel arrived, but scooted closer to the window.

A seventy-four hour ride suddenly seemed like a lifetime.

The worst of winter fell away mile by mile as Mabel left the only town she'd ever known behind her. It felt like a kind of molting. She was still herself, but newer.

Old skin left behind with old worries.

The journey on the train made her wish that she *were* a writer. It would have been a most artistic way to memorialize it. The route took her through places that had only ever been small red dots on faded maps: Richmond, Raleigh, Atlanta. And later a change to a new train that took them due west through Mobile, Beaumont, Houston. Their names inspired memories of long-ago school classes: the burning of Richmond and *Gone With the Wind*. They rushed past in too much of a blur to see, but for once the impossibility of seeing such places in her lifetime seemed utterly within reach.

Even as her newest seatmate remained tight-lipped, Mabel found other amusements on the train. An observation car with even larger windows. Desks on which to write letters.

*Dear Ginger*, she wrote on a postcard, one in a stack of gold embossed ones intended for the use of the first class passengers. A scene of the train emerging from a tunnel in a mountain. *I am seeing how very extraordinary this country is and I hope that someday you can join me on an adventure such as this!*

Even the dining was exceptional. China plates, iced lemonade in crystal goblets, white napkins that put the clouds to shame. She'd never had a filet of beef in her life, but she was certain now that it was the best thing in the world.

All the wonders occupied her attention during the daylight hours. But when the sun fell, the conductor rearranged the cabins—as if by magic—into sleeping berths. The seats were flattened into beds and upper bunks were pulled from the ceilings. Sheets were arranged and pillows procured.

It was in the darkness of her bed that all the new experiences stilled. She could hear the heavy breathing of the other passengers despite the weighted curtains offering privacy. Troubles laid to rest for the night. Except for Mabel. Guilt rose like bile as she chastised herself for these indulgences. *My mother and Robert lay in their graves. Buck might be freezing on a jungle floor, for all she knew. And Pops*—she could only hope that he'd found shelter in some charitable establishment.

It didn't matter that Mrs. Koehler had paid for it all, or that Mabel hadn't asked for such an extravagance. The world was suffering outside the opulence of these train cars and it couldn't be forgotten.

She did wonder, however, just who was Mrs. Koehler that she could afford this? Was she some kind of eccentric that she would send for a girl she'd never known for a job that was not fully described?

In her enthusiasm to escape the confines of Baltimore and start a new life, she'd given little thought to where she was actually going.

*How*, she wondered, *how on earth have I been chosen for this job?*

Her letter had been genuine. She recalled the words, having honed them in draft after draft before sending it:

*Dear Mrs. Koehler,*

*I am not a writer. But I have always been told that I have excellent penmanship and good listening skills. And I became head secretary at Clipper City Fabrics, quite young for being nineteen years old. I am without family, the war having dealt its blow to mine as it has to many. So I am free to be at your disposal day and night and I promise to be most diligent in my work. Every writer had to start somewhere, so maybe this is my own beginning, if you will take that chance on me.*

*And I won't deny that I'm quite intrigued by your location. Baltimore is so terribly cold at this time of year, and though it's all I've ever known, I have never made peace with its chilly temperatures. I should like very much to be welcomed into a warmer climate such as yours.*

*I am shy a hundred words of your request, but I don't believe that truths have to be elaborated upon when the simple case is this: you will not find a more hard-working and eager girl to consider for this position, and I hope you will extend the opportunity to one who is so in need of it.*

*Sincerely,*
*Mabel Hartley, Baltimore*

Her heart had sunk after she'd slipped the letter into the blue metal postal box at the corner of Albermarle and Watson. It wasn't perfect. And the photograph showed a crooked smile, the flash having gone off one second later than she'd anticipated. Still, her hair had been set in thick curls and she'd taken great care with her few cosmetics. The picture had been intended for Artie, as a memento. But shortly after she'd picked it up from the developer, she'd received his letter and seen this advertisement, and she was happy to be rid of the reminder of what didn't come to pass.

This Mrs. Koehler must be some kind of character to have chosen hers out of so many letters. Or *were* there so many? She could have been competing against three or three hundred or three thousand. There was no way of knowing.

So it was a remarkable surprise to receive the response saying that she was hired, though it prompted the painful task of sorting through her family's possessions and turning over the keys to their landlord, Mrs. Molling. They'd agreed on a small storage fee to keep the most sentimental of the few pieces until further notice. The rest she donated to charity.

She'd brought only what she could it fit into her suitcase and hoped that it would be enough for a new life.

As the fourth day began, the conductor came through the cabin rustling the passengers so that the bunks could be remade into the tidy seats that served during the daytime. He announced that San Antonio was the next stop, a mere forty minutes away. Mabel was grateful for a tip from the waiter in the dining car that the shower stalls were more available in the evening, so she'd washed up the night before. She quickly slipped out of her night-gown into the pale pink dress that she'd saved for this morning, a feat of contortion in the coffin-like space. She'd stitched the frock from a seldom-used tablecloth that she'd found as she sorted household items. Simple lines, but nevertheless new. She fastened the last button with hurried fingers and opened the bunk's curtain.

A streak of sunlight cut through the windows and she felt its warmth on her bare feet. It stood in contrast to the chill on the window pane. A similar dichotomy revealed itself as the train slowed on the tracks. Though the hour was early, they'd arrived at Sunset Station.

Mabel smoothed her hair and ran her hands across the dress. She pinched her cheeks in an attempt to brighten skin that hadn't seen much sun these past winter months.

A crowd was gathered behind a gate. Waves and hugs and greetings took on a symphonic tone. Familiarity abounded and Mabel felt the acute stab of aloneness.

She caught the eye of a woman, aged sixty or so. She had a set jawbone that contradicted the bright floral dress she wore. And an expression that was just as rigid.

The woman held a cardboard sign:

MABEL HARTLEY

There was her name in dark blank ink, written in letters that seemed to have been set straight with a ruler. Her heart clenched. This was really happening.

Mabel walked toward her, feeling the return of a trepidation that had quieted amid the luxury of the first class rail car.

"That's me," she whispered. "I'm Mabel Hartley."

The thin lips that responded didn't allow a smile. "And I'm Helga Siegfried," she said with a thick German accent. Mabel's shoulders tightened at the woman's glare and she had to hold her breath to keep from shaking.

"I hope Mrs. Koehler hasn't make a mistake with you."

> **SEEKING MOTIVE
> IN KOEHLER CASE.**
> SAN ANTONIO POLICE
> UNABLE TO FATHOM
> AFFAIR.
>
> *The Houston Post headline,
> November 15, 1914*

# CHAPTER SIX

TODAY HELD HOPE akin to the Christmases of Emma's youth. Where Papa dressed as *Weihnachtsmann* and candles were clipped to tree branches and the anticipation of opening the wrapped presents was enough for a child to burst. Helga had left an hour ago to pick up the girl from Baltimore, beginning the final chapter of Emma's unusual life.

She watched the cars turn from West Main Street to North Ashby, waiting for a particular one to make its way to the house.

It was an old, forest green Ford, purchased five years ago, and not even new then. Emma's acquaintances found it amusing, even endearing, that she didn't buy something more in keeping with her status, even if she wasn't the one who drove it. At one point, the Koehlers had been among the wealthiest couples in the city, worth thirteen million dollars if you counted Otto's investments in an Idaho mine, a Mexican railroad, and the Texas Transportation Company. Not to mention his pet project, the once-grand Hot Wells resort an hour away.

Dear Adolphus Busch had warned Otto that such broad responsibilities would keep him from running the brewery as well as he ought and encouraged him to enjoy his money a bit rather than working all the time.

Emma's sentiments exactly. But Otto had difficulty remaining faithful to just one enterprise.

And just one woman.

At last, Emma saw the rounded nose of the car stop at the intersection and turn left toward the house. It was easy to spot it from this vantage point. Otto had chosen this lot on which to build their elaborate mansion because of its astounding views. From here, he could see the San Antonio Brewing Association building and watch the smoke rise from its tall red stacks. The color of the smoke would indicate the level of productivity happening at any given moment and he watched it with the reverence of Catholics awaiting a papal conclave.

The tires made a crackling noise as they arrived at the driveway, a sound that reminded Emma of the pop of barley when it was heated in the steel barrels.

Brown, withered leaves blew onto the threshold as Helga and Miss Hartley stepped inside. The girl set a suitcase on the wood floor and though Emma's eyesight was not what it was in her youth, she assessed the newcomer in a quick second.

Leather bag, old but tenderly polished. The stitching touched up with a skilled hand, though with a different colored thread than the original. Miss Hartley was thrifty, but capable.

Her wool coat appeared to be well worn and overly thick for this climate. But then, she had come from the northeast, so it was surely a standard part of daily attire for much of the year. If she lasted in Texas long enough for the summer to descend, perhaps she would find that the city's charms offset the hot misery that residents wilted in.

The girl stepped forward and spoke with a voice that sounded older than she must have been.

"Mrs. Koehler? I'm Mabel Hartley. I'm so pleased to meet you."

Emma wheeled her chair closer and adjusted the glasses on her nose. Mabel bent her knees so that she could face Emma eye-to-eye, a gesture that the older woman appreciated.

"Miss Hartley. Welcome to Texas. I hope your journey was not too difficult."

"No, Ma'am. Long, but more than pleasant. And the accommodations were more than generous."

Emma squinted her eyes and looked into the tired ones before her. She had to admit that the girl had gumption to venture out in such a way and then treat it as if it were a trifle.

"Miss Hartley, if this goes as planned, you and I are going to get to know one another quite well. I don't stand on formalities. Look at me, " she pointed to the wheels at either side of her hips. "I actually don't stand much at all. My friends call me Emma and you will be expected to do the same."

The girl nodded and remained in what must have been an uncomfortable position. "Then please call me Mabel."

"Fair enough." The niceties were out of the way, and in the German fashion of her ancestors, Emma saw no need to spend undue time on chatter.

"Helga, please show our guest upstairs. Give her the French room." She saw Helga wince at the order, a harbinger of what Emma's family was likely to think about this newcomer and her placement in the choicest of suites. But it was no matter. It was her own business and they would have to abide by her wishes.

"Mabel," she continued. "We will have dinner at eight this evening. I know that may be late, but we run things according to brewery hours here and that is after the day shift ends. It's nothing fancy on the week nights, so don't expect a banquet."

"Of course not. Thank you, Mrs. Koehler. I mean, Emma."

As the footfalls of the two younger women began their ascent up the grand central staircase, Emma looked after them. It had been so long since she herself had seen the rooms on the second and third floors. Their magnificent views. The brocade curtains and the lace coverlets that she'd chosen in all of their world travels. Silk sheets from China. Wool rugs from Turkey.

And the nursery with its wooden toys from England and Holland.

How she'd wished to fill it up with children. To hear the echoes of laughter through the halls. And even the cries. Emma would have kept her children close to her own bedroom, and though she could have afforded it, she would not have had nannies fussing and bustling about.

Instead, that part of her heart had been closed and she'd made an adequate substitute by opening wide the doors of her home to the migration of family. They needed her and this house needed them and Otto needed a wife who would aid him in producing enough beer to flood the river that wound its way through the lower street levels of the city.

What Emma needed was never anyone's consideration.

This city was named for the patron saint of lost items. Apt. Because Emma had lost much.

NOTICE: The funeral of Mr. Koehler will be held at the family home tomorrow afternoon at 3 o'clock. Members of the office force of the San Antonio Brewery Association, of which Mr. Koehler was president, will be pallbearers.

*The Houston Post, November 15, 1914*

# CHAPTER SEVEN

IN THE MORNING LIGHT, Mabel was better able to see the room she'd been given. The space was nearly the size of her entire Baltimore apartment. She felt like Rapunzel in a tower from this third-floor height. A bench seat curved around the nook in the turret, covered in cushions made of paisley chintz, with shelves beneath them offering a variety of books. A quick inventory of them showed that none of the spines had seen a bit of cracking, but they were meticulously dusted. The kind meant more for display than for reading. In the middle of the room, she'd slept in a four-poster bed made of a whitewashed wood. Blanket upon blanket was piled upon it, all white, and topped with a down covering that was comfortingly warm.

Even the washroom was luxuriously appointed with an iron tub boasting enormous claw feet and an elaborate mirror that hung above the sink. Fashioned after one at Versailles, Helga had told her. An imitation. But an expensive one.

Mama would have loved this, she thought. Ginger, too.

After a breakfast of oatmeal and toast with strawberry jam, she tucked her notebook under her arm, stashed a pencil behind her ear, and made her way to the drawing room minutes before eight o'clock, as she'd been instructed.

"I like a girl who appreciates the importance of timeliness."

Mabel jumped at Mrs. Koehler's voice. She hadn't expected her to be here already, but then she noticed blankets and a pillow stacked neatly on a sofa across the room. Is this where she slept?

Mrs. Koehler cleared her throat and folded her arms, resting her elbows on the side of her wheelchair. "Are you ready to get started or am I interrupting a daydream?"

Mabel pulled her hair back with two hands and tied a ribbon around her blond hair. She shook her head.

"I'm ready."

She was surprised at the lack of a *hello* or *how do you do* but thought it best to adapt to Mrs. Koehler's manner.

"Good. You may sit at that desk in the alcove, where the light is best. We'll work for a couple of hours or until I'm tired and need a rest. There is much to cover."

"Yes, ma'am."

She smoothed her skirt and sat in the high-backed chair by the window. It was not comfortable, not as much as the sofa might have been, but she could last for two hours or so. Perhaps it was meant to keep her awake.

"Let's begin." Mrs. Koehler wheeled herself over to the other side of the desk, taking great care over the plush rug. Mable wondered if she should offer to help, but something about the woman's demeanor indicated that she neither needed—nor wanted—assistance.

Mabel pulled out the fountain pen she kept for the purpose of writing shorthand. She'd been trained in the Pitman method, its phonetic symbols drawn out through thick and thin strokes. When she'd first seen the system, it looked like the scribbles a child might draw, but as she understood that sounds replaced letters, she appreciated the brilliance of its simplicity.

Mrs. Koehler cleared her throat again. "I'm an old woman, Mabel Hartley. And when one gets to my age, you start to reflect on the life you've lived and what your time here meant. I have no illusions that by this time next year, I'll be six feet under the dirt and there will be nary a flower on my grave."

Mabel's throat tightened. The reaper was a familiar visitor, having wielded his sharp sickle too many times in her small family. Though she'd only just been introduced to the woman in front of her, she did not care to imagine her end being as near as she implied. She began to protest, but was cut short.

"To that point," said Mrs. Koehler, "I've given a great deal of thought as to what I want to say. My family is set for money and I will leave with little worry on financial grounds. But these are trying days for women and I believe I have a story that may offer hope."

Trying times indeed. Men were off at war, women were holding up the home front, feeling its precariousness in their blood. Like a tower of playing cards that would tumble in the wind. If Mrs. Koehler, shriveled by age and handicap, could be a source of inspiration, Mabel was happy to be the instrument through which it came to light.

She pressed her pen against the yellow, lined notebook.

"Where shall we start?" she asked.

"In the middle."

Mabel looked up, confused, but Mrs. Koehler explained.

"Yes. It's an odd place to begin one's story. I'll give you that. But a necessary one. You see, Mabel, my husband died almost thirty years ago. We'll get to the sordid details of that at another time. He enjoyed successes in many endeavors. But brewing beer was his great love. And mine. It was part science, part art, and lacking children, that building you see off in the distance became the only offspring we had. We nurtured it, sacrificed for it, fed it as one would for any child and it was poised to grow into something quite magnificent."

Mabel nodded, scratching out every other word, trying to keep up. She could write a clearer copy later in her bedroom.

"Otto and I spent long evenings on the porch talking about

our plans. And though he was the named president, a good number of the ideas he presented were at my suggestion. Our marriage was quite a partnership. If not in romantic ways, at least in business."

Mabel paused and bit her lip at this admission. She would have imagined the owners of this magnificent mansion to have a love story that equaled it. But if Mrs. Koehler had any intention of expounding on that statement, she didn't say so. In the matter-of-fact way that Mabel had already begun to witness in her, the woman pressed on. She picked up her pen once again and took down the dictation.

"When was the first time you imbibed, Miss Hartley?"

Mabel looked up. Emma's expression was stern: she expected an honest answer.

"Imbibed?"

"Yes. Drank alcohol. When was the first time you tasted alcohol?"

"I—I never have." It wasn't merely that she was two years shy of the legal age. It was that drinking had consumed her father, body and soul. For all she knew, it tasted like the nectar of angels. But his foul breath and irrational temper under its influence was enough to render her a teetotaler.

But she couldn't say these things. Not to a stranger.

Mrs. Koehler grimaced. "Exactly. My parents were German and in their day, babies suckled beer almost more often than mother's milk. So when the first stirrings of Prohibition came about, we thought it quite ridiculous and dismissed the possibility. But as their cause gained ground in Texas and later across the nation, Otto and I traveled to St. Louis frequently to confer with Adolphus Busch, who ran the mighty Anheuser-Busch brewery. It was predicted that brewers across the country would be bankrupt if the dry craze swept the nation as it began to look like it would."

Mabel wondered if she would have sided with the prohibitionists if she'd grown up at that time. Perhaps such a crusade would have saved other families from all hers had endured. It was not a question she'd ever pondered. Yet in front of her sat a woman whose very life and legacy had been built on a foundation of hops and yeast and barley.

Mrs. Koehler voiced what Mabel didn't. "Are you against it, then? The drink?"

What could she say to this? She had to choose her words carefully.

"I suppose not in *every* circumstance." She shifted in her seat, trying to conceal her discomfort.

"So you would have voted wet back in the day? You'd have been on our side?"

Mabel held her breath. It was too soon to head back to Baltimore.

"To be honest, I've never given any thought as to how I would have voted."

This was true, at least.

"Hmph." Mrs. Koehler pulled her wire-rimmed glasses from her face and rubbed her eyes. Then she squinted, and Mabel felt naked under the scrutiny.

The old woman pressed for more. "Would you have voted to put thousands and thousands of people out of a job? Hundreds at my brewery alone?"

She hadn't thought of that. Her father had been ruined by alcohol, but how many fathers had been equally ruined by its prohibition? Things were never as simple as they seemed.

"I'd never want to see anyone out of a job."

Mrs. Koehler—for she could not think of this formidable woman by her Christian name—put her glasses back on and rested against the back of her wheelchair.

"That's the problem with young people today. You don't know your history. If we'd learned something from the last war, we wouldn't be in the current mess, but no one studies the past as they ought. Look—"

She wheeled herself closer so that the armrests butted up against the desk. She tapped a knobby finger on the glass-topped wood.

"I was in charge of the livelihoods of hundreds of people in my employ. That's husbands with wives and children who relied on *me* to make the brewery succeed. I didn't do it because I needed money. Otto left me more of that than I could spend in ten lifetimes. I did it because I could not bear to see anyone starving and anguished. Worrying over how they would bring home the next meal. I grew up that way, in my littlest years. I could not inflict that on anyone."

Mabel nodded. "But that was out of your control. Prohibition wasn't your fault."

"Maybe. But there is much in life that is out of our control. The answer is not to give up and crumble. The answer is to find a way around it, no matter the difficulty. No matter how impossible the obstacles."

Running a large brewery, even as its sole product was deemed illegal, seemed like an insurmountable task. But that, perhaps, was the very story Mrs. Koehler wanted to tell.

"So what did you do?"

The first smile of the day spread, thinly, across Mrs. Koehler's face. "Ah, what did I do? My dear, that is the exact meat of what I want to have you record for me. Because I didn't lose one single employee during that time. Not one. All this while being told that women didn't have the heads or stamina for business."

Mabel set the pen on the desk and intertwined her fingers, resting her chin on the perch they made. She looked at the older woman, the topography of wrinkles spread across her ancient face. How many times had she passed women of that age in the street as she hurried to work? Their secrets hidden beneath the vicious mask of age that robbed them not only of their beauty but of the regard of later generations?

She considered it in a new light. And it saddened her. She would never know her own mother this way. Mama died while there was still sparkle in her eyes, while her perfect skin was lovingly cared for with morning and evening doses of Noxzema moisturizer.

Mama's story would not have been as grand as that at which Mrs. Koehler hinted. But listening to the older woman, in a way Mabel couldn't explain, could let her do what she'd never be able to do for her mother.

She rubbed her temples, picturing the enormity of the responsibility Mrs. Koehler had taken on after her husband's death. A woman running a business—an *empire* of sorts—was unthinkable today, let alone thirty years ago. To steer it through the double storms of Prohibition and the Great Depression was miraculous.

No, not miraculous. *Heroic.* To say otherwise was to deny Emma Koehler all the credit due for accomplishing something of that magnitude.

Mabel suddenly found this job very intriguing for its own sake. Not only as an escape from Baltimore and all the blows it had dealt her.

"Emma," she started, though the familiar nature of it still sat uncomfortably on her tongue. "What is your goal with having me here? Do you intend for this to be an article? A book?"

*Dear God, please don't let her say a book.* Mabel felt inadequate enough as it was and the idea of having a narrative of that magnitude sit on her inexperienced shoulders was daunting.

"What do *you* think it should be?"

Mabel paused. Mrs. Koehler wanted *her* opinion? No boss—certainly not Mr. Oliver—had ever wanted to know her thoughts. A myriad of possibilities came to mind, but it was difficult to settle on exactly the right one.

"How about ... how about we don't settle on anything yet? I just take notes and we can decide from there."

Mrs. Koehler smiled again, this time wider than the first. Mabel had the feeling that she'd passed some sort of test.

"Quite prudent, my dear. You would have made a good brewer. It takes patience and a watchful eye. No need to rush any decisions."

Mabel felt her cheeks warm, sensing that Mrs. Koehler didn't distribute compliments loosely. It gave her the dose of confidence she needed, having worried that Mrs. Koehler would regret choosing a girl so inexperienced in this field.

"So," she started, flipping back through three pages of notes. "If that is the middle, should we now continue with the beginning?"

Mrs. Koehler nodded and wheeled her chair back to the edge of the rug. Her rose-scented perfume lingered.

"Yes. The beginning. Pick up that pen. We have a lot to cover."

# TO THE MEMORY OF MR. KOEHLER

With simple ceremony and only a few words of consolation by life long friends, Otto Koehler, president of the San Antonio Brewing company and multi millionaire, was buried this afternoon in a plot in the Mission Burial Park. No religious services of any kind were held either at the home or the grave. The funeral cortege was the largest held in San Antonio in many years. More than 150 automobiles, 100 carriages and the large white auto hearse were in the procession. Fully 2000 people paid their respects to the memory of Mr. Koehler at the Koehler home and more than 3000 people witnessed the ceremony at the grave. The body of Mr. Koehler rested in a heavy bronze casket in the southeast parlor of the Koehler Home. The floral contributions were many and beautiful and were received from every part of the state.

*The Houston Post – Houston, Texas November 16, 1914*

# CHAPTER EIGHT

*1886*

"TEXAS?"

Otto might as well have said that he wanted us to move to the moon. It was as foreign to me as the Germany of my parents' life before they each immigrated. I'd been told stories of the small house Papa grew up in. The one that boasted magnificent views of Alps. I'd only seen mountains in picture books and in the tears my mother shed when she thought I wasn't looking. She'd never felt settled despite the expansive community of "our own people." She'd even been robbed of her language, pressed upon by my father to learn English and to expunge every trace of an accent that marked them as foreigners.

Of course, she was my second mother. The one my father married when I was only five years old, having lost my birth mother three years prior. I was the eighth and last child of that union, born to Helen, whom I could not remember, but whose eyes and chin mine were said to resemble. She was a ghost to me, known only in photographs, just as the mountains were.

Marianna came along and became the one who inherited "Mama" as a term of endearment. But only from me. Married at the age of forty-three, she was much too old to give my father more children. And as he was nearing sixty himself, that was fine with him.

My other siblings called her Bertha, a secondary name she abhorred. Which was probably why they used it. They all remembered our mother, having been born early enough to recall the sound of her voice when she sang lullabies like Guten Abend, gut' Nacht. I heard those only as cast-offs. Second-hand, never as good as my mother was supposed to have sung them. Johanna, Catherine, John, Caroline, Anna, and Herman made special mention at Christmas of our mother's Plätzchen cookies. Which, though she tried, Marianna could not replicate even half as well.

Only my sister, Dorothy, remained silent about poor Marianna. But that's because she'd died the same year as my mother and they were buried next to each other under the shade of a large elm tree at Bellefontaine Cemetery.

So I had two mothers. The one who was supposed to look after me as an angel in heaven and the always morose one I knew in the flesh and who never ceased to pine for her homeland of Hanover.

As the youngest, Papa treated me like his prinzessin. He would hoist me upon his shoulders when my little legs were too weary to continue our walk along the banks of the Mississippi. And from that vantage point, I imagined myself to be a giant: all-powerful, undefeatable. Sentiments he encouraged. I grew up unaware that the world would look so unkindly upon my gender.

Still, I was a product of an age that made me feel the sting of obligation to follow where my husband led and when my own Otto glistened with enthusiasm for the opportunity to manage a brewery nearly a thousand miles away, I could not refuse.

But I was appalled. What could San Antonio possibly hold that my beloved St. Louis did not?

Even our namesake was more illustrious.

St. Louis was named after a king of France. San Antonio, after a poor Italian friar.

But, Lord help me, I loved my husband. And that, more than the affection for my city or the marital contract sealed at the altar, compelled me to adopt his enthusiasm for what this new life promised us.

It's what drew me to him in the first place. Otto strove to be the best at *whatever he endeavored. In our neighborhood, he became an excellent stickball player only days after first taking it up. I have no doubt he could have played pitcher for the Cardinals if it had been his ambition. But while his body was made for athletics, his mind was made for business.*

*And not only business, but that particularly reckless variety of it: entrepreneurism.*

*Otto figured out from a young age how to turn one penny into two, a nickel into a dime, a quarter into a half-piece. He'd buy a dozen roses from a flower seller for a dollar and thirty cents, only to separate them and sell them around the corner for twenty-five cents each. He'd approach a man walking with a woman on his arm, Otto holding a single, long stem— any wilting pedals removed and discarded—counting on the man's chivalrous nature. Or his unwillingness to look like a cheapskate in front of his companion.*

*Little did the man know that he'd saved himself more than a dollar because surely the flower seller would have accosted him in the same manner just steps later. Suddenly, the quarter would seem like a minor investment in keeping the woman happy.*

*Otto understood that it was not the quantity of roses that mattered to the woman. It was the fact that she was remembered at all.*

*It was only one of Otto's schemes, though with some thought, I might choose a better word. Because "schemes" make it sound like he was up to no good when only the opposite is true. A whole pie purchased at the baker would be repackaged and sold as slices while it was still warm and aromatic. He constructed tables along busy streets that sold water on hot days, hot tea on cold days. And between school hours and the hustle du jour, he worked the old-fashioned way: couriering messages between businesses, cleaning restaurants after hours, and working in his brother's general store.*

*Otto had two ambitions in life: to be rich and to marry me. In that order.*

*Ours was not a conventional courtship. It was not built upon my ability to thread a needle or roast a chicken or to achieve any of the wifely attributes my friends aspired to. Rather, we met on a July day by the Mississippi when he tried to sell me a tepid cup of water and I reasoned that if* he bought a block of ice from the icehouse, he would be able to charge three pennies more for the luxury of its chill. I could see the numbers run through his head the same way they did through mine: that a block of ice cost fifty cents and it would take only seventeen cups to break even, minus some loss for what melted before it could be finished.

He recognized me as an equal and quickly asked me to join him, figuring that we could not only double our clientele with our dual efforts, but we could take turns running to the ice house to replenish our supply. When I further calculated that we could pay a young boy a nickel to fetch the ice for us, thus freeing me up to sell at least ten more cups of water, I knew that an engagement ring would follow as soon as we were both old enough.

On my seventeenth birthday, my instincts proved correct. By then, Otto had secured a position as a bookkeeper for Anheuser Busch, attracting the attention of the owners. He demonstrated his care for every aspect of the business, even spending some hours on the brewing floors washing hops before they were turned into beer.

He labored as if the brewery was his own.

I could tell he'd been working with the hops when he arrived at my home, the musty-sweet scent of the small green pods attached to his shirt, his hair, his fingernails. It was pleasant; it had become Otto's de facto cologne, and it's a smell I loved until the day he died.

When he got down on one knee, me standing on the porch, my stepmother peeking through the window, I half-expected the velvet box he presented to contain a chip of a diamond bought, in all likelihood, at a flea market for a good price.

But he surprised me. Inside was an emerald ring, the stone rounded like a large pea, and it shone with brand-new brilliance. Though I knew little of jewelry, I recognized its extravagance. Especially for a man who'd worn the same pair of shoes for the past six years rather than spend a cent on a new one. A cent that could be reinvested into two or three.

His words were clumsy. There was no flowery preface. No mention of the color of my eyes, the sweetness of my lips, or other flatteries that girls in my position so treasured. Just a simple, "Let's get married." With the same tone that one might say, "Let's have sauerbraten tonight."

*I did not need sentiments. The ring had told me all that I needed to know: that he valued me at least as much as he did money. And that marrying me was an investment in his future.*

*Our future.*

*My stepmother flew out of the house, handkerchief in hand, wiping away joyful tears instead of her usual laments. I had not even said "Yes," yet—though I intended to. She wrapped one arm around me and the other around Otto and long-dormant German words came flooding from her lips as if her happiness for us required the native tongue in order to encompass the many feelings to be had on this occasion.*

*As we walked along the river later that evening, a young boy with a rose in hand approached us and held out a flower. Otto's eyes met mine and his jaw tightened. I knew that he did not care to spend hard-earned money on something that would perish in days. And though I shared that opinion—Otto admired my practical approach to such things—the moment felt like an omen.*

*To my surprise, Otto bought the stem and even tipped the boy an extra nickel! The man had clearly lost his mind.*

*When I returned home that evening, I plucked the pedals one by one. An echo of a silly girlhood chant repeated through my head. "He loves me. He loves me not."*

*And as I set them aside to be pressed between the pages of my family Bible, I reached the last one.*

*He loves me.*

Mr. Koehler was considered one of the most active workers for the development of San Antonio. He was one of the supports of the chamber of commerce, both financially and personally, and never was he called on to aid that he failed to give substantial support. In charities he was also foremost, but many of his charities will never be known, for he said little about them.

*The Houston Post, November 15, 1914*

# CHAPTER NINE

THE OLD WOMAN'S eyes began to droop. Her words took on the drowsy slur that might have indicated drunkenness in another person. But Mrs. Koehler did not seem to be the kind of woman who was easily enticed by the excesses of her own product.

"Go over there," she told Mabel, pushing herself to continue and pointing to one of the many bookshelves in the parlor. "Pick up the large red book."

Mabel rose, relieved to escape the uncomfortable chair and have a chance to stretch her legs. She found the book easily; it was the biggest among thin, individual volumes of the tragedies of Shakespeare. Embossed gold letters indicated it to be the Luther Bible.

"That's the one. Set it over here and open it up."

Mrs. Koehler was now slumped in her chair like a deflated balloon, but she seemed determined. Mabel placed it on the desk and turned to the first section. The pages released a scent that reminded Mabel of mothballs and fireplace embers. Sweet and smoky at the same time, the signature odor of items meant to outlast their owners' comparatively brief lives.

The first things she noticed was that the text was written in both German and English, which accounted for the heft of the tome. Pages alternating between the languages, repeating the same passages.

Births and baptisms and marriages were recorded in varying shades of faded ink in handwriting that was distinctively European. Dates went back nearly two hundred years. The last child recorded was Emma Bentzen on February 25, 1858, though the name of the church had been obscured by water. Mabel wondered if they were formed by raindrops or tears.

The union of Emma Bentzen to Otto Koehler marked the end of the marriage records, and lines extending from their joining remained blank: theirs had not produced any children.

Mabel's finger traced the emptiness of the barren page and looked up to see the rigidity in Mrs. Koehler's face as she watched the action.

"Turn to Exodus," she instructed.

Mabel knew little about the geography of the Bible, but recalled that Exodus contained the story of Moses, and surely that happened somewhere near the beginning. As she passed Genesis, her hunch was quickly confirmed, for in the second book, she heard the crinkle of waxed tissue and saw the darkened, dried rose petals flattened on the page opposite the Ten Commandments.

Her eyes fell on the fifth, as if she was meant to see it: "You shall honor your Father and your Mother, so that you may live long in the land that the Lord your God gives you."

A bitter taste gathered in her mouth, accusing her of neglecting this edict. She'd been a good daughter to her mother, but had left her father on the streets of Baltimore to come here. She pursed her lips and reminded herself that she'd tried time after time, night after night, to get him to give up the drink and return home, if he could even be found.

How far did filial duty extend, especially to one who rejected it?

Mrs. Koehler's yellowed fingernails tapped the desktop, impatient.

"You see those?"

Mabel brushed her hand against the pressed petals, preserved under the translucent paper. She nodded.

"That was the first and last rose I ever received from Otto."

Silence descended as the two women looked at each other and Mabel waited for her to continue, but no further explanation came. She supposed it was the one he'd given her after they'd become engaged.

What had happened to change everything?

Mabel stepped into the crisp January air and pulled the scarf tighter around her neck. Had she been in Baltimore, she would have had to hold it against her face, bracing herself against the biting wind and allowing the wool yarn to warm the breeze before breathing it in. Her lungs had always been sensitive to the cold, having suffered a near-fatal case of bronchitis as a child. One more indication that she was meant to leave her hometown for points south.

So far, winter in Texas was downright balmy in comparison, despite the vapors forming as she breathed.

She slipped her fingers into worn leather gloves, every tiny, unknown muscle aching from the hours spent writing down Mrs. Koehler's dictation. And later, cleaning it up on fresh paper.

Now she found herself outside, more curious than ever about her aged employer.

The grounds of the Koehler Mansion were vast and her ankles turned downward as she stepped carefully across the sloped lawn toward the sidewalk. The view from the bottom of the hill was obscured. No wonder Otto and Emma had built the house where they did: it reigned over the growing city, a white marble crown atop the neighborhood. A greenhouse sat on the north side of the house. A red fox ran across the lawn and hid in the bushes.

Mabel looked left and right, noticing that more cars drove to the west of the house, so she walked that way. She passed a synagogue with the large red dome and went a block further to the busy San Pedro Avenue. There, catty-corner from her stance stood the most magnificent park. The trees were bare, sleeping away the winter months. But she could imagine the lush scene when the leaves would grow and wondered if spring would find her still in San Antonio.

She hoped so.

Mabel crossed the street and walked along the paths that cut into the lawn. The occasional squirrel stuck his head out from fallen branches. She was reminded of reading the Narnia books with Mama. Though wintry, it was a land so removed from anything she'd ever seen. In the middle, a large concrete hole sank into the land like a fissure. A one-story building sat on the other end.

*San Pedro Springs Swimming Pool*

If the summer months in Texas were anything close to what she'd heard them to be, she was sure this was a welcome respite for the locals. Though the image of Mrs. Koehler or Helga frolicking here made her laugh. It was unlikely that either of them visited this place.

A voice startled her.

"You're not from around here, are you?"

Mabel turned and saw a man sitting at the edge of the empty pool, his legs swinging. He wore a gray knit cap that was frayed at the front, and a burgundy scarf around his neck. His nose was red from the cold, as hers probably was.

She wrapped her arms around her waist and took a few steps toward him.

"How could you tell?"

"You have that look of wonder that can only be worn the first time you see such a place. Unless you're an actress. Are you an actress?"

Mabel felt her cheeks warm. The idea of being mistaken for one who would have such a glamorous profession!

"No. I'm—" What exactly was she? Until a few weeks ago, she'd been the assistant to Mr. Oliver and now she worked for Mrs. Koehler in a position that was still quite beyond definition.

"I'm just me." She flushed with embarrassment as she said the words. What a childish thing to say. But something about him made her nervous. In the very best kind of way.

The man curled his knees up to his chest and pushed himself up. As he came closer, Mabel noticed his deep blue eyes and the creases that formed at the corner of them as he grinned. "Well, Just Me. I'm Erik. Erik Garrels."

He held out a gloved hand and she unfolded her arms to do the same. Though two layers of wool and leather separated them, she felt a shiver run down to her toes as they touched. She looked away as he kept his gaze on her.

"Do you go by *Just* or do you prefer *Miss Me*?"

He paused, raising an eyebrow as he continued. "Or is it *Mrs.*?"

Mabel couldn't help but smile. It was the kind of jest that Robert would have made, picking up on such little statements and poking fun at them in a humorous way. Though she would have expected to be saddened at the thought of her brother, something about Erik made it impossible to feel anything but cheery.

"*Miss* Hartley. Mabel."

"*Mabel was a good lass. Raised with a touch of class. 'Til a boy came around and she declared herself found and they married in Cork in a flash.*"

"Is that a poem?" She'd never heard something with her name in it.

"A lyric. From a vaudeville show I worked on. And it wasn't Mabel, it was Moira. But they're interchangeable. Two syllables, starting with M. Easy switch."

His voice shook as if he were not quite as confident as he pretended to be.

"You're an actor?" she asked.

"A stage hand. Though I've had the occasional walk-on part and minor understudy roles when they were in a pinch. I also build sets and tinker with the lights."

Mabel had never attended a live theater production, though she'd seen plenty of movies since the Senator Theater opened in Baltimore a few years ago. She and Ginger would catch Saturday matinees. Artie liked to take her to evening shows, though. It was where they had their second kiss, beneath the flickering lights of *Mrs. Miniver*. And their third. And their fourth. She would leave the theater not knowing any more about the movie than when they'd arrived. Ginger had been right. Artie had been too fresh too fast and Mabel would be wise not to make the same mistake again.

No matter how blue the eyes of this one. But she couldn't help herself from continuing the conversation.

"What theater do you work at?"

"It's right over there. SALT. Or, rather, San Antonio Little Theater." He pointed north, past a particularly thick grove of trees, but devoid of their leaves. She was barely able to see a building through their trunks. "It's why I asked if you are an actress. We get quite a few aspiring ones come by looking for a part."

"I'd like to go sometime."

She bit her lip and wanted to take it back. Like putting a fresh sheet of paper in the typewriter. She hadn't meant *with him*. Merely that she'd like to see a theatrical show.

Or was she fooling herself? Ginger believed that our first thoughts were our truest ones.

"We're rehearsing *Green Grow the Lilacs* right now. Opening night is next month. But I could always sneak you into a dress rehearsal."

A dress rehearsal! The idea was tempting. To see the inner workings of a theater before the public saw the show. Would that be better, she wondered, than seeing the polished, final version?

Maybe she would take him up on it.

But then she remembered Artie. She couldn't let herself say yes so easily. Instead of accepting, she recalled a newspaper article she'd read a few months ago.

"*Green Grow the Lilacs,*" she repeated. "It sounds familiar."

"It should be. It's seen a resurgence in the past few months. Rogers and Hammerstein adapted it into a musical and it's opening on Broadway in two months as *Oklahoma!*"

That's where she'd heard of it. A color advertisement had run in the Baltimore Sun around Christmastime, selling train tickets to New York to see it. Bright yellow with pink and green dancing figures graced a half-page spread, difficult to miss. A write-up opposite it had referenced the 1931 play it had been based on.

"Anyway," he said, perhaps sensing her reluctance. "It should be a good show. Harry Turner is playing Curly to Donna Pride's Laurie. They started seeing each other at the beginning of rehearsals, but they've already broken it off and it's been a hoot watching them jump in and out of character. But they'll pull it together for the show. They're professionals."

Mabel nodded, desperately wanting to go, but leery of giving him hope. "Maybe," she said.

He turned toward the direction of the theater.

"Well, I've got to get back. I only came out to clear my head and awaken the lungs a bit. I don't usually run into anyone out here. Not at this time of year. But I'm needed inside for a terribly important task. I'm the only one brave enough to climb the scaffolding and paint the top of the proscenium." He grinned.

She had no idea what a proscenium was, yet couldn't help but be impressed by the thought of him doing what no one else wanted to do.

He looked down at his shoes and then back at her. If she didn't plan to see him again, at least she could glance at those eyes one more time. It was difficult; shyness wanted to pull her away. And good sense.

"Anyway," he said, "If you decide you want to come, give them my name at the box office. Tell them you're Erik's guest and they'll get you in."

"Thank you," she managed to say. "That's very kind of you."

He lifted his right hand to his head, as if to tip his hat to her, only to realize that it wasn't so graceful a gesture with a knit cap. He laughed and she couldn't help but do the same.

"Until then, Mabel Hartley."

She watched as he turned and walked away, surprised that the absence of one who just minutes ago was unknown to her could already be felt so keenly.

## THE TWO HAD BEEN
# INTIMATE

Miss Burgemeister is a beautiful blond, petite, vivacious, with regular features and an appealing smile. She is a trained nurse and is said to have received many visits from Otto Koehler in her little cottage during the last few years. It is known that the two had been intimate.

*The Winnipeg Tribune, December 5, 1914*

# CHAPTER TEN

*I'M THE ONLY ONE. I'm the only one who left St. Louis.*

The words were whispered through trembling lips.

Mabel set her notebook down and placed a hand on Mrs. Koehler's liver-spotted arm. Her skin was paper thin and wrinkled, and cold to the touch.

"Catherine!" the old woman cried.

The formidable voice of Emma Koehler had given way to fear-filled ramblings.

"Who is Catherine?" asked Mabel gently. She pulled her hand away and raised the blanket so that it covered Mrs. Koehler's arms.

"My sister. I left them all to follow Otto."

As she said his name, her eyes lost the glazed look they'd adopted, as if he was some kind of touchstone that grounded her even all these years later.

She began to speak once again in a lucid tone and seemed unaware that she'd spent the last half hour mumbling incoherent words. Mabel sank back into the firm cushion on the chair, relieved that things were getting back to normal. It was frightening to watch someone vacillate between child and old woman and if Helga hadn't warned her that this was becoming a frequent occurrence, she might have panicked.

Mrs. Koehler sighed and readjusted the blanket, folding it over in a straight line across her lap. "I've outlived all my siblings, Mabel. By decades. I wonder sometimes if I have angered God in some way. To take Otto, to leave me without children, and even to lose my brothers and sisters. Money is no substitute for loneliness, I assure you."

"What about your nieces and nephews?" Mabel had met several as they came in and out of the house. It seemed impossible to be lonely when she shared her roof with so many others.

"They're quite a bunch," she said. "Some good eggs and some bad ones. But I don't feel like talking about them right now. Where did we leave off?"

Mabel knew this by heart, but she made a show of flipping through the last pages of her notes. Despite Helga's assurances, she'd found the morning unnerving.

"Otto had proposed to you," she started.

"Yes. Then let's continue from there."

*1886*

*Otto convinced me that our move to Texas should happen right after the wedding. His enthusiasm was such that I feared he would go without me if I refused. An offer from Anheuser Busch to open a brewery in San Antonio was like catnip to him and he became enraptured with the hope that they might add his name to the masthead someday. An unlikely notion, to be sure, despite the mentorship he received from Adolphus.*

*But he was to be rewarded, at least, by heading their new Lone Star brand.*

*Any thoughts of living in the familiarity of St. Louis were too limited for Otto's insatiable ambitions.*

*His work became his first mistress, though I was too love-struck at the time to realize it.*

*During our last week in my beloved hometown, we sat in his apartment on the wooden trunks that held our few possessions. As if Otto doubted my commitment to our move, despite the evidence surrounding him, he grinned* and said that he had a surprise for me.

"Close your eyes," he insisted, leaving no room for hesitation. Already, I'd learned that obedience kept him happy.

So I complied.

He crossed the room to the small kitchen and opened a cupboard. I heard the fizzing sound of bottles opening and in the enclosed space, I smelled the familiar scent of beer.

Otto returned and put a warm bottle in my hand.

"Drink this," he said.

I took a large sip, grimacing at its temperature. Beer always tasted best when cold, but we'd already drained the icebox in preparation for our move.

"Now this one," he said.

"When do I get to open my eyes?"

"It's not about what you're seeing. It's about what you're tasting."

At first, there was little discernable difference. Beer was beer was beer, some sweeter than others. But that night, Otto began the patient process of teaching me to differentiate between the brands and explained how their water content directly affected their final product. In time, he insisted that I learn the variations of lesser ingredients like hops, corn, rice, and barley malt. It was an education in geography and chemistry more thorough than anything I'd learned in a classroom.

And a skill that would serve me well later, though at the time its only meaning to me was the intimacy it created between us: one on one in those sparse rooms with the man I was about to marry. I would have sat riveted at the most mundane of dissertations, so content was I to be alone with him.

A bride adoring her groom before time unfolds its inevitable turns.

And so we set out for Texas, armed with an eager sense of adventure. I shed lavish tears and accepted promises of correspondence from my brothers and sisters. My father had died shortly before our wedding, a loss I've not recovered from all these years later; but I visited Bellefontaine Cemetery before we left and set flowers on his grave and my mother's and sister's.

*Would we ever return?*

*Like me, Otto came from a large family, one of ten to my eight. Though few of them had immigrated: only his twin, Karl, and their sister Joanna. So his extravagant goodbyes had happened many years ago and he had only these two siblings to part with this time around.*

*We took the train to San Antonio. Coach class, though we were only one car away from the first class dining car. Smells of roast beef wafted through the doors as conductors walked back and forth between us, prompting my mouth to tingle with an anticipation that went unfulfilled. Silverware chimed like bells and the pop of champagne bottles being opened sounded like gunshots. In contrast, we nibbled on the scant dried apricots and walnuts that I'd brought.*

*Our stopover in Dallas was more of the same. We stayed at a humble boarding house across the street from a far more luxurious hotel whose name I have forgotten after all these years.*

*Those two nights became our honeymoon. Prior to our marriage, I'd let Otto's hands roam a bit more than my stepmother would have considered proper. But with the blessing of a marriage certificate, I discovered a side of Otto that I hadn't even known to hope for. His regard for me and for my happiness nearly erased the pangs of my homesickness. I transformed from girl to woman in mere days and felt dizzy with the newly discovered power of femininity that had been dormant until then.*

*Otto was eager to hear my opinions about life, work, and lovemaking, and regarded me as a partner in everything.*

*For a time, at least. And for that time, it was glorious.*

*As we strolled the gaslamp street after dinner on our first night, he took my hand and pointed to the palazzo across the street. "We're going to stay there someday, my darling. I don't intend to remain in the station of life I was born into. I will build you a fine house and you will dine in the best restaurants and we will stay in the most glamorous of hotels."*

*He lifted a finger to my lips when I whispered that I didn't need fanciful things, silencing my protestation.*

*"Hush, my darling. We are going to have it all."*

*From the moment we arrived in Bexar County, Otto set out to prove* that the Busch family had placed their trust in the right man. He left the old apartment we'd rented before the sun rose and returned long after it set. By then, he was too exhausted to do more than eat the meal I'd prepared hours earlier and give me a peck on the cheek. The only time I saw my husband during daylight hours was on Sundays. And if the brewery hadn't closed at two o'clock on those days, I have no doubt that Otto would have confined himself to its grounds until dark. As it was, I had to muster all my powers of persuasion to keep him from using his key to go into the office, even for a few hours.

To fend off boredom during some of the other six days and to contribute to our income, I became a companion to an elderly woman. The widow of an early investor in barbed wire. I read the daily newspaper to her, which I found to be more beneficial to me than it was to her. It was an excellent way to learn about the unfamiliar city. I also helped with minor household tasks. Mrs. Terroba hailed from Mexico and I became enamored with her command of its culture and the language. So lively compared to my stilted German.

Despite her poor vision, she learned to read me early on.

"Emmazita," she said, calling me by the pet name I'd somehow earned in a short time. "I'll tell you the secret to keeping a husband happy."

Desperate to recapture even a few hours with Otto, I was ready to listen.

"It's all in the afrodisiaco. The aphrodisiac."

I'd never heard the word, either in Spanish or English.

"The sex, my dear."

Heat rose to my cheeks as if a match had been struck. I couldn't believe she'd said that word aloud. I had never heard my stepmother say it, not even when I began menstruating. I'd come home from school convinced that I was dying after I saw the trickle of blood and she couldn't bring herself to tell me what it meant. It was my sister Anna who wrapped her arms around me and explained to me the mysterious wonders of being a woman. But not even she had been as brazen as Mrs. Terroba.

She leaned her cane against the large mahogany table where we'd been writing letters to friends of hers. She grinned, the wrinkles around her mouth disappearing and showing a glimpse of the beauty she must have been as younger woman.

"You have to show your husband how much better it would be to come home to you. To leave the office for the pleasures that await. But as lovely as a woman may be, the wise one is not too proud to secure certain aids that keep him happy. The foolish woman, though, thinks that it is about the bedroom."

She held up a bony finger and waved it.

"It is about the kitchen."

The kitchen! What was she suggesting? The image that came to mind was too shocking to speak of. But her next words calmed my nerves.

"You see, it's what you give him in the kitchen that affects what happens in the bedroom. In Mexico, we señoras have several secret weapons."

She leaned in further and I did the same, feeling like the gravity of some ancient secret was about to be entrusted to me.

"The first—chocolate. But not any kind of chocolate. We add chili to it. Individually, they bring out—how should I say it—the romantic inclinations of a man. But together ...."

Mrs. Terroba brought her fingers to her lips and kissed them. "Together, they are irresistible."

"How do I serve them?" I asked. I could only imagine asking the grocer for a block of chocolate and then sprinkling chili powder on it. It sounded unappetizing to me.

"You serve it hot," she answered. "You melt the chocolate and add cream. Then a pinch of the powder. Just a pinch, though. You Germans don't have the stomach for the heat that we do and I wouldn't want you to kill him."

I looked at my wristwatch and wondered if I could get to a grocer before they closed.

"The second thing," she added, as if I'd forgotten that she'd hinted at several suggestions, "is scent. It's overlooked but so very important. Most women douse themselves in rosewater or gardenia oil. But those appeal to the female nose. Instead, you have to think like a man."

She pulled herself up on the cane and took slow steps to the kitchen, *beckoning me to follow. She opened a cabinet and pulled out waxed paper. She unfolded it with care. Inside were three long, brown strands.*

*"Vanilla," she said. "These are vanilla beans. Smell."*

*She held them up to my nose and I inhaled, immediately drawn in by their luxurious scent. "They're not only for cooking. Look!" Mrs. Terroba rubbed the strands in her hand until the oils from it seeped out. Then, she touched either side of my neck.*

*"When your husband comes home and kisses you on the cheek, he will not miss this scent. It will bring up warm memories of home and comfort."*

*The vanilla scent was enchanting and I knew that Otto would immediately love it. I could already envision the turn our new marriage could take from this. "Thank you," I whispered, still astonished at how unabashed she was.*

*Mrs. Terroba refolded the paper and put it into my hands.*

*"You take this," she said. "And some of these." Another cabinet produced a small block of dark chocolate and a tiny bag of red powder.*

Mabel put her pencil down and looked at Mrs. Koehler, who was smiling.

"For a while, Otto rarely worked past six o'clock after that," she said. "And never on Sundays."

Miss Burgemeister has been placed in Baylor hospital under police guard and Miss Daschiel is being held under surveillance. Miss Burgemeister is a blonde with regular and pleasing features, is not more than 35 years old and is declared to have come to San Antonio from Germany, her native land, four years ago in company with Mr. and Mrs. Koehler on their return from one of their periodical visits to Europe.

*The Daily Times, Davenport, Iowa*
*November 13, 1914*

# CHAPTER ELEVEN

SUNDAYS WERE SACRED in Mrs. Koehler's mansion and whether it had anything to do with the story she'd last told Mabel or not, it was clear that it was a day like no other.

Frieda the cook began working an hour before dawn, baking rolls and pies, needing that extra time to let the dough rise. The maid dusted the formal dining room, which was left untouched on other days. She took great care to wipe each crevice of each scroll on each chair. Even Helga came more alive, offering to help both of the women. Emma tried to do the same, but Mrs. Koehler waved her hand to brush her aside.

"Sunday is your day of rest, my dear. I insist upon that."

"But I want to do my part," she objected.

"Oh, you will, I promise. You'll meet my extended family over dinner tonight, and that will be work enough for you."

"What do you mean?"

"Mabel Hartley, you will be here for several weeks and maybe more. Every Sunday night, the family comes to dinner. Those who occasionally stay in the rooms upstairs and those who live around town. And it is wonderful in a way. But you will, no doubt, arouse their curiosity. Arm yourself, for they will be full of questions."

Like some kind of trial? Mabel wondered.

"I am a stranger to them," she said aloud. "Surely it will be natural for them to want to know why I'm here."

Mrs. Koehler nodded. "The young men will find you pretty and be curious for all the best of reasons. The young women will find you pretty and become envious. The older ones—the married ones who know what a struggle it is to make a living and keep up with the bills—they will wonder if you've wormed your way into my life for the purpose of winning some kind of favor and stealing a piece of what they see as their rightful inheritance."

"Surely not!" Mabel answered. The idea was abhorrent to her.

The old woman shrugged. "You don't get to be where I am by being naïve about people's intentions. I'm quite a rich woman whose estate will be passed on a very short time from now. They have almost all come over from Germany at one time or another, Bentzens and Koehlers alike, and given me their time on Sunday evenings in the hopes that there would be a payoff in the end. Some of them, at least. There is one nephew I think particularly highly of and I think you will, too. But I'll let you judge for yourself. The lot of them."

Mabel let pass the comment about the nephew; it was absolutely not her intention to be romantically matched and was surprised that Mrs. Koehler had even hinted at such a thing.

She pictured the cacophony of a large Sunday dinner. She'd had only her small family to gather with and couldn't imagine what it must be like for Mrs. Koehler to have so many people depend on her. It was a burden to be wealthy, she thought for the first time. Everybody wanting something. Never being sure who might visit for the most sincere of reasons—or not.

"If I may ask, then," she said, "why do you invite them every week if you feel that way?"

Mrs. Koehler shifted on the plush sofa, arranging pillows at her back. "Because good or bad, there's nothing more important than family. I am under no illusions that if I'd been able to have children they would miraculously have been perfect specimens of human beings. Not one of us is. My legacy will be not only what I did at the brewery but what I gave to my community and to my relations. And beyond money, what I can give them is the gift of each other. It's not easy to come from a different country and make a life here. But if they have each other to lean on, they will have a far better foundation than most."

The drum of family again, following the commandment she couldn't get out of her head: *Honor your father and your mother.*

She shook off the guilt that still beset her for leaving Baltimore. She'd left the Texas address with her landlord in case her father ever returned home or her brother was found. But did that mitigate the fact that she'd set off on her own?

Despite the admonition from Mrs. Koehler to take the day off, Mabel slipped into the kitchen to help Frieda. She simply couldn't imagine relaxing when she knew all the preparations that must be taking place.

She crossed through the dining room toward the powder blue door that was supposed to lead to the kitchen. Frieda was singing, in German, of course, and the clang of pots and pans offered accompaniment. She opened it to find a room in which no expense had been spared in its building, despite being the domain of servants. The tiled floor boasted a mosaic pattern of white and brown and blue shapes. The white cabinets were topped with wooden block counters that were glossy enough to see one's reflection.

Frieda jumped back when she saw Mabel.

"Miss Hartley! *Es tut mir leid,* I did not see you come in."

"I didn't mean to startle you. And please call me Mabel."

The cook picked up a knife and started to cut an onion into paper-thin slices.

"You have a beautiful voice," Mabel told her.

Frieda shrugged, but Mabel saw the corners of her lips curl up, pleased.

"I'd love to help. What can I work on?"

Frieda had no compunctions about accepting the assistance and pointed to three yellow onions. "You can cut those into quarter-inch slices, and after that, peel the potatoes in that bin." Her accent sounded similar to Helga's, but with a softer tone.

Mabel took an apron off of a hook and tied it around her waist and neck.

"How is it that you can put on such a spread when there is rationing going on?"

The cook leaned against the counter. "Mrs. Koehler survived the Great War, Prohibition, *and* the Depression. This is no different."

Though the answer lacked the details Mabel was curious to know, it occurred to her that wealth afforded privileges that were far beyond the common person.

As if reading her mind, Frieda continued. "But there is no person more deserving than Mrs. Koehler to get ahead in a few ways. She has supported more people than you or I could ever imagine. And not only the family. But the whole of San Antonio."

Perhaps that was the justice in it. And it wasn't as if Mrs. Koehler hoarded the food for herself. It looked, from the spread in the kitchen, that she would be serving quite a crowd tonight.

For ten minutes, neither woman spoke, focused on their work. Frieda began to hum the song *White Christmas*, though the holiday had passed a few weeks ago. The weather outside was cold enough to still feel festive. Mabel joined her, humming it in harmony. Then, Frieda moved on to the melody of *Silent Night* and Mabel followed, two notes lower. Mama had taught her to harmonize everything from *Joy to the World* to *Puttin' on the Ritz*. Music had a way of connecting people, no matter how different their lives or languages.

But there had been no more music in their house after Mama died.

Tears began to gather in Mabel's eyes, and she wiped them away with her sleeve.

"*Zwiebeln!* The onions! They are making you cry." Frieda covered them with a towel and put them aside. She walked over to the sink and washed her hands. "I can finish those later."

The truth was too painful to share.

"We can boil the eggs for the meatloaf instead," said Frieda.

Mabel had never had boiled eggs with meatloaf and was eager to see how that came together.

"So you're writing Frau Koehler's story?" the cook asked. "For a book?"

Mabel set aside the onions and began to wash the potatoes.

"I don't really know," she answered. "I'm taking notes, but she's not told me what the purpose is."

Frieda nodded her head. "It's a good story. Frau Koehler, she is ... I think you would say, a *remarkable* woman?"

"Yes. Exactly. Though she's only just begun to tell me about when they first moved to San Antonio. It's my understanding that the truly *remarkable* things happened after her husband died. Did you know Mr. Koehler?"

She shook her head. "*Nein.* It was so long ago. Almost thirty years."

Mabel felt embarrassed by her mistake. Frieda couldn't be more than forty. She would likely have been a child.

The cook didn't seem to take any notice, so Mabel continued.

"Did you ever hear any stories about what kind of man he was?"

Frieda took a deep breath, seemingly careful with her words. "I was told he was a good man. And a busy one. He had many, many businesses. But after Frau Koelher's car accident, he became very different."

"A car accident?"

"Yes. They were visiting Germany when it happened. There was a brewery that Herr Koehler wanted to visit. Frau Koehler didn't want to go; she was going to visit with her mother's sister, but Herr Koehler insisted and she agreed. But in the rain, they slid into a tree. Frau Koehler was quite wounded, as I've heard it. Though she was spared the *lähmen* that would have happened if she'd hurt her spine."

"*Lähmen*?" asked Mabel.

Frieda placed twelve eggs into the boiling water and turned down the heat. "Forgive me, sometimes the English words are still difficult. *Lähmen*—ah, where if her spine had been hurt, she wouldn't get to walk?"

"Oh, paralyzed?"

Frieda lit up. "Yes! That is the word. Pa-ra-lyzed. The doctors said she was so close. It was a long time before she could walk. Her hip was broken and also her legs. It was two hours before a *krankenwagen* could get her to a hospital. She lost a good deal of blood, and it's said that Herr Koehler was quite upset. And very angry with himself."

"What happened after that?"

"She was in the hospital for many weeks, but her muscles didn't work because she hadn't been using them. So she was put in a rolling chair on the ship back to America. Mr. Koehler hired a nurse to care for her. Emma Dumpke was her name at that time, before she married. But it was an unfortunate decision."

"Why?" Mabel wondered if Mrs. Koehler would ever tell her these details.

"Because Fräulein Dumpke and Herr Koehler had an affair soon after he'd hired her. And in the end, that was the first step that led to his murder."

**PROBABLE THAT THE CHARGES WILL NOT BE PRESSED**

Friends of the family have intimated that a prosecution of Miss Emma Burgemeister and Mrs. Emma Daschiel, both of whom were arrested relative to the death of Mr. Koehler is not desired and it is probable that the charges will not be pressed.

*The Houston Post – Houston, Texas November 16, 1914*

# CHAPTER TWELVE

THERE WERE FIFTEEN people gathered around the table for dinner, though it was set for twenty. Mabel was astounded to learn that what normally fit eight seats could expand into more than double its size. Frieda showed her the secret as they set out the place settings.

"It's a German design," she said with pride. "You pull it out like this." She tugged on one end and as if by magic, leaf after leaf rolled out on perfectly oiled tracks until it stretched to its full length, taking up most of the room.

"Then, you need to set down the legs." Frieda walked to either end and unlatched a lock that, when undone, released supports that were attached by hinges.

"That is amazing," said Mabel. Even more so was how it looked after they'd set out the bone China plates and the silverware that Frieda said she polished after every Sunday dinner. Linen napkins in powder blue matching the kitchen door were folded into swans—Frieda showed her the trick to it—and crystal goblets sat ready for the drinks. There were three at each place: one for water, one for red wine, and one for beer.

"Usually, the third would be for the white wine," the cook explained. "But Frau Koehler orders a batch of the latest brew from Pearl every week and enjoys commenting on quality."

Mabel bristled. After a lifetime of watching what alcohol had done to her father, she'd avoided even so much as a sip and didn't want to start now. But how could she avoid offending the family whose very life had been shaped by it? She was already going to be under a great deal of scrutiny.

By six forty-five, the room had filled with strangers who prattled on in their native tongue, none of them giving her more than a sideways glance and air of suspicion. The mirrored buffet against the wall left the impression that there were double the number of people than what had been planned for. Mabel felt distinctly lost, but figured that it was to her advantage. Maybe she could pour the drinks into a nearby plant without anyone noticing.

Helga entered with the matriarch on her arm. Mrs. Koehler's steps were feeble but determined and her expression held its usual formidable shape. There was no doubt that she was the strongest person in the room: in will, if not in body.

She had to be. Frieda said that Mrs. Koehler never showed up to Sunday dinner in her wheelchair.

"*Stoppen*," she said, holding up the hand that was not hanging onto Helga. Everyone quieted at the sound of her voice. "I want to introduce you all to Miss Mabel Hartley of Baltimore, who will be my guest here for awhile. I expect you all to make her welcome and to speak in English so as to not make her feel left out."

Fourteen sets of eyes turned toward Mabel. Only Frieda did not look her way, but she was flitting back and forth, setting out small bowls of lemon wedges at every third seat.

Mabel could tell that Mrs. Koehler's assessment of her family was exactly right. The young men smiled at her, the young women groused. The older ones glared at her with the piercing suspicion that the old woman had anticipated. Mabel hoped that she would be seated in the corner by the kitchen, where she could slip in and out after Frieda and be of some use. Anything to escape the quiet judgment they'd already placed on her.

But to her chagrin, Helga escorted Mrs. Koehler to an empty chair at the head of the table, and in turn, Mrs. Koehler gestured for Mabel to come join her to her left. Mabel flexed her hands back and forth into a fist, hidden in a pocket. She took a breath that she hoped was unnoticeable and took her place.

The chair to her left was empty.

"Where is Bernard?" she asked to no one in particular. Her voice was weary, but determined.

Mabel wondered if that was the nephew she'd spoken of. Because even among the few young men gathered around the table, there was not one that she could imagine Mrs. Koehler feeling a particular affection for.

A stunning woman at the opposite end of the table spoke up. "He sent over a message earlier saying that there was a problem with the temperature control at Pearl and he hopes to make it by dessert."

Mrs. Koehler pursed her lips. "Just like Otto," she said under her breath. But Mabel heard the disappointment in her voice. Her hostess leaned over. "That is Ernestina. She's a sharp one. A distant cousin on my late husband's side. One of the ones who would have you for lunch if she could. But to your face, she'll be sweet as pie."

Already, Mabel felt intimidated, but if she was going to make a success of this, she needed to have the wherewithal to speak up and learn all she could. She reminded herself to use Mrs. Koehler's given name, as she'd been instructed. "It would help me so much, Emma, if you could give me some hint as to whom I should befriend and whom I should avoid."

Mrs. Koehler's finger shook as she lifted it to eye level and answered. "I'm not suggesting that you avoid any of them. They are all intriguing in their own ways. But it's best to know who to trust and who to be cautious with. See that one there?"

She pointed, discreetly, to a couple at the other end of the table. "The man with the mustache and the receding hairline is my nephew, Otto. Otto *A.,* we call him, for *Andrew,* in order to distinguish him from *my* Otto. He oversees the brewery now. He's the son of my late husband's twin, Karl. The woman next to him with the long jaw and thin mouth is his wife, Marcia. Until recently, she excused herself from our Sunday dinners, citing her philanthropic duties. But now that my health is failing, she shows up, all smiles. She's already redecorating this house, room by room. In her imagination, at least. She has it in her head that they are the natural heirs to the mansion. "And," she leaned in closer, "they're right. But it's a great deal of fun to keep her guessing."

Mabel grinned at her hostess. Though she'd seen signs of senility in the past few days, Mrs. Koehler was, at most times, completely sharp.

The meal was splendid, course after course. Frieda had outdone herself: garlic soup, meatloaf, Wiener schnitzel, turkey. Mabel could not believe that they ate like this every Sunday evening! She thought again of her father. How he would have loved it all. She vowed to ask Frieda for the recipes and, whenever she returned to Baltimore, try to entice him home with recreating them. Maybe by then, Buck would have been found alive. They could have a family dinner like they all used to do, or something as close to it as they could given that two were gone. Looking around the table, she remembered how very important that was.

Frieda entered with a steaming plate of hot cookies and a tub of vanilla ice cream. Mabel could smell the molasses and her mouth began to water. She waited until everyone had been served and took her first bite. The sweetness of the powdered sugar on top hit her tongue first, a prelude to the rich taste of the dessert.

"Ah! I got here in time for my favorite—Frieda's *pfeffernüsse* cookies."

Mabel had not heard anyone come in, but she looked up when he spoke.

It couldn't be! There stood Erik, the man from the empty pool in San Pedro Park.

His eyes, brilliant blue even in this dim light, found hers right away, and it was only then that she realized that some of the powdered sugar had landed on her chin. She took the napkin from her lap and wiped it away, teetering her water goblet when her elbow hit it. But she steadied it before it could spill.

If he was as surprised to see her as she was him, he didn't show it. Or maybe he didn't remember.

"Ah, Bernard," said Mrs. Koehler in as soft a voice as Mabel had ever heard. The old woman tried to push herself up from the table, but in two strides, he came to her side and placed his hands on her shoulders to keep her seated.

He kissed her cheek. "Auntie Emma, you're looking especially beautiful today."

"I've told you to see the doctor about your eyes, my boy." But the pride in her smile was unmistakable.

Mabel was certain that he'd introduced himself as *Erik*, which only added to the confusion of what his connection was here. He'd also said he worked at the Little Theater, but Ernestina had announced that he was coming from the brewery.

Mabel was glad that this dessert course was the last and that he'd only arrived. She hoped for a chance to talk to him afterwards and get some answers, but if she'd had to sit through a whole dinner wondering, she feared she would have lost her mind.

Mrs. Koehler gave an introduction, but it did nothing to answer Mabel's questions, nor did it hint at anything Bernard—*Erik*—had told her.

"There's a place for you right there," the old woman told him, pointing to the empty chair next to Mabel. There was an impish look in her eyes and Mabel could see the familial similarities between them.

"This is my nephew, Bernard Garrels," she said. "He's the only one in this bunch who is related to me on my mother's side. The rest are either Bentzens like my father or Koehlers like my husband. Or branches off those. And, in truth, he's a cousin, but everyone else calls me *Aunt*, so it seemed fitting."

Garrels. Yes, he'd used that name at the park.

"You make me blush, Auntie," he said, grinning. "Getting promoted to nephew like that."

She wagged a finger at him playfully. "You deserve it, my boy."

To Mabel, she leaned in and said, "There's not a harder worker at Pearl than this one."

Mabel forced herself to look to her left. She set her hands in her lap, gripping them together to keep them from giving away her nervousness. She didn't want him to know that being so close to him had that kind of effect on her and barely wanted to acknowledge it to herself.

"And are you going to tell me who your lovely guest is?" he asked Mrs. Koehler. "Wait—I want to guess. If I'm right, I get a second *pfeffernüsse*. Seems fair, wouldn't you say?"

Mrs. Koehler sat back in her chair and crossed her arms. "Oh, you're a wily one. Five dollars says you'll never get it."

"Never mind the five dollars. Frieda's cookies are worth way more than that. And you know I don't make wagers."

He turned to Mabel, the silly game an excuse for him to look her over again, this time in much closer proximity then when they'd been at the empty pool. She could smell on him something like the description of the hops that Mrs. Koehler had spoken of in reference to her husband. It was pleasant: somewhat sweet. It distracted her from feeling as jittery as she had when he'd walked in. She sat up straighter as he began guessing.

"You seem like the wholesome type," he quipped, rubbing his chin. Mabel became keenly aware that the table had quieted again and all eyes were on this interaction.

"So," he continued, "I'm going to guess Mary. I've never met a Mary who wasn't a very nice girl."

Mrs. Koehler laughed. "You're not so far off. That's a good start."

He switched hands and rubbed his chin with the other. He

grinned at Mabel, the smile reaching his eyes. He was enjoying this and she felt heat in her stomach rise to her cheeks.

"So I'm close with Mary. Ma– Ma– Ma, how about *Margaret?* It's a solid name. A sturdy name. A dependable name."

He emphasized *dependable* and furrowed his eyebrows as he said it. Mabel found herself mirroring his expression unintentionally. It was not exactly every girl's dream to be called "sturdy" and "dependable". He'd done that on purpose, maybe to get a rise out of her.

Mabel could see Mrs. Koehler looking back and forth between them. Surely she was picking up on the unusual nature of this conversation. She spoke again. "You're still close, Bernard. Quite close. Almost as if you already knew. "

Exactly. Nothing got past her.

"Are you calling me a cheater, Auntie Emma?"

"I'm calling you nothing of the sort. It's just uncanny that you're so near the target."

"Well, that's a pretty big hint and if I get this right, I'm not going to feel like I earned a cookie, but a deal's a deal, so I'll keep going."

He looked at Mabel again, his eyes getting slim as he appeared to really concentrate. He was so believable that Mabel began to doubt herself. It even crossed her mind that he could be an identical twin of Erik's instead of the man she'd met, so convincing was he. They ran in the family.

"I think I've got it!" He announced. "In fact, I'm sure of it. Your name is—*Mathilda.*"

Mathilda! It sounded even *sturdier* than Margaret.

Mrs. Koehler let out a robust laugh. "You were so close. So close. You had me believing that you actually knew. In fact, her name is Mabel Hartley. Of Baltimore. She's a writer who has come to help me record my story."

Bernard—*Erik*—had looked at his aunt, but at this, his head snapped back toward Mabel.

He put out his hand to shake hers, and Mabel obliged. The touch of his skin on hers, this time without the impediment of gloves, made her feel dizzy and she wondered if the racing of her pulse could be felt by him. She hoped not. It would be the height of embarrassment.

"It's nice to meet you, Mabel Hartley, the *writer* from Baltimore." Then, he pulled her toward him and whispered in her ear. The heat of his breath against her skin made it tingle. Not even Artie had made her feel like this.

"Just so you know, I hadn't forgotten your name. No need to share our secret rendezvous with this cloying bunch, though. I'd love to talk with you after dinner. Will you meet me on the porch?"

The words were quick and it seemed like he'd pulled away as soon as he'd gotten close. Perhaps he was as aware as she was that they had an audience. A captive one. Even without turning to the rest of the table, she could feel their attentive eyes. Erik continued to look at her, waiting for an answer. She nodded.

Then he turned again toward Mrs. Koehler. "Was I close enough, Auntie, that I earned a cookie anyway?"

She picked up the tray that had been set in front of her and slid it over to him. "You can have all you want."

Conversations among all the guests began again, but they were far more trite than they'd been over dinner, and Mabel wondered if it had anything to do with their exchange. If there were any jealousies of her before, they could only be heightened by the display of attention given her by Mrs. Koehler's *apparently* favorite nephew.

She focused instead on her ice cream, already softened by the delay and pooling around the edges of the bowl. She convinced herself that she was imagining things. Surely they could not be so concerned over such a simple conversation. When she dared to look up, nearly everyone had resumed their prior behaviors, most smiling and enjoying their ice cream as well. But two were chilly. Chillier than the dessert.

Marcia Koehler and Ernestina. They looked at Mabel and then at each other. Marcia shook her head and kept from speaking.

Ernestina, however, had no such reservations.

"Bernard," she said, nearly shouting from the other end of the table. He looked over at her. "Silly me, the lights are out on my car and I wouldn't want to drive home at night without them. Could you bring me back to my apartment when we're finished?"

Mabel saw his jaw tighten as well as the grip on his spoon.

"But you live past King William."

Mabel had no idea where King William was, but it must have been far enough that he didn't want to drive there. Or maybe he didn't want to drive Ernestina particularly.

Dare she hope? But that was wishful thinking. Ernestina was beautiful to the point of being glamorous. What man wouldn't want to spend time alone with her?

She countered him with a pout that was so exaggerated it could have found a home in a comic strip. "You wouldn't have me driving there without proper lights, would you? Be a sport?"

Mabel watched his shoulders slump.

"Sure."

"Wonderful." She stood up. "I'll get my coat."

"But—" he started, obviously surprised at her abrupt readiness to leave. Before he could continue, though, Marcia was at his side, cornering him about something to do with the brewery. A batch of yeast gone bad. All the guests began to push their chairs back and put on their jackets. Frieda entered from the kitchen and began picking up the plates.

Mabel took advantage of the many good-byes being bestowed on Mrs. Koehler to slip out of the dining room, taking as many plates with her as her arms could carry, and pouring the remainder of her drinks in a nearby planter. She grimaced at the waste when there were so many soldiers who would crave even a sip, but it had already been served and there was nothing to be done about it.

After such a long day on her feet cooking, she couldn't believe that Frieda had all these dishes to do as well, and not one person had offered to help. Laden with eight plates balanced on her fore-arms and two goblets in each hand, Mabel turned around to place her back against the swinging door that led to the kitchen. When she looked up, she could see Erik watching her from across the room, a whole head taller than nearly everyone else. Marcia Koehler was still speaking to him, but he didn't turn toward her. Instead, he had a look of disappointment in his eyes that matched what Mabel was feeling.

Then, a sad smile that seemed to tell her that their own conversation would have to happen another time.

She hoped it would be soon.

## Love, passion, AND MURDER.

Miss Burgemeister's tragedy suggests the tense gloominess of an Ibsen play. As a glimmer of light being cast on its mysterious details, all the southwest finds its attention drawn by the drama of love, passion, and murder.

*The Scranton Truth —
Scranton, Pennsylvania
November 23, 1914*

# CHAPTER THIRTEEN

MABEL FOUND A NOTE under her bedroom door on Monday morning, written in Helga's precise script:

*Mrs. Koehler is feeling unwell this morning. She requests that you postpone your work together until after lunch today.*

It was a bit of a relief. Although she'd already bathed and dressed, she looked forward to a leisurely morning. Last night had been one of the most restless she'd experienced in a long time, her mind reviewing the memory of yesterday's dinner like a gramophone needle stuck in a groove.

If she had been able to think on their first conversation by the pool and the jovial nature of it, she might have slept the sleep of a baby. Instead, too many questions challenged even the most arduous sheep counting. Why had he introduced himself as Erik? Why had he said he worked at the theater when it was clear that he worked at the brewery?

There were probably simple enough answers for those questions, but one image could not be erased no matter how tightly she shut her eyes: Ernestina cast a glare that could burn an ant through a magnifying glass, and Mabel had the distinct impression that she herself was the unfortunate prey. Though they gathered as family, Mrs. Koehler had indicated that Erik was the only relative

One o'clock arrived faster than she'd anticipated. She'd rested her head on the leather-topped desk after writing the letters and fell into a deep sleep. When she stopped in front of the mirror to brush her hair before heading downstairs, she noticed indentations on her face: a circle where she'd rested on her wristwatch, a rectangle from the ink pen.

Writing the letters had been just the remedy to set her mind elsewhere and she vowed to do so more often. And to keep them from being as bland as this batch, it was high time she explored more of her new city during her off hours. Ginger and Mrs. Molling deserved far more interesting correspondence than what she'd offered so far and she knew that both were eager to hear of what they'd referenced as her Adventure in Texas. Mrs. Molling had never left Maryland save for the wedding of a friend across the Pennsylvania border in Shrewsbury. Ginger had once taken a train into New York City to see a Broadway show with her mother, but when her pocketbook was stolen in Penn Station, Ginger was forbidden from ever going again. So the great unknown state far west of them held much hope for vicarious living.

Hungry after having missed the midday meal, Mabel nevertheless smoothed the wrinkles from her dress, pinched her cheeks, and headed down to the parlor.

Mrs. Koehler had already wheeled herself in, and from the vantage point of the stairs, Mabel could see faint swatches of baldness underneath the braided bun that adorned her employer's head. It said something of her character that even at this age she had a degree of vanity.

"There you are," she said as Mabel entered the room. "I hope you took in some fresh air this morning. Before I was bound to this thing for a majority of hours, I used to enjoy brisk walking around the area. Good for the blood flow."

Mabel didn't want to admit to such a lusterless use of her time, nor did she care to lie. "I had a good morning, thank you. Shall we get started?"

She settled into a Queen Anne chair that faced Mrs. Koehler's current position on the Oriental rug.

"What did you think of my Bernard?" the old woman asked. Her eyes were piercing, despite a faint twinkle. At his name, though it was one less familiar to her than the one he'd introduced himself with, Mabel felt the beat of her heart even through her hands.

She steadied her voice. "He was very pleasant company. How disappointing for him that he had to miss all the excellent food that Frieda prepared."

"It *was* excellent, but dear Frieda puts on a similar spread every single Sunday, so he has that to look forward to again in six days. And, unlike most of my family, he has come every Sunday for as long as he's lived here. Far before it was known that the Grim Reaper would be paying me a visit sooner than later. That's how I know he's a good boy. He asks me for nothing."

Mabel could hardly ask about the name *Erik* or about the Little Theater without giving away their previous acquaintance. She was tempted to try to steer the conversation back to the job at hand, but curiosity got the better of her.

"What does he do at the brewery?"

Mrs. Koehler smiled. She seemed to like that Mabel was asking about him.

"A little of everything, just like my Otto did. He started in bookkeeping and had a minor talent for it. Then he advanced to a position where he hired people for jobs throughout the brewery. But they weren't the best fit for him. He's far more active than deskbound positions allow and when we promoted him to be a floor manager, he was much happier. He was always going from container to container testing the samples, analyzing the water, checking the temperature, and even making repairs. He's not one to sit on his hands."

"Do many of your family members work at the brewery? Ernestina?"

As soon as she'd said it, Mabel flushed. She hadn't meant for the woman's name to escape from her head to her lips. There was no reason to bring her up other than the fact that she's the only person whose name she remembered from last night, save for Otto A. and Marcia.

Mrs. Koehler's eyes lit up at the name, but not with affection.

"So you noticed the tension between them? I had hoped it wasn't so obvious. It's a sore point within the family. Yes, Ernestina works there. She is a liaison between Pearl and the other breweries around San Antonio. And even beyond. She travels frequently to Austin, arguing for and against laws that would impact our industry. She's a sharp one. And, as you could easily see, she imagines herself to have quite a territorial hold over my nephew."

Mabel's heart sunk. It would be impossible to stand out against one so elegant and accomplished. To speak regularly in the halls of government, especially as a woman! It was an impressive feat.

"I can see why he might be drawn to someone like her."

Mrs. Koehler gave a wane smile, but shook her head. "Oh, you may be a bit too young to see what goes on beneath the exterior of good manners, but Bernard is most decidedly *not* drawn to her. Oh, there was once a kind of understanding between them and at the time, we thought there might be wedding bells. But Ernestina—well, her behavior was less than desirable, and I fully supported him in breaking things off."

Mabel wondered if it was selfish to be happy that something had happened to separate the two of them.

"What about you, dear?" asked Mrs. Koehler. "Are you romantically attached? I should think not, if you came here, but is there a young man back in Maryland pining for your return?"

It did not hold the tone of casual conversation. Mrs. Koehler spoke with intention.

Mabel's first thoughts went to Artie, having not yet broken the habit of thinking of him as her fiancé. So the old wound, not yet scabbed over and healed by happier days, reopened to fresh pain. She shook her head, and looked down at her fingernails. They needed polishing, though such frivolities were scarce during wartime.

It was a distraction to keep her from answering the questions, but perhaps addressing it would be the much-needed salve she needed.

"I was engaged to a soldier until recently," she whispered. "But he fell in love with an English girl."

It was still bitter to speak of. Though as she said it, she surprised herself with the realization that it was not Artie particularly that made her heart ache. It was what being engaged to him represented: the promise of family again. Children. A future.

And the possibility that she would never have these things.

She wanted to turn the discussion around to deflect it from herself. No sense complaining to a dying woman about her own woes. But Mrs. Koehler was determined.

"There is hope for you, Mabel. Maybe you can understand these things better than I thought, though I'm sorry that one so young as yourself has already had to experience betrayal. In the case of Bernard and Ernestina, she became involved with her counterpart at Behrend Brewery. We discovered that their trips to Austin had become about more than business."

"Poor Bernard." Mabel was careful to use the name that his aunt called him by. To call him *Erik* would give rise to questions she didn't want to answer.

"Yes, he was devastated. But only briefly. When it was discovered that her lover was associated with the *Auslands-Organisation,* with her full knowledge, no less, Bernard told me that he was glad to have ended things. He has no tolerance for Nazi sympathizers."

"Ernestina is a Nazi sympathizer?" Mabel felt slack-jawed. Though the war overseas affected nearly every aspect of the homeland, the photographs of some of the atrocities coming out of Germany were so abhorrent that she couldn't imagine anyone here supporting it in any way. Certainly, she'd never met one.

Mrs. Koehler pursed her lips. "No, I would be stretching the truth to say so, and despite my feelings toward the girl, I will not besmirch her name unnecessarily. I think she was blinded by love for that troublemaker and chose to ignore—or at least minimize— his involvement. And I can't really say to what extent he was vigorously loyal to Germany. But I do know that he received a recruitment letter to return to the motherland and join the *Wehrmacht* to fight against the Allies. He didn't understand that our families owe a tremendous loyalty to this country that gave us a new start. We may have all the trappings of being German, but we are Americans first."

Mrs. Koehler pulled a handkerchief from her long sleeve and swatted at a fly that had entered the room.

She continued. "But before he could respond to the recruiter, he was taken by the police to an internment camp at Fort Oglethorpe in Georgia. They'd found enough evidence of his per- suasions to hold him. I don't know what they will do with him when this unfortunate war ends. It hardly seems the thing to do to release him back into regular life in the United States. But it would also seem unwise to deport him and let him get into the kind of trouble there that could hurt our interests. No doubt the experience has embittered him even further."

Mabel's chest felt heavy hearing these things. Her own English lineage, with a touch of French on Mama's side, deemed her safe. But if a German immigrant could be interned, even though there appeared to be just cause in this case, what did it mean for people like Mrs. Koehler's extended family? For Erik? If, indeed, he was foreign-born like many of the others. He had no accent that she could detect, so it was difficult to be certain. But the mere threat of it worried her.

In all likelihood, this beau of Ernestina's had merited the detention, but Mabel had read of thousands of Japanese descen- dants sent to similar camps merely for having the blood of a land that was an enemy of this country.

"Is your family safe, Emma? I hadn't considered it before, but the sentiments against German immigrants are substantial in some circles."

Helga peeked in and spoke in her unceremonious manner. "Coffee for either of you?"

Though the offer was a welcome one, Mabel was sorry for the interruption.

Perhaps coffee was another resource that her employer had special access to. Mabel knew that a ration of one pound every five weeks was not enough even for one cup a day. It occurred to her that she should offer her ration card to Frieda. So far, she'd been fed breakfast, lunch, and dinner every day and it was only fair that she contribute to it with her own allotment.

"Yes," answered Mrs. Koehler. "Extra sugar for me today, Helga. I'm still quite tired after last night."

"I'll take mine black, thank you," said Mabel. Before the war, she'd added at least three teaspoons plus milk to cover up her dislike for the flavor. She'd never taken to coffee as anything other than a pick-me-up before heading to work, a necessity to get through the day. But as the rationing began, she used less and less until she'd gotten unexpectedly used to its bitter taste. Now the idea of putting so much sugar in it sickened her.

When Helga left, Mabel returned to her question. She did not mean to delay Mrs. Koehler in telling her story—the job she was here to do—but the reality of being surrounded by so many foreign-born people and their descendants was an oddity to her and she wanted to know more. And considering that there must have been similar challenges in the previous war, no doubt it would be part of Mrs. Koehler's narrative.

"I was wondering," she said again, "how safe your family is from having the same fate as Ernestina's lover?"

It felt scandalous to say such a word so casually, but Mrs. Koehler had used it first and there really was not one that served better.

Mrs. Koehler removed her glasses and rubbed her eyes. The words she spoke were flavored with a burdened weariness.

"The government couldn't round everybody up if they wanted to. They already have their hands full with the Japanese and the Italians living here. There are over six million Germans and descendants in the United States. And most of them, like my family, have been here long enough to have assimilated and prove themselves productive members of society. Even those who have not yet been granted citizenship are still entwined in their communities and give no reason for concern. For my part, as I was born in Missouri, I have no such worry. And I have properly filled out the sponsorship paperwork for each of my relatives who have immigrated. If the authorities were to come knocking on my door, they would have more than just me to reckon with."

She paused and spoke with pointed deliberation. "I have powerful friends."

Of that, Mabel had no doubt. It was part of the story she was eager to learn. But she shouldn't distract Mrs. Koehler from that anymore.

"I'm sorry to have sidetracked us," she offered. "Shall we begin?"

She looked through her notes. She could tell that the shorthand of each day's entry grew sloppier by the end. Not so much that she couldn't transcribe it, but she vowed to be more diligent with her neatness.

"I believe we left off when you and Mr. Koehler arrived in San Antonio so that he could work for the Lone Star Brewery and that the chocolates and chili peppers ..." she blushed thinking of its implications, "assisted you in keeping him from working long hours."

"Yes," started Mrs. Koehler. But Helga knocked on the door and entered with a tray of two steaming cups. She set it down on the table between them.

"I've had a telephone call from Mr. Garrels. He said that he can pick Miss Hartley up around nine o'clock tomorrow morning to tour the brewery as you requested."

"Not later in the week?"

"I asked him, but he said that it is the best day for him if you don't mind."

In this household, the brewery was spoken of in devout tones, voices softening with affection as if it were a member of the family, flesh and blood instead of brick and stone. She was eager to lay her eyes on this legendary place. All that could be seen from the mansion were its smokestacks. Surely it would be magnificent, befitting a woman as formidable as Mrs. Koehler.

She tried to convince herself that this was the only reason that merited the excitement she felt. But the mention of Erik being the one to show her sent a flush to her cheeks.

Mrs. Koehler took a sip of her coffee and nodded. "Ring him back and tell him that we'll make it work. Miss Hartley and I can skip a day. No doubt she'd rather spend the time with a man like Bernard than with an old lady such as myself."

Mabel opened her mouth to protest, but was cut off. Mrs. Koehler raised her finger even as she slipped her glasses back on.

"Don't pretend that's not the truth. I may be older than Moses, but I remember what it was like to be a girl your age. You'll be going and I won't entertain any dissent."

Helga left the room and before Mabel could speak up, Mrs. Koehler jumped right into her story.

"So, yes. Otto came home to me more often in those first months. But it wasn't long before he reverted to his old habits. And soon after that, he left Lone Star. Rather high and dry, I might add. It was quite a scandal. But you see, he received a visit from his lawyer that changed everything. For the rest of our lives."

## INSANE ASYLUM IF SHE REMAINED IN TEXAS

For six weeks after the death of Koehler she (Burgemeister) was in jail, but then bail was arranged for her. Only $7500 was demanded — a small bond for so serious an offense. Then, she says, lawyers told her to flee from the State, as the San Antonio county authorities were bent on avoiding the scandal of a trial, and would seek to put her into an insane asylum if she remained in Texas. This frightened her... and she came to New York.

*St. Louis Post-Dispatch – St. Louis, Missouri October 10, 1917*

# CHAPTER FOURTEEN

MRS. KOEHLER WAS ONLY half an hour into the day's narrative when the doorbell rang. Moments later, Helga entered the parlor.

"Ann Mauerman is here. She said she has an appointment with you at two o'clock."

The old woman sighed and once again rubbed her eyes. "I'd forgotten. Send her in."

It wasn't like Mrs. Koehler to be unaware of the time, though the constant interruptions couldn't be helping. The minutes on the clock pulsed through her veins as steadily as blood. Mabel knew her well enough by now to worry about this decline, though Helga and Frieda had seen signs of it for some time.

She turned to Mabel. "The mayor's wife. She's purportedly here to discuss plans for the Battle of Flowers Parade. But as I'm in no condition to accept an invitation to march, I have no doubt that she's sniffing around for funds to cover the expense."

An elegant woman entered wearing a green floral dress with a matching hat, a peacock feather standing tall from its velvet band. A whiff of jasmine followed her. More than a whiff. A shower of it that tickled Mabel's nose.

She walked into the room as if it were her own home, pulling fitted gloves from her fingers one by one and settling onto the sofa without formality. "Emma, dear," she said in a voice that filled the parlor, "you're looking like a marvel today."

Mabel looked at Helga, who was rolling her eyes behind Mrs. Mauerman's back.

Helga cleared her throat and held the door open. "Miss Hartley?"

It was Mabel's invitation to leave and she had a feeling that Helga was rescuing her from it, though she would have enjoyed staying for the saccharine encounter.

"They're all like that," she whispered, leaning in to Mabel as she closed the door of the parlor. "And yet she never says no."

It fit the impression of Mrs. Koehler that Mabel had formed. Someone with a tough exterior and a soft inside. Like a turtle. Or a porcupine. Yet neither was quite accurate. A turtle was too simple. A porcupine too bristly. Emma Koehler was really her own creature, beyond definition.

Mabel returned instead to her bedroom to straighten up her notes, disappointed that she'd not yet gotten to the heart of the story. All she possessed so far were a lot of facts, and those were at Mrs. Koehler's direction. She recalled her eleventh grade English teacher pressing her students: "Who's your audience? What is the purpose of what you're writing?"

Mabel had complied enough to get good grades, but had not thought about it since, as none of her work required more than the automation of listening to dictation and taking it down. She reread what had been told to her this morning, but the purpose in all of it continued to elude her.

*Lawyer named Oscar Bergstrom told Otto K. that stock in association called City Brewery was going up for auction.*

*Sherriff's sale happening because an employee named Belohradsky embezzled two thousand dollars*

*Financial trouble for brewery*

*Oscar wanted Otto to invest. Begged him.*

*Otto risked security and the goodwill of Anheuser and Busch families for venture that had no promise of succeeding*

These facts came from Mrs. Koehler's own lips.

But Mabel had taken to making observations of her own.

*Mrs. K. spoke of Oscar Bergstrom with agitation. My imagination? Or no?*

*What was two thousand dollars worth at the time? Better narrative if I can learn that information.*

*When did relationship with Anheus./Bus. get repaired? Recall Mrs. K. mentioning continued friendship/communication with that family.*

She added these to her previous notes and set her papers on the desk. Released for the day, she decided to clear her mind and find a Walgreens. Her face cream jar was almost empty and she had to use a fingernail to scrape the last bits of her favorite lipstick out of its container. She'd hardly indulged in more frivolities than those back at home as she reasoned that there was no sense spending money on them when sacrifices could be made instead for the war effort.

But it would not keep the Bucks of the world from coming home if she purchased a little mascara, a little rouge. Why not look her best for her tour of Pearl Brewery? She tried to convince herself that it had nothing to do with seeing Erik.

The cosmetic counter made it difficult to deny, though. It was four shelves wide, colorful boxes and bottles promising instant beauty for pennies and romance if you cultivated luscious looks.

Pond's called their new lipstick *Beau Bait.*

Seventeen's powder created the *Natural look men go for.*

Flame Glo *Keeps you kissable.*

Jergens suggested that you *Be his pin-up girl.*

Maybelline said there would be *More flowers for the lady with beautiful eyes.*

That was only the beginning. Barely a package could be found that didn't convince a woman that a man would love it.

The effect of seeing them all displayed so outlandishly hit her in a new way. Was it so impossible that a woman might want to look her best for herself and for no other reason? Should her aspiration be to look exactly like Judy Garland or Irene Dunne?

What was wrong with being Mabel Hartley?

Ginger knew her way around a cosmetics counter better than anyone else and had a talent for shaping an eyebrow and outlining a lip. Mabel had given it little thought until she'd met Artie, but something about getting to know Mrs. Koehler made her consider things she'd never thought of.

Would there be a future where a woman could be celebrated for her abilities rather than how she might look in a cocktail dress and pearls?

A flush of excitement raced through her. Maybe that could be the angle in which she would view Mrs. Koehler's story! A woman owning a business in a time when it was unheard of. And not any woman. A widow. A widow in a wheelchair. Mrs. Koehler's story was interesting, yes. But more than that, it offered hope to girls who were only beginning to see a world where opportunities were available to them that were never there before.

Suddenly, mornings of dry dictation took on a new meaning and her fingers ached with an eagerness to get back to work. That's how she needed to look at the tour of the brewery. Not merely a chance to spend time with Erik—why pretend that she wasn't looking forward to that—but to get inside Mrs. Koehler's world in the most literal way. Marveling at what she'd accomplished. Inspiring young women like herself with what they were capable of.

How funny that the revelation could come in an aisle of a Walgreens, but it did. Like lightning striking.

She made her purchases and returned to the mansion on Ashby with a sense of lightness. One that she couldn't remember feeling since childhood. The war had weighed her down and she had let it. She'd run away from her troubles in Baltimore, but maybe that had not been the case at all. Maybe she'd been running *toward* something and hadn't realized it.

Mabel found it difficult to sleep when she went to bed that evening. Her mind was bustling at this renewed excitement and her scalp was sore from the Tip Top button curlers she'd purchased. The packaging had promised that they were "soft to sleep on" and that she would be able to "make pin curls easily," but neither had proved to be true. Pink plastic dug into her skin and she didn't have any aspirin on hand.

Beauty was pain.

This was still a man's world and women had to look good in it. It would not change overnight and until that happened, she would slip her legs into hosiery, stuff her toes into pointed shoes, and pin her hair like her life depended on it. Certainly doors had opened for Ernestina because of how she looked. It was just the way it was. But Mabel would find ways to chip away at these notions as best she could. Perhaps through telling Mrs. Koehler's story.

Mabel unsnapped the round discs and laid them on the bureau next to the bed. She ran her fingers through her hair and took a deep breath before looking into the mirror. Ginger would have been proud. They were nearly perfect, cascading down her back in light blonde waves.

She brushed them out a little more to soften them and conceal the impression that she'd gone to as much trouble as she had. Trying too hard was irrelevant if looked like you were trying too hard.

She dabbed a light pink lipstick on, having decided against the sultry red shades advertised at the store. That would have been too much.

Her wristwatch said eight fifty-eight.

With the punctuality she'd come to admire in the short time she'd lived in this household, Erik ran the doorbell precisely at nine o'clock.

Helga made it to the door first.

"*Guten morgen*, Herr Garrels."

"Good morning, Helga. Is Miss Hartley ready?"

Mabel reached the bottom of the stairs and turned the corner. "Hello, Mr. Garrels," she said. Such formalities to maintain when everything in her body felt so askew.

He held out his arm to her, and she took it, hoping that Helga didn't think that the gesture was anything but chivalrous.

Erik had pulled his car up to the house, taking the long curved driveway that started at the gate. In front of her was a shiny Ford Deluxe convertible, a model whose name she knew only because Robert had always spoken of getting one when he returned from the war. This one was baby blue with a camel-brown cover that was open despite the January date.

"I hope you don't mind," he said as if intuiting what she was thinking. "It's a few degrees warmer than it was yesterday and there's no breeze. I haven't been able to take the top down in months and I can't think of a better occasion on which to do it."

She smiled and didn't even try to keep it small and modest. It would be a true joy to ride in it, a bright spot in the sadness of losing the brother who would have loved it so much. Even if the weather had been frigid, she would have welcomed the chance.

Erik came around to her side to open her door and she slid into the creamy leather seats. When he returned to his seat and started the engine, it sounded like a robust purr: strong and smooth.

"This isn't the best way to start a friendship, but I have something to confess," he said. "I was not entirely truthful to Helga when I called yesterday."

Mabel turned toward him, but his eyes were looking ahead, beginning the curve toward the bottom of the driveway.

"What do you mean?"

"I told her to tell Auntie Emma that I was only free to give you a tour of the brewery this morning instead of later in the week. But that wasn't true. I just didn't want to wait any longer to see you."

If Mabel had been the one driving, she might have slammed on the brakes when he said that. She'd thought about seeing him again ever since they met by the empty pool in the park. Then he showed up at the family dinner. And now he was suggesting that he'd been thinking the same things.

Women's advancement didn't have to exclude romance. It was the most fundamental building block of existence. But even this, she saw with new eyes: she could have a romance because she *wanted* to. Not because she *needed* to.

She should be cautious. Such enthusiasm so quickly, on both their parts. But even if Artie had turned out to be a heel, it didn't mean that all men were like him.

"That is so kind of you to say," she began. Simple and safe.

If her restraint disappointed him, she couldn't tell. His face was turned left toward West Ashby, waiting for the traffic to thin. She knew that the drive would not take long and decided to ask what was on her mind straightaway.

"So, why did you tell me that your name is Erik when your aunt and everyone else calls you Bernard? And, while we're at it, why didn't you tell me when we met that you work at the brewery?"

He came to a stop sign and glanced over at her. "I figured that would cause some confusion. Though in my defense, when we met at the pool, I only knew you to be a fellow soul enjoying the winter beauty of the park. I had no idea until I showed up at Auntie Emma's dinner that you had any connection to her. I was as surprised as you no doubt were."

He gassed it again and continued driving.

"Anyway, the first is easy. I'm Bernard Erik Garrels. My initials are BEG. How's that for a lousy monogram?"

She laughed. "Not the best. Though mine is hardly better. Mabel Elizabeth Hartley. MEH."

He returned her good spirits, his own laugh reaching down to his shoulders, which were shaking. "We're an unfortunate pair, if you go by our names. *Beg* and *Meh*. Not the most inspiring. We can do better than that. What would your ideal initials be if you could name yourself?"

Mabel had never considered such a question, but it was a great game to even think of the possibilities. After rejecting a few, including FUN which sounded far more suggestive than she would have meant by it, she settled on one that suited her best.

"SUN. I think those would be nice initials. We never get enough of it in Baltimore and I crave it."

"You'll get your fill of it in Texas, I promise you that. I like it. SUN."

"How about you?"

"ACE."

"ACE? Why that one?"

"Well, this will sound silly. Like in a deck of cards. My dad is a gambler. I like the ace because in Twenty-One, it can be either the top card or the bottom card, whatever it needs to be for a particular hand. I'd like to think that I can be what I need to be, no matter what I'm dealt."

Mabel let out a breath, impressed by the explanation.

"*I* never gamble, in case you were worried," he said quickly. "I only know about it because of him."

Erik grew quiet, seemingly lost in thought. He'd alluded at dinner to never making a wager, so it was clearly a sore point for him. If his father was a gambler and hers was a drunk, they'd no doubt experienced similar woes and would have stories to tell should their friendship ever grow deep enough to share the secrets that children of such troubled paternity kept.

She knew all too well that the first symptoms of that kind of upbringing were to pretend, *always*, that things were better than they were. To keep up a façade of happy family life even as it was cracking to the point of breaking. And to avoid the offending vice at all costs. One might presume cowardice in those choices, but she knew them to be the baselines of survival when one was wounded by the very person who was supposed to protect you.

"But," he continued, changing his tone. "That really didn't answer your question. Why did I introduce myself as Erik? I wish I had a more exciting story for you, but it's simply that I've always preferred it. Auntie Emma insists on using my name as it was given to me and no one dares to cross the great Queen of the Pearl."

"And the other part?" Mabel could now see the smokestacks and knew that their drive would soon be cut short. "The part where you didn't mention that you work at the brewery?"

He shrugged. "More wishful thinking. The brewery is something I do because there is no one in the world I admire more than Auntie Emma. She pulled me out of a tough situation at home to come work for her and I don't ever plan to let her down. It's a good way to make a living. But it's not what I love the most. She took me once to see a play at the Little Theater and I was immediately enraptured. Not only by the acting. It was the *hows* of it: how the lighting came together. How they scrolled through backdrops for the different scenes. All of it. So I try to volunteer on several shows a year. It sustains me. Do you have any hobbies?"

Mama had tried to teach her the art of lacemaking when she was younger, but it was already a dying practice and a difficult one for little fingers. And after she died, it was too painful a memory for Mabel to continue with that work. Mama's shuttles and threaders had remained in the upper drawer of her bureau until Mabel moved to Texas and cleaned everything out of the apartment.

Her interests had not rested in handiwork, even if that's what her friends did.

"I'm almost embarrassed to say," she told him, "because it's not supposed to be a girl's hobby."

The corner of Erik's mouth wrinkled. "I don't believe in that kind of thinking. A girl—a woman—should be interested in anything she likes."

She smiled. Artie had never said things like that. He'd told her he wanted her to improve her cooking by the time he came back from the war. She'd mastered a perfect chicken soup since then—her secret was lemongrass—but the kitchen was not her natural domain.

Mabel looked out the window. "I like baseball."

She felt Erik's eyes on her. They'd reached another stop sign and the shadow of the smokestacks sent a line of dark gray across the car. They were at Pearl, but he seemed to be in no rush to get her there.

"Baseball?" He grinned.

"I told you it's not a girl's hobby."

"Playing or watching?"

"Both."

"I like that, Mabel. You shouldn't be ashamed of it."

She turned back to him and read the sincerity in his face. "My dad used to take my brothers and me to Oriole Park. My mother came sometimes, too, and those were the best days. The five of us, cheering them on. My parents first met at a baseball game. Babe Ruth was playing."

"I thought he was with the Red Sox. I'm sorry—I haven't followed much of the sport, though many of Auntie Emma's other family members go way back as St. Louis Browns fans."

Mabel felt the animation of her voice. Talking about baseball opened up a place in her that had long been closed off because after the boys went off to war, they'd never been to a game since.

"Most people know Babe from the Red Sox, but he's actually from Baltimore. I even have a 1914 baseball card. Signed. It was my dad's most prized possession."

It sat in her suitcase in a small pocket, safely in Koehler Mansion. She would not have left it at Mrs. Molling's for anything.

"Show me how to play some time?"

Mabel's smile widened. "I'd love to."

Erik looked up and Mabel's gaze followed. The brewery towered in front of them, more stunning in person than she could have imagined when it was a mere dot in the distance. Golden bricks set in intricate patterns. White arched windows that looked like the eyebrows of an old soul. A black cupola sat nine stories above like a pointed cap piercing the sky.

"We're here," he said. There was a tone of apology in his voice. If he was sorry that their ride had been so brief, she had to agree. The Ford had served as their own private world for all of ten minutes.

Mabel felt goose bumps run up her arms as if the ghosts of all the people who'd worked here before were passing by. But it was more likely the sensation of coming face to face with the place that was the very reason she was in San Antonio. The heart of her newfound mission.

This was the progeny of Emma Koehler. The one whose story she had only begun to learn.

She turned back to Erik, and he smiled as he swept his arm out.

"Welcome to Pearl."

# Otto Koehler Park

As a Christmas gift to San Antonio, Mrs. Emma Koehler, widow of the late Otto Koehler, has deeded the city the 11 acres of ground included in the tract of land popularly known as Madarasz Park. The city commissioners accepted the deed at a called meeting this morning. The park is to be named "Otto Koehler Park" in memory of Mrs. Koehler's husband, who often expressed a wish to deed the property to the city.

*The Houston Post – Houston, Texas December 25, 1915*

# CHAPTER FIFTEEN

UNEVEN PAVERS WERE laced with old metal train tracks but Erik seemed familiar with each divot and imperfection. He placed his hand on Mabel's elbow, guiding her across the path of the vast grounds.

She knew it was just a gesture of chivalry and reminded herself not to lose her head.

He pointed ahead to a dump truck whose contents were spilling over.

"We're tearing up the old road, as you can see. When Auntie Emma was in charge, she was loath to spend money that didn't have to do with production. She's a sentimental one underneath that stodgy façade. But our trucks were getting too many blown tires. Life changes and we must change with it."

Mabel understood that well enough.

She pulled away and turned toward him. "Erik, I'm worried about something."

His eyes held the same jovial look that they'd had since she first met him, but they grew serious when he saw her face.

"Are you all right? Are you too cold? I'm afraid it won't be too much better in there. We have to keep it pretty chilly."

"It's not that. It's...."

She sighed. This was a more difficult admission than she'd anticipated.

"I've never tasted a beer before. Or wine for that matter. But I didn't know if that would be expected of me here."

She waited for a flicker in his eye. The one that would tell her that he thought it was funny. Artie had called her a child when she ordered a Coke instead of a beer when they went out.

But Erik's face remained serious, and his voice dropped. "I would never ask you to do something you didn't want to."

He looked down and she saw a sincerity in his expression that made her face tingle with the onset of tears. She pursed her lips and held them back.

"If you will satisfy my curiosity, though, is it a religious belief?" he asked. "I've heard of that, of course. Just not in my family circles. Germans have a long history of drinking the stuff like it's water."

Mabel shook her head. She'd never told anyone about her father's problems with alcohol. Not even Ginger or Artie. Though Ginger had certainly seen the Hartley family shatter. Some secrets weren't easy to keep.

But she didn't want it assumed that she was some kind of tee-totaler on moral or even political grounds. The Koehlers had surely seen enough of that during Prohibition.

Her worry was that she was afraid that whatever weakness made her father depend on it so greatly might lay dormant in her. Waiting for her to succumb to its lure. Could even one sip awaken that kind of monster?

She took a deep breath. He'd told her that his father was a gambler so perhaps he would understand. "My father—he ruined his life through drinking. I'm afraid of turning into what he became."

He folded his arms and looked down at his feet before glancing back at her.

"I am so sorry," he whispered. "I've known people like that.

They fall on hard times and blot it out with alcohol. I can't imagine the pain they must feel. But like anything, it's how you use it that matters. Water quenches your thirst, or you can drown in it. Fire warms you, or can rage through a forest and kill everything in its path. Alcohol has medicinal and social benefits, but can ruin lives if misused."

Mabel had never considered the comparisons to water and fire, two substances that anyone alive used frequently. Perhaps there was nothing to be frightened of, but she wasn't ready to start now. She'd endured too much from its poisonous side. Cleaned up too many times after her father, sick from overuse.

"Thank you for understanding, Erik."

His voice lifted. "Tell you what. There is plenty you can learn from smelling the brews or from crumbling the hops and barley in your hands. Taste is only one sense but there are four others. And, if you wish," at this he smiled, "you can try some of our *La Perla*. It's our non-intoxicating brew. The one we ship to the army. That way, our soldiers get all of the taste and none of the effects."

If only Pops had known about something like that! A beer with no alcohol. But she suspected that it was not the taste he was after. It was the very sensation of washing away problems with drunkenness. The numbing of heartbreak.

They'd reached the door to the main building and Erik held it out for her and followed her in. "We ferment the yeast, which releases the sugars in the wort, which converts it to ethyl alcohol and carbon dioxide."

"So to make something like La Perla, do you stop the process before fermenting the yeast?"

Erik had been right. The temperature inside the building was quite cold. She flexed her fingers, already feeling stiff.

"No. That would be a lot less costly. In fact, to make near-beer, as we call it, we have to take it through the entire process. But while the regular Pearl gets bottled, the near-beer gets reheated, burning off everything that would give it that intoxicating feature. Then, it's chilled again and bottled."

"So," she offered, wrapping her arms around herself to stay warm, "if I try La Perla, it will taste almost the same as the Pearl brew since it went through the same process?" She hoped so. She wanted to understand Emma Koehler's story and that meant understanding the brew that was so beloved by her.

"Close enough. It's a little bit lighter. Auntie Emma was one of its pioneers, you know. She and Uncle Otto traveled up to St. Louis a couple of months before he died to visit with Adolphus Busch. They and a few other brewers could see the writing on the wall with Prohibition coming and they had the idea to burn off the alcohol."

She slipped her hand in her jacket pocket, but she'd forgotten to bring a notebook. She hoped she'd remembered the details when she got back to the mansion. This was her chance to ask the things that Mrs. Koehler might not volunteer.

"Your aunt suggested that there had been some bad feelings between Otto and the Busch family after he left Lone Star to invest in the San Antonio Brewing Association with his lawyer."

She followed Erik down a red-tiled hallway. He stopped before a door with a glass cutout, and put his hand on the knob.

"Oscar Bergstrom is the man you're thinking of. He left Otto high and dry not long after that and went to New York City for newer opportunities. Adolphus and Uncle Otto might have grown close again given some time, but Adolphus himself died of dropsy during one of their trips to Missouri."

"Oh, how terrible!"

"Yes. Auntie Emma said that there were thirty thousand people at his funeral. And another one hundred thousand lining the streets. I think it made her pine for St. Louis again. Seeing how that community came together. I often think how different our lives would all be if she'd left Pearl and gone back to St. Louis after Otto was murdered."

*Murdered.* The word was not a surprise to Mabel, but it was still so difficult to imagine that it had happened.

Mrs. Koehler had not nearly gotten to that part of the story.

"Anyway," Erik continued, despite her hope that he would elaborate on the more sordid details of the Koehler saga. "The Busch family never held Auntie Emma accountable for Uncle Otto's defection all those years before. Adolphus Busch II carries on quite a nice correspondence with her even to this day."

Mabel paused to look around her. They were standing on the end of a long corridor with many doors on either side. In the distance—it sounded as if were off to the right—was a steady hum of machinery. The air smelled like a cross between a bakery and a garden shop.

A door to the left opened and the click clack of high heels echoed down the tile floor. A woman walked with determination and as she approached and it was only when she grew close that Mabel recognized her. Her nerves bristled.

Ernestina.

She glanced at Mabel, her eyes assessing her down to her shoes, but turned to Erik.

"I need to speak to you privately," she told him.

"I'm giving Miss Hartley a tour right now." Mabel could see his jawline tighten.

"This will only take a minute and we don't need to bother Miss Hartley with it."

"She's here at Auntie Emma's invitation, so anything that needs to be said can include her."

"Emma Koehler no longer works here and I don't need to abide by the dictates of a woman who probably won't live past Easter."

Mabel clenched her teeth. Mrs. Koehler's nepotistic ways had certainly brought some characters into the brewery. She knew it was not Ernestina's job to be conciliatory. It was her job to look out for the best interests of the company and Mabel could hardly begrudge her that. But it didn't seem necessary to deliver her words with such animus.

Erik was quick to defend his aunt and Mabel heard a fearsome tone in the voice that had only ever been pleasant when directed toward her. "Pearl wouldn't be here if it weren't for Auntie Emma. And your family never would have been able to come over here or pay for your schooling if she hadn't arranged for it. Show her at least that much respect."

This, oddly, mollified her. She bit her lower lip, on which Mabel had detected the tiniest quiver.

Ernestina sighed and turned to Mabel. Her voice pooled into sweetness like warmed honey. "Of course, he's right, Miss Hartley."

She took one step closer to Erik, narrowing the space between them to a hand's width gap. "It's nothing urgent. I just need to review an issue I'm having with the congressman from the fourth district. Come by my office later?"

She placed a well-manicured hand on his elbow, but Erik shrugged it off. "I'll be there at three."

Ernestina, a half-head taller than Mabel, narrowed her eyes at her. "Sorry to have interrupted, Miss Hartley. I *do* hope you'll forgive me."

"Of course," Mabel stuttered. But Ernestina had already turned back toward whichever door she'd come in from. When it closed behind her, Erik gestured for Mabel to follow him down the hall. He stopped at a set of stainless-steel doors with rounded glass windows.

He grinned. Are you ready to see where the magic happens?"

"I solemnly swear that I was born at Berlin, Germany on or about the 11th day of October, 1879; that I was naturalized as a citizen of the United States before the Western District Court of Texas at San Antonio on the 5th day of May, 1913; that I am domiciled in the United States, my permanent residence therein being at San Antonio in the State of Texas, where I follow the occupation of trained nurse; that I have been residing temporarily abroad since Feb. 1915 in Germany; that I last left the United States in January 1915 arriving in Genoa, Italy, in February 1915; that I am now temporarily residing in Berlin; and that I intend to return to the United States within two months with the purpose of residing and performing the duties of citizenship therein. I desire a passport for the purpose of returning to America."

*Emma Hedda Burgemeister, U.S. Passport Application Sworn at the American Embassy at Berlin, 2 July 1915*

# CHAPTER SIXTEEN

EVERY SUCCESSIVE ROOM was a wonder.

The first housed the hops. The temperature was near freezing and the green pellets were stored in boxes that reached to the top of the tall ceiling. They were labeled with words like *Perle, Hallertau, Mount Hood,* and *Liberty.*

Erik gestured for Mabel to come over and smell the *Perle* variety. A pungent scent tickled her nose.

"They're bitter, aren't they?" he said. "They have to balance the sweetness of the barley malt, or it would be undrinkable."

"Kind of like life," Mabel thought. Though in the last few years, it had been far more bitter. It was long overdue to change in her favor. And for the first time, she had reason to hope that it might happen.

"Do you like history?" asked Erik.

It had been one of her best subjects in school.

"I do."

He smiled and leaned his arm against a stack of boxes, his breath forming wisps as he spoke. "Then you'll love this. Guess why hops beer became so popular with the Germans. I'll give you a hint: it has to do with religion."

Religion? Mabel tried and tried to think of what that connection would be, but nothing of substance came to mind.

"I don't know."

"I didn't either, until Auntie Emma took me through for the first time and told me the stories."

He cleared his throat and continued. "A vast hop yard was owned by Pepin the Short, the father of Charlemagne. Until then, anything resembling an early ale was flavored with something called gruit. Gruit was a combination of herbs such as mugwort, ivy, and sweet gale."

"Sounds appetizing," she said with sarcasm.

"Doesn't it, though?" He crossed his arms and widened his stance. Mabel could tell how excited he got by talking about it. His theatrical instincts apparently kicked in when he got to explain, even to this audience of one.

She loved that this was her job right now, however temporary it might be. It beat typing letters for Mr. Oliver a thousand times over.

"The Catholic Church was the local authority at the time and had a monopoly on the supply of gruit, taxing it heavily. Hops, however, were grown privately and were not taxed. So the Germans started making their brews almost exclusively with hops to save money and it became the new standard in brewing. Even to this day."

Erik checked his watch before she could respond. "We should move on. There's a lot to see. And if I keep you here, you might turn into a Mabel Popsicle."

She laughed at the image.

Mabel couldn't remember the last time she felt this happy. Life had been bleak, falling far short of the things she'd imagined for herself. Being with Erik made her feel like those neglected parts of herself, the ones that had only begun to bloom when her mother died, were getting their chance to emerge again.

The next room was markedly warmer than the last, set well above room temperature. After stepping through the double doors, Mabel found herself on a ledge that overlooked a cavernous space filled with huge steel containers with glass tops. The scent in here was quite different from the previous room. This one smelled musty and thick, the aroma quite welcoming.

"What are those?" Mabel asked, pointing down to the room below.

"Those are called mash tubs," Erik explained. "We mix barley malt with rice and water and cook it. That's why it feels warmer in here. In fact, let me take your coat."

Mabel unbuttoned her wool jacket, already perspiring from the sudden change in heat. Erik stood behind her and held it up by the shoulders as she slipped her arms out. She turned around to take it from him, but he'd already slung it over his arm along with his own coat. Although she could have done it herself, it was nice to be looked after. No one had looked after her for so long.

"Thank you," she said.

They looked through a glass window to the floor below and Erik pointed to something on the side.

"You can see those mechanical arms going back and forth making sure that none of it stagnates. Back when the brewery was built, they didn't have that kind of automation. In fact, it's a fairly recent addition, set in place by Auntie Emma and finished by Otto A. I believe you met him at dinner, along with his wife, Marcia."

"Yes. Does anyone ever get them confused when talking about them? The two Ottos."

"Not now," he answered, "though I would imagine that some-one just learning about them would need to pause to consider who was being mentioned when hearing the name. As for myself, I wasn't around when Auntie Emma's husband was alive, so the only Otto I know firsthand is the one running the brewery now. But decades ago, when his father, Karl, died, and he came over as a youth to live at Koehler Mansion, it must have been confusing. Two Ottos under one roof. And three Emmas."

It was exactly the opening she needed.

"Three Emmas—your aunt and the two nurses?"

His eyebrows arched. "Ah, yes. So you know about our little family scandal. Crime of the century. Headlines around the world and all that. The other two Emmas only lived on Ashby a short while before Otto bought them their own house. But they still spent a great deal of time at the mansion caring for my aunt."

"Didn't one of those Emmas murder Otto?" Of course, she knew the answer, but she hoped he'd tell her more.

He stepped forward a few feet to where the glass ended, and leaned against the railing. Mabel stayed where she was. She felt lightheaded at the height.

"Yes. Emma Burgemeister. But I'm not going to spoil Auntie Emma's tale. She doesn't like other people talking about it. Especially those of us who weren't there. She says we invariably get something wrong."

So the most salacious parts would have to wait.

Mabel turned back toward the steel bins, keeping a good two feet between herself and the railing and returned her thoughts to the tour at hand.

"Ok. What happens after you cook the barley and rice?" Add some beef and carrots, and it sounded like a recipe her mother used to make.

"We drain it. See the darker-colored parts down at the bottom?"

She couldn't tell from where she was standing and took a hesitant step forward, now with only a railing to stand between her and a fall. Erik must have sensed her trepidation, because he put his arm around her shoulder, and a hand on hers.

"I know it's a little daunting. You're not the first person to feel anxious here."

The feel of his arms around her gave her an entirely different sense of vertigo, but one that was far more welcome. It emboldened her. She didn't want to appear a coward in front of him and very much wanted to see how things operated down at the bottom of the room.

"I can do it," she said.

He stepped forward with her, inching toward it and letting her lead as her comfort allowed. His presence calmed her more than she would have expected.

"Those giant mesh sifters strain out the solid parts and send the liquid through those tubes into the next room. At that point, it's called *wort*, which is a fermentable sugar that gives the beer its amber color."

Mabel took in the spectacle of each of the huge tanks and the vast tangle of pipes leading into the walls.

She pulled back, and Erik followed, but he didn't let go of her.

She turned toward him to speak, but lost her words when she realized how close he was. He looked down at her and moved his hand only to raise it to her cheek and brush his thumb down to her chin. They stood like this for what must have been seconds, but seemed like hours, hundreds of unspoken words passing between them. The sense of understanding that they were two souls planted here, far away from where they each came, forever changed by fathers whose failures had shaped them for better or worse. Though they'd only hinted at each of their stories, there was something of a gravity between them, thick as the scent of barley that permeated the room.

Erik's face inched toward hers. It was impossible not to make a comparison to Artie's fervent, insistent overtures and what seemed like a gentle advance by Erik. One that sought invitation in her reaction rather than assuming it was what she wanted. She didn't want to break the silence with even one word and hoped that the look in her eyes, one that she was certain matched his, told him that this was welcome.

The double doors opened and a chill blew in from the adjacent room.

They pulled away from each other, almost on instinct, and saw that Ernestina had entered.

How much had she seen? Mabel wondered. Probably too much. There were glass panels between the two rooms.

"You're wanted on the telephone," Ernestina said to Erik. Her voice matched the coldness of the room behind her.

Erik sighed, breathing the frustration that Mabel felt. "Is it something that can wait?"

"Not unless you want the temperature in the fermentation room to fail again. It's the mechanic you called in on Sunday night. He thinks the electric panel won't last more than a few weeks and wants to talk over the options for ordering a new one."

Mabel was more upset by her presence than she wanted to be and wondered why Ernestina had taken on the role of messenger. It seemed out of the purview of her job.

Erik held up a finger. "Tell him I will call him back in five minutes."

Ernestina seemed determined. "Do you think that's wise? It was hard enough to get ahold of him on Sunday, and this is the time of year when heaters are failing all over town. You've got him right now. I wouldn't risk it."

He folded his arms. "I'll be there in one then."

They spent five of those sixty seconds staring each other down, but Ernestina finally turned back and left them alone.

Once she'd gone, he faced Mabel again, and put his hands on both of her shoulders, squeezing them slightly. "I'm so sorry," he said. "I do have to take this call. And it will be awhile, I'm sure. He's the best in town, but I usually have to spend far too much time on the phone with him talking him down off the price. He starts impossibly high. I think he hopes that one of these days, I'll cave and pay his ransom."

Disappointed, she nevertheless respected how important Erik was here and his dedication to preserving what Emma and Otto had begun. "I understand. I can walk home and we'll finish the tour another time."

Do you know how to drive?"

She'd never owned a car, but Robert used to make deliveries for an icehouse and he'd taught her in his off hours.

"Yes," she answered.

He pulled keys from his pocket. "Take my Ford back to the house. I'll come pick it up tomorrow afternoon. I'm working early tomorrow and should be finished by three o'clock."

"You don't have to give me your car. It can't be more than a mile and a half and I wouldn't mind the walk." Still, the idea of driving the car that Robert would have loved so much gave her an all-too-rare sense of connection to the brother she'd lost.

He took her hand in his and placed the keys in them, the tender gesture reassuring her that Ernestina was not the threat she'd initially feared. "I would never hear the end of it from Auntie Emma if I didn't behave like a gentleman toward you. And, regardless of what she'd say, *I* insist."

She appreciated that. Robert and Buck would have done the same thing. And though Mabel believed that the capabilities of women needed more recognition, it shouldn't be at the expense of the age-old chivalry that caused a girl's knees to weaken.

And her knees, indeed, felt liquid as Erik stood so close.

So close.

The one minute had passed, but he hadn't turned to go yet.

No need to give Ernestina more reason to chastise him. So Mabel accepted the keys and he let her out a side door that was a short distance from the parking lot.

"I'd walk you to the car myself, but I do need to get to the phone."

"Nonsense. Go. I'll have it waiting for you tomorrow afternoon."

He leaned over, his face almost as near as it had been when they almost kissed. "If you don't have plans then, I'd like to take you somewhere."

Her heart beat faster. She could see the outline of where a beard would be, the stubble leaving a shadow a shade darker than his light skin.

"As long as Mrs. Koehler is finished with me by then."

He laughed. "Auntie Emma has taken an afternoon nap for as long as I've known her. Your afternoon will be free."

### A CONSTANT VISITOR AT THE SAN ANTONIO COTTAGE OF THE GERMAN NURSE

Miss Burgemeister plans to sue Koehler estate for $21,000. It is her intention to sue the Koehler estate for $21,000 on two notes of $10,000 each, bearing interest, which Koehler gave to her. In this matter, she will make Koehler's widow, executrix of the estate and State Senator Carlos Bee, lawyer and nephew of Postmaster General Burleson, defendants. Bee, she alleges, was given the two $10,000 notes to collect, but has sent only three remittances – $750 and $2500 in 1915 and $1000 this year. Koehler was a constant visitor at the San Antonio cottage of the German nurse, who, although well into her 30s, was much younger in appearance. What trouble grew between them never has been clearly told. One reason given for the reluctance of the San Antonio authorities to put her on trial for murder lies in an avoidance of putting the Koehler family under the light of such publicity as a murder trial would involve.

*St. Louis Post-Dispatch – St. Louis, Missouri October 10, 1917*

# CHAPTER SEVENTEEN

EMMA CONTINUED the next day, a stretch of lucidity sending Mabel into her second notebook.

*I felt alone once again, the sting of neglect piercing more than sharp words might have. Any words, any glance from my husband would have been welcome. But Otto's only focus was this new brewery of his.*

*Our apartment was cluttered with sketches made on every available scrap of paper, Otto's ideas for this venture overtaking the counter, the sofa, the icebox. On the evening of our first wedding anniversary, I set out white linen napkins that had been a gift from my oldest brother. Otto hardly touched the beef I'd marinated as he drew out a budget for new equipment on his napkin before reaching across the table to continue on mine.*

*The stains would not wash out.*

*I had not moved across the country to be widowed. For that is how I felt. I'd lost my husband to his manic attention to the business.*

*Otto changed the name of City Brewery to San Antonio Brewing Association and I used the first dollars he earned to buy new table linens.*

*Expensive ones.*

*He didn't even notice.*

*Determined to make a success of our move, I adopted a notion to take a walk along every street in town, the hellos and how-do-you-dos of* shopkeepers and passersby more plentiful than the words that passed between Otto and myself. It was a naïve plan, for I soon learned that San Antonio was experiencing a boom and was expected to become the largest city in Texas by 1900. Still, I purchased a map, eager to learn as much as I could about this new place I lived in.

In the evenings, I would return home and mark my routes with a pencil. Within a few weeks, I'd covered the scale of two square miles in leaden lines. Within months, I'd gone as far as the source of the river that ran through the city, four miles north.

It began as a brook, a trickle of water rising from the mossy green bed of leaves. I'd learned that it stretched all the way to the Gulf of Mexico, widening along the way into a wild, rushing force. I imagined that I could be that river. Right now I sat little and unimportant, but my father had always told me that I could be anything I wanted. I had to believe that he'd been right.

I wrote to my stepmother from that quiet place, and to my sisters and brothers, elongating facts until they resembled something far more exciting than what my life had actually become. I could not bear for them to know that I was unhappy. And even more, I could not bring myself to cast Otto in any light except a complimentary one. I was stubbornly loyal, whether he deserved it or not.

Or maybe I just refused to acknowledge failure, especially in my marriage.

To that end, I never gave up. I renewed my efforts during the city walks by looking for things that might persuade my husband to leave work for a bit and join me.

I'd thought that the movement of an entire building five blocks from its original location would pique his interest, given that he was constructing an edifice of his own. The Fairmount was a "drummer's hotel," frequented by traveling salesmen who hocked clothing across the country. Otto declined, but I still elected to watch as workers removed beds, tables, and chairs, followed by the windows, doors, and beams. Eventually, it was a mere framework of bricks and metal, and those were hoisted upon thirty-six hydraulic dollies, supported by a crane and six trucks full of stabilizing gravel. Until the final day when it was lifted from its foundation and a visit from the people at the Guinness Book of World Records named it the largest hotel ever to be moved.

The reinvention of something old, a shell ready to be filled in a new place. I felt a kinship to that strange old building.

And slowly, slowly, my homesickness abated as San Antonio wooed me with her river waters and ambitious plans of greatness. She was a lush and vigorous place, growing by the day.

In contrast, Otto grew wane and pale and I became concerned for his health. But any mention I made was met with a retort that I was not being supportive of his vision for the future. His office was without windows—too expensive to add them, he said—and his skin never saw the sun. He rose before it did, and slept long after it had set.

He'd grown immune to the charms of vanilla oil and chocolate and chilies. And me.

Everything he made was put back into the business and I was compelled to become thrifty with our money if we were to survive. I added water to soup, salt to inferior cuts of meat, and mended our clothes in the daylight so as to avoid the overuse of candles. Another husband might notice how I skimped on dinners, but Otto ate with perfunctory quickness. Filling his stomach before falling asleep, never commenting on the taste.

One evening in December, he came home later than usual. I'd piled three quilts on top of my shivering body. The heating oil had run out and the landlord had been unavailable for days. I heard the bedroom door close. Otto removed his coat, vest and shirt, letting them drop to the floor, unheeding of my continual request for him to lay them across the chair. But when he slipped in beside me, the heat of his skin warmed me, and awakened something that had been left dormant for far too long.

His fingers brushed my leg and fanned out across my hips. At last! Too much time had passed since we'd lain like this and I was happy to sacrifice the sleep. I turned to face him, kissing the cold wisps of his bristly mustache, eager to welcome him back to what we'd enjoyed so much at the beginning. But he turned his face at my approach, burying it in my neck as he laid me on to my back and pushed my flannel nightgown up to my waist. I pulled *at the hem, lifting it higher, trying to wrench it over my head.*

*I craved his skin on mine, nothing between us. Not the flannel. Not the business. Not the last year in which we'd grown so distant.*

*He stopped my hand. The garment gathered in folds upon my chest, painful in the way they sat bunched against me as Otto turned over and enveloped my body with his own. Again, my mouth sought his: the kiss always being our most exquisite intimacy. But the girth of my nightgown remained an obstacle. Instead, without warning or tenderness, I felt him maneuver between my legs, exhausting himself in seconds before I'd had a chance to join him in this bliss.*

*He turned without a word, facing the door and breathing deeply before even a minute had passed. Leaving me to stare at the ceiling, convincing myself that I should be grateful for the scrap of time he'd given me.*

*I wondered if other women were left feeling so unfulfilled. Was it wrong of me to wish that lovemaking lived up to its lore? I could hardly ask the advice of my sisters, even through letters. It simply wasn't discussed and as I browsed bookshops for the scant amount of titles relating to marriage, I found none that addressed this topic. Only those that discussed the proper way to keep a home.*

*The Otto of our honeymoon ceased to exist now that the brewery had stolen him from me.*

*I occurred to me: if I wanted a share of Otto's attentions, I had to enter his world, for he had abandoned the one we'd started to create for ourselves.*

*As dawn shed its first light over the plaster cracks in our walls, I came up with a plan.*

*I began to prepare lunches for him and bring them to the office. I did not pinch pennies on this. I took in a bit of sewing, enough to pay for a better quality bread, tastier cheeses. I included an apple and, when I had enough jobs to do so, a piece of cake or chocolate.*

*I went in every day, including Sunday. Because I'd made it so convenient, I succeeded in talking Otto into sitting outside with me as we ate. In time, his color returned and he gained enough weight to remove the gaunt look that my phantom husband had sunken into.*

Though I dotted our conversation with details of my walks around the city, I curated them to be items that he would find most interesting. And if there was some way to tie them into business and brewing, all the better. Soon, he began to dispatch me to restaurants that served rival beers, giving me a modest budget to do so. At least once a week, I ate at excellent establishments, always careful to ask waiters for their opinions on what to drink and reporting to Otto about my impressions of the taste and the enthusiasm of the one serving it. I even ate at alehouses, often the only female save for barmaids. My favorite among them was the White Elephant, situated on the same plaza as San Fernando Cathedral.

As I became a regular at the alehouses, I was often invited to join card games and light up cigars.

I declined both—a worrisome penchant for gambling had claimed the fortunes of several branches of my family—but I did sit and watch. It is amazing how alcohol and tobacco combine to loosen lips and it was here that I often got the most honest take on anything I wanted to know.

It was at the White Elephant in which a conversation with the barkeep led to my first discernable impact on Otto's work.

"Mrs. K, back again," said the man. He had a patch over one eye and a graying beard that hung two inches below his chin. "Here to peddle that sewer juice your husband makes?"

It was a well-worn jest. Jeb Booker liked the brew almost as much as I knew he liked me and he took every opportunity to have a laugh at Otto's expense. I never responded in kind, loyal to my husband and to our fledgling brand.

"Not today. I'm sampling the competition. What do you have for me to try?"

He set a cold glass on the counter, the froth spilling out over the rim. "Lone Star has been working on a mighty fine new ale. I think it will be up to your exacting standards."

I took a sip, enjoying the taste of the Anheuser Busch offering, reminiscing about friendships that had become strained after Otto's defection.

Jeb set his elbows on the bar and leaned in. His cigar-saturated breath crinkled my nose. "The problem is not the taste of Mr. Koehler's beer. It's *the name. Lone Star says Texas. We feel like it's ours. Likewise, City Brewery had a long history here. If you ask me, throwing out the name was a mistake."*

*I spent the next week asking around at the other saloons and was met with unanimous agreement: in trying to create his own new empire, Otto had eliminated the familiarity of the company that had been a homegrown favorite of San Antonio.*

*And to my surprise, Otto acted on my findings.*

*First, changing name of the brew back to its original title. Then, I made suggestions on the taste. On the packaging. All gleaned from conversations as I continued to tour the city.*

*Sales increased as San Antonio embraced our beer.*

*Initially, Otto attributed it to luck. Far be it for a woman to actually have a talent for business. But my predictions and commentaries were too correct too frequently to be chalked up to anything but acumen.*

*An opportunity came our way and I could see Otto's eyes glean at the possibilities. The recipe for Kaiser-Beck's Perle beer was up for sale, and I convinced Otto that the growing German population in San Antonio would enthusiastically receive its light flavor. The owner of Kaiser-Beck had named it such because he likened the bubbles that formed when poured to little pearls, and it was an image I was convinced we could sell here.*

*The other investors agreed with our belief that not only would the brew become a popular one, but the name—Pearl in English—would be well received.*

*Though I couldn't say so at the time, I had ambitions to bring Pearl to women. Why was our advertising focused on only half of the population?*

*Women, as always, were forgotten. But not by me.*

*And thankfully, not by my brother, John. Concerned that Otto and his investors might not be able to pull enough money together for a bid, I wrote in secret to John in St. Louis and asked him for a loan of five thousand dollars.*

*Otto would have been mortified to reach out to my family, but he'd been denied a loan by Trader's National Bank. The idea that such a sum could be needed for something as seemingly minor as a recipe nearly got* us laughed out of their offices. Little did they know that the actual sum needed was far more, but it was as much as we dared to try for from any one entity.

So I asked for John's assistance, risking Otto's shame and anger. But when my brother came through with not only the five thousand dollars but twice the amount, my husband could not help but be elated.

I was in his good graces. For the time being.

To my delight, Otto asked me to accompany him to Germany, where he intended to bid for the recipe in person at the Kaiser-Beck brewery. The competition for it was considerable and he believed that our presence together would be persuasive.

I reveled in what I might be able to contribute.

We traveled by train from San Antonio to New York and at every stop, Otto checked in with the stationmaster to see if any messages had come from the office. When they had, he sent telegraphs in response. I rued the day when communications like that became possible. Had I ever had the occasion to meet Mr. Alexander Graham Bell, I would have told him that his invention was a bane to the institution of marriage.

We sailed on a brand new German liner called the Kaiser Wilhelm del Grosse, hailed as the most luxurious ocean liner of its kind. Even as second-class ticketholders, we were treated to tapestries so intricate that they looked like paintings until one came up close to marvel at their tiny detailing. Gilded scrolls at every turn. Portraits of the Imperial family. The entirety of the ship, over fifteen hundred passengers, could be seated at once in an upper level dining room topped with a vast domed ceiling.

But my enjoyment of it was short-lived. As the first morning dawned, I fell ill with a nausea and fatigue so powerful that I could not lift my head from the pillow. Otto was unusually attentive, bringing me peppermint tea and ginger biscuits.

Though the words did not pass our lips, I believe he hoped what I did: that I was at last with child.

On the third day, however, the monthly scourge of women came about and I was cast yet again into the despair unique to those who desire a child so ardently and are disappointed time after time. Left to wonder at the cause of their brokenness or their failure in God's eyes.

Our arrival in Germany came at last, and I was relieved to have several days on solid ground before subjecting myself again to the rough North Atlantic. If only one could have attached wings and flown far above its turbulent waves!

But welcome news took away any preoccupation I had with the return. We successfully won the bid to purchase Pearl beer as well as the mother yeast from Kaiser-Beck. Otto explained that the recipe was only half of the equation. The ingredients all added their own flavors to the final product, but the main component—the most essential one—was the original yeast that gave each beer its distinct flavor. Using a different one, even one of close composition, could be the death knell of a brewery. The many German immigrants who had relied on the consistent flavor of the Perle they'd always enjoyed would surely detect the difference if the mother yeast were not used. And though the waters of the San Antonio River would be different from the waters of the Weser River, the minerals could be adjusted to match it as closely as possible.

"You are my yeast," Otto whispered as we left the negotiation table. Which, from the mouth of anyone but a brewer would sound distinctly unromantic. But I understood it exactly as he meant it.

It meant that I was essential. That I was the most important thing.

It was a morsel to someone ravenous for her husband's affection and I was happy to have it.

Otto took me to the most glamorous restaurant we'd ever been to and even ordered champagne.

"You are my lucky charm," he said over dinner, a variation on the earlier praise that actually made me nostalgic for the more original one that was so perfectly descriptive of what we meant to each other. "I was certain that the group from Philadelphia would win."

I cut into my sauerbraten, the most delicious thing I'd ever tasted. Though I suspect now that my senses were greatly influenced by my happiness, a more powerful flavor than any combination of spices.

"Yes, they made quite a case," I answered. "They seemed confident because they had offered the most money."

"Did you see the face of the man from Philadelphia when Heinrich Beck announced that we'd won?"

I giggled, intoxicated with joy. "His eyes! They were so red! Fiery red, like his hair."

Otto took my hand and held it across the table, rubbing the back of it with his thumb. His eyes never left mine. "Herr Beck knows that it's not about how many Deutchmarks he has in the bank. It was your testimony that secured our place. The way you told him about how Pearl would become a part of the very culture of San Antonio. About our German population that aches for a touch of the motherland. You told him a story, and that is a far more effective approach than mere numbers."

My cheeks tingled at these words. It was unlike Otto to be so complimentary of my talents. He never degraded them; they simply weren't noticed or mentioned. I felt warm from my toes to my ears at this onslaught of rare praise.

"It is all the walking I have done and the people I've gotten to know. I dearly wish, Otto, that you would get out of the office and join me some time."

He pulled his hand away. "I don't see how that will be possible. Now more than ever, I'll be spending a great deal of time at the office. I will rely on my darling wife to be our voice and face in the community. No one wants to see me, anyway. Not when they have you to look at."

This cocoon of bliss continued for the weeks it took to journey home. I basked in the confidence Otto had in me and felt—almost—like an equal. And I was so very excited at filling the role of community liaison when we returned. For once, I understood Otto's preoccupation with nearly living in the office. Suddenly, my thoughts were filled with plans for the future and ideas for introducing Pearl to America.

Every night, we relived our honeymoon and I could imagine that this, at last, was what the rest of our lives would look like.

It was a nice dream.

If only life hadn't woken me.

# Justification for the
# KILLING

When the case was called by District Judge W.S. Anderson, the defendant failed to appear. Her attorney, State Senator Carlos Bee, read a letter from Miss Burgemeister in which she said she was going to Germany to nurse the wounded soldiers. Judge Anderson thereupon declared the bond forfeited. Nothing was heard of the defendant until about a year later. October 28, 1917.

In her petition she alleged that she was forced to leave San Antonio as the result of threats of county officials. She alleged that she had not requested any bond be made for her; that the names signed to the bond were fictitious and that she did not know the signers. She said she wanted to come back to San Antonio to stand trial – to plead before the world her justification for the killing.

*The Topeka State Journal – Topeka, Kansas January 14, 1918*

# CHAPTER EIGHTEEN

MRS. KOEHLER ENDED the session on that ominous note, and Mabel knew that her life and Otto's had been anything but idyllic. She'd heard enough snippets from Frieda and Erik and Helga to piece together a picture of great heartbreak and tragedy.

But also with a dose of heroics. Mrs. Koehler had yet to relay the part in the story that most fascinated Mabel: her ability to lead Pearl Brewery after Otto's murder and to carry it through Prohibition.

Helga knocked and peeked in through the arched doorway.

"It's time for your medicine and nap, Emma."

Mrs. Koehler waved her arm. "Sleep is the best medicine. I don't need pills. I don't want to spend my last days feeling ill from the way they turn my stomach."

"But Dr. Weaver said—"

"If President Roosevelt himself appears at my front door and implores me to take them, I will tell him the same thing."

Helga looked over Mrs. Koehler's head toward Mabel, but Mabel shrugged. She certainly didn't have any sway with their mutual employer, and even if she did, she couldn't imagine forcing an old woman near the end of her life to do something she didn't want to do. It just didn't seem right.

Helga stepped forward and wrapped her hands around the wheelchair's handles. "Whatever you say. But I'm not going to be the one to tell Dr. Weaver."

"He'll figure it out at my funeral."

Their bickering faded as they walked down the hall toward Mrs. Koehler's room. When Mabel had first arrived in San Antonio and heard her speaking in such ways, she recoiled. Talking about death so casually was initially appalling. But once she'd had a chance to think about it, she realized the opposite was true. After all, Mrs. Koehler had led a life that was quite full, very influential, and had helped untold numbers of people. She was old by anyone's measure, and would likely perish from natural causes. If one could design the end to their days, these were certainly hallmarks of a well-spent life. What, then, was there to hold on to when the end would bring a cessation of pain—the physical and the emotional kind—and a possible reuniting with loved ones who'd gone before? If one believed in that.

Mabel had known early losses, lives taken too soon.

She glanced at her wristwatch, eager for distraction. Erik was due in half an hour to pick up his car. And to take her somewhere, according to the last thing he'd said.

The doorbell rang, and Helga walked in from Mrs. Koehler's bedroom to open up. If it was him, he was early. She rushed upstairs and put thicker stockings on to stave against the cold, careful to not rip them. They were akin to gold amid the rations.

The beautiful weather of yesterday now seemed like a distant mirage.

Grabbing her coat, she walked downstairs in slow steps that belied the anticipation that threatened to make them unsteady.

Erik looked up and she felt her pulse quicken.

"Hi, there," he said, smiling. "It's a cold one today. Do you have a warmer jacket?"

"Yes—it's on the coatrack behind you."

He turned around. "The dark blue one?"

"Yes. Thank you."

He lifted it off its hook and held it out so that she could slip her arms through its sleeves.

"That's a different one than what you had at Pearl."

She was surprised he'd noticed. As close as she'd been to her brothers, neither of them had made a mention of the time she chopped her long hair into a bob, let alone the color of something she was wearing.

"Back home, you have to have several, depending on the severity of the weather."

"Matches your eyes," he murmured. She pressed her lips together to keep from grinning.

"I'll have her back by suppertime," Erik promised Helga as she held the door open for them.

"It's none of my business," she answered. "You know your aunt doesn't stand on ceremony."

"I told Miss Hartley that I am a gentleman and I plan to live up to that."

"I've known you for many years, Bernard," she smiled. "I could tell her a thing or two."

Helga's smile was all the giveaway Mabel needed to know that she was teasing him. Usually, her mouth was set in such a way that would have made the Mona Lisa seem positively exuberant.

Erik had that effect on people.

As they walked toward the immense driveway, Mabel took the keys from her pocket and handed them to Erik.

"How did you like driving it?" he asked.

"I loved it," she grinned. The car itself was a beauty, and she could imagine the exhilaration of driving it faster down a deserted road. Wind in her hair on a warm day. What she did not tell him is that she almost pulled over blocks away from Mrs. Koehler's house because of the tears that welled up in her eyes when she imagined how much her older brother would have enjoyed taking it for a spin.

"It's my one extravagance. I live in a small apartment nearby. One room for living and sleeping. And I have enough clothes to get me through the week before laundering them again. But my little Ford—I couldn't resist."

"Why don't you live with your aunt? It seems that so many others do at different times."

They'd arrived at the car, but he put the keys into his coat pocket and gently pulled her by the elbow toward the gate. "We're walking to where we're going."

The crunch of the gravel underneath Mabel's boots sounded like popcorn cooking in a kettle, reminding her that she'd not had lunch.

"I used to live with Auntie Emma," he continued. "When I first moved here. But, " he looked away, toward a grove of trees, "that had its difficulties."

Erik didn't elaborate and Mabel wondered if it had anything to do with Ernestina. Had she lived in the mansion at one time, too? But she couldn't bring it up. It might still be the kind of memory that stung. And he would know that she and Emma had been talking about him.

"Anyway, I'm still close. I walk to the brewery, as long as the weather is not scorching."

He turned back to look at Mabel and opened the wide iron gate to let her through.

"If I owned your beautiful Ford," she answered, "I would drive it everywhere. Even the few blocks to work."

"As soon as the war is over, I will. But gas rationing makes short drives an impossible luxury. Unless there's a pretty girl to take with you."

Had she looked into his eyes, she would have been lost. No one had ever said that kind of thing to her; at least not with such sincerity.

They passed the gate, and walked the route past the synagogue that had taken her to San Pedro Park last week.

"I hope this isn't an inconsiderate question, but why were you not drafted like other men your age?"

As happy as she was to be here in this moment with him, it hardly seemed fair when so many young men in their generation were oceans away. And he didn't seem like the type to have run away from an obligation.

A dark look came over his eyes and he stopped walking.

"I tried. But they're suspicious of native Germans. Afraid they might be spies. I guess I can understand that. I applied for citizenship a few years ago and Auntie Emma was all set to sponsor me like she has for so many others. But then the war broke out and there was a moratorium on granting it to Germans, Italians, and Japanese."

So, he *was* foreign-born. She was glad she didn't have to ask. One didn't know when rudeness might take over curiosity.

"Mrs. Koehler told me that a friend of Ernestina planned to join the German army."

His jaw tightened. "That man is a traitor to a country that has shown him nothing but generosity and Ernestine should have had better sense than to cavort with his kind."

He turned toward her and his voice softened. The shadow of the synagogue's red dome was cast diagonally across his face, which might have been comical were their conversation not so grave. And so timely, given the faith of the building they stood before.

"It's an odd position to be in," he continued. "No longer loyal to a homeland that has been taken over by a tyrant. And not fully embraced by a country I long to become a part of. No matter how hard I've worked to eradicate my accent, a stray word comes out now and then that sounds foreign and someone will invariably look on me with suspicion. I used to volunteer at the USO canteen on Commerce Street, but it was clear that they were uncomfortable with my presence."

Mired as she'd been the past few months in her own series of heartbreaks, she'd never considered how the war had affected those besides the families of the ones serving. Or the families of the lost. She'd heard of internment camps and other injustices, but grief had a way of blinding one to all but the identical grief in another, rather than seeing all the shades of it. For too short a time, being engaged to Artie had lifted her from all of that, only to have his betrayal send her back to its grip.

Until the newspaper ad that Mrs. Koehler had placed. A rope in the deep well she'd sunk into.

"I'm sorry," she said, words that felt as insignificant as the breath with which they were spoken. But it was through sharing what bruises the war had left on all of them, and was leaving every day with each new headline, that they could triumph over it. And survive.

Erik took her hand in his, glove to glove, interlacing their fingers. She turned toward him, no longer able to dismiss the pull she felt. His blue eyes met her own with a gentleness that softened every safeguard she'd built for herself. It was all she could do not to cry.

"You have nothing to be sorry for, dear Mabel," he whispered. "You've given me the gift of your friendship, new as it is, without prejudice."

He turned and continued walking toward the park, but he did not pull his hand away. Nor did she want him to. Talking like this filled her with the first traces of peace she'd felt in a long time.

Crossing San Pedro Avenue, they continued on Ashby, away from the empty pool of their first meeting. The day was cold and warm breath crystallized at its touch, so they walked the rest of the short way in silence.

They walked on toward the theater and approached by the front, where the walls were made of smooth stones. A pointed roof and two Doric columns graced the front. Nods to the theater tradition that meant so much in the Greek world. She was glad to finally see it up close.

Erik unlocked the large wooden door at the front, the metal key making a deep groaning sound as the latch turned. It was sheltered from the elements by the roof covering, surely meant to provide welcome shade from the blazing summer sun she'd heard so much about. In this winter, however, it only served to make the landing colder, and Mabel shivered.

Darkness awaited them inside and Erik stepped in first. He ran his hand along an interior wall and some lights came on, illuminating the front part of what appeared to be a hallway that extended horizontally to either side. At the far left was a concession stand where Mabel could imagine enjoying popcorn and sodas before seeing a show.

Erik reached out for her hand again and she took it, the action feeling more natural with each successive time. He led her toward another set of double doors.

"I can't wait to show this to you," he said.

Like before, these opened into darkness, but this time when he switched on the lights, she saw the theater itself.

Its name, San Antonio Little Theater, was appropriate. Though she'd never been to see a show in Baltimore, she knew the Hippodrome on Eutaw Street to be renowned for its magnificence. She'd walked past it many times, under a bulb-lit marquee and seen throngs of tuxedoed and sequined patrons passing their tickets to the box office attendants. In comparison, The Little Theater seemed to hold about three hundred people and had no adornments to speak of.

But Erik looked very excited to be here.

"Come this way," he said with an enthusiastic smile.

He led her to the front row. The chairs on the end were labeled in brass. He pulled down a red velvet seat for her to sit on.

"Stay right there and close your eyes."

Mabel could hear him leap onto the stage and listened as some kind of equipment shuffled across. She was tempted to peek, but didn't want to spoil his surprise.

When the sounds abated, she heard the distinct click of lights turn on, which echoed through the empty space.

She felt Erik pull down the seat next to her.

"Ok. Now open."

What had been a blank void was now a small cabin on the plains. A painted canvas spanned the back of the stage, depicting fields of corn six feet high with a blue, cloudless sky atop it. Sunlight was a mere suggestion, with the blue fading to near-white at the top.

The cabin had a front porch with a white rocking chair and red and white gingham curtains in the windows. To the left, a cutout of a horse was attached to a carriage with a fringed top. The horse was recognizable by shape only: it had no mane, no eyes, no hooves.

It was as if Mabel had been planted in another time and place entirely.

"What do you think?"

She turned toward Erik, awed by what she was seeing.

"Did you do all of this?"

He smiled. "Not all of it. I designed it. And oversaw it. And I'm particularly proud of acquiring the carriage, which was not as easy to find as one might think. But there are several people who bring it all to life."

He shifted on the chair, tucking one leg under the other. "You see. It's not the biggest theater. It's not the most impressive one. But when you bring people together with a similar vision, something beautiful comes from it."

It was a sentiment aimed at the humble space, but one that could be spoken in a number of settings. Mabel wished she'd adopted that philosophy sooner. She could have been volunteering all this time with the USO, sharing that similar vision of support for the troops; but instead, she'd survived tragedy the only way she knew how: working many hours in a job untouched by war so as not to be reminded of all she'd lost. Meanwhile, Ginger and other friends worked in munitions factories and other endeavors that aided the war effort, putting its reality in front of them every day.

But faced with Erik's enthusiasm, and the very *wonderfulness* of him, she saw a different path. One that promised that even if she was late to arrive at it, she could still find a way to do some good.

"Erik, there are no words. This is marvelous work."

He smiled even wider and his eyes shone. Maybe it was the effect of the stage lights, but she thought not. "I'm so glad you like it. It's not finished. You can see that the horse still needs to be painted. In fact, that's why I brought you here today. I thought you might like to help with it."

"I would love to!" Buck always had an artistic heart. He'd painted a watercolor once of Oriole Park and they'd hung it over the fireplace of their bungalow. It was one of the items that Mabel had left in storage, too afraid that it could get damaged in her move to Texas. But wherever she settled someday, she would go back for it and for the other items stored underneath Mrs. Molling's staircase. She wanted to keep sentimental things that conjured the sweetness of their memories, not their sorrows.

Erik stood and bounded up the stairs to the left, looking back to see if she'd followed. She was right behind him, buoyed by the idea of the project ahead of them.

Up close, the set had less luster than it did when it could be viewed in its entirety from the velvet seats. But this view held its own kind of magic: looking back to the empty theater, she could imagine the people who would sit in those seats, setting aside their own worries for a couple of hours to lose themselves in the story being played out.

"Where do we start?" Mabel asked.

"I'm going to take this guy off the hinges of the carriage and we'll lay him on the tarp."

Mabel took off her coat and laid it on the edge of the stage. She rolled the sleeves of her sweater up to her elbows. When she turned around, Erik had already detached the horse. He pulled a dark wooden box from the carriage and set it on the floor.

"Do you want an apron?" he asked.

"Are you going to wear one?"

He looked down. "Nah, I'm not wearing anything I can't spill on a bit. But you—you're a vision. I wouldn't want you to spoil your clothes."

It was a considerate offer. She couldn't afford to ruin a perfectly functional outfit when she had so few as it was.

"Thank you. I'll do that."

"Good idea." He rummaged through the boxes and pulled some out. "You can have your pick. There's this beauty. " He held up a green and blue plaid one with red paint splatters that would look like blood if you didn't know it was paint. "And you can't go wrong with this." The second was a pale pink with layers and layers of lace around the edges, as if someone had used it for sewing practice.

"Oh, goodness," Mabel laughed. "They almost make me want to take my chances without them."

"Mabel, Mabel," he said, clutching his heart. "You wound me. I lay these gifts at your feet and you reject them."

She took them from his hands and held them up. "Well, I'm going to let you pick, then, since you're the one who will have to look at me in it. I can either look like the victim of a murder or an old woman's tablecloth."

He scratched his chin and considered it. Looking back and forth, he said, "I'm going to go with the plaid one. If you wear the pink, I think I'm going to laugh the whole time and we'll never get any work done."

"Plaid it is." She reached behind to tie it at her neck. Erik leaned over and wrapped his hands around her hair, holding it up to make her task easier. She finished it in a double knot, but he didn't let go.

He looked into her eyes as she moved her arms down to tie the other strings behind her waist. Only then did he release her hair, running his hands slowly down the long, straight strands that she hadn't bothered to put in pin curlers last night. Mabel held her breath and tried to still her jitters. Erik's closeness, the way he looked at her, the aloneness of being in this enchanted place with him, overwhelmed her.

"We should get to work," he said in a whisper that was barely audible. But he didn't make a move to step back.

"We should." She could see small flecks of brown in his ocean blue eyes, giving them a sense of depth.

A light bulb flickered overhead and they both looked up. It was better, at least, than an interruption from Ernestina would have been. But it reminded them of their surroundings and the task they were there for.

"Work," he said again. This time, he pulled back. He sat down on the tarp and gestured for her to join him.

She sat down, arranging her skirt over her knees, her heart racing at how near he'd been. They danced around their feelings, each with their wounds at the hands of their fathers and of their former loves. Hesitant to love again, yet aching for one who would understand the other's soul.

Erik picked up a brush and opened a can of paint. He took a deep breath and spoke of the task at hand. "I thought I'd make this guy brown to contrast with the white carriage, but if you think that's too boring, feel free to speak up. We're a democracy here at the theater."

Mabel thought back to pictures of horses she'd seen and considered what might look best when the bright lights above were shining on it. "I like the brown," she conceded. "But I wonder if it will contrast too much with the white spotlights. When they're focused here, for example," she pointed to the length of its body. "I can imagine that we'd see two circles and that could be distracting."

Erik clapped his hands slowly. "Spoken like you've been a set designer all your life," he said. "What do you suggest?"

Mabel grinned. Mama had always thought her daughter had an eye for art, but Buck was older and there was only enough money for one of them to take classes after school. Her parents promised that she would get her turn when she was fourteen. But after Mama's death, Mabel had taken on her role of looking after the men in the family. Soon she'd buried the interest so deep that she'd forgotten about it. Until now.

"I've seen pictures of American Quarter horses that are more of a golden-brown color. With white manes and tales. And look—your backdrop has lots of blues and greens. I think he would stand out nicely against those."

"I wonder if they had American Quarter horses on the plains of Oklahoma in the last century," he said.

"It doesn't have to be that breed precisely. It was just one that came to mind."

Erik began to mix some white paint with the brown, and as he stirred, a perfect shade began to emerge.

"Do you really think someone in the audience would comment if the breed was wrong for the time and place?"

He nodded. "Oh, Mabel. You surely have enough manners that you would attend a performance and enjoy the effort and if you noticed an inaccuracy, you would keep it to yourself."

"Has that ever happened to you?"

"A few times. The manager once passed on a letter to me from a horticulturist who'd seen us do *Show Boat* and claimed that the kind of grass we painted on the backdrop never grew on the shores of the Mississippi River."

"Wow! That *is* splitting hairs."

"The funny thing," he smiled, "is that I wasn't aiming for any particular variety of grass. I was just painting thin green strokes. If it depicted anything specific, it was purely accidental."

Mabel hoped she'd never be like that when she was older.

Though it occurred to her that if she'd continued to live in Balti-more and dwell on all that was unfortunate, it would have become a habit. Given a few more decades, she could well be one who would be so ensconced in her own bitterness that something so small could prompt her to complain.

Mrs. Koehler and her nephew had thrown life preservers to her and they didn't even know it.

Erik handed her a small can and a large brush. "Here is the cream color. Shall we put you in charge of the tail, mane, and hooves?"

"That's probably best. I'm new at this." She took the pieces and began to work on the tip of the tail.

They worked in silence at first. As she covered the tail with the paint, she began to see how adding some dimension might make it seem more realistic. She rummaged through the box for a thin paintbrush and dipped it into the darker brown can. She began at the top of the tail and gently painted strokes down it, blending the streaks with the still-wet lighter color. When she was finished, she stood up to look at it with a little more distance.

To her delight, it had given the exact effect she'd wanted. She glanced over at Erik, surprised at her eagerness for his approval, but he was facing away from her, hovering over the neck of the horse. He'd mixed the colors until they were the perfect shade of golden brown, and already it looked terrific.

Erik must have felt her eyes on him. He stopped and turned toward her, causing more than a little embarrassment that he'd caught her staring. "Will you come to one of the shows in a couple of weeks? I can't describe the feeling you get when you watch all of your work come together."

She'd been thinking the very thing. "I can sit in the audience and enjoy the beauty of my horse tail."

"Oh, there is much more to do than that if you're game. We still have enough work that you could pinpoint something in nearly every scene that would have your touch on it."

Her evenings were quite free, if that's when most of the work was done. Mrs. Koehler was always tired by midday and had missed several suppertimes this week, leaving Mabel to eat in the kitchen with Frieda. It would be an enjoyable diversion, especially with the outdoors so bleak. There was little else to do, save for exploration of Mrs. Koehler's book collection. But a quick glance had shown her penchant for old tomes. Like the ones in Mabel's bedroom, the house boasted many leather-bound volumes that looked beautiful on a shelf but held very little appeal to a reader beyond its aesthetic.

"I'd like that, " she said. Satisfied with the tail, she scooted down the stage and began on the hooves. Erik returned to the neck, taking care with the details. He used black paint to add shadows, and even from here, Mabel could see that the result was that the horse had discernable muscles.

"What would you like to name him?" Erik asked, keeping his eyes on his work.

"The horse?"

"Yeah. He doesn't have a name in the script. But you could name him. It would be our secret."

The idea flushed Mabel with a sense of belonging, of having something she was connected to. Even something so silly as a wooden horse could make her feel like she was tied to this place.

But no matter how much it fulfilled her, she would never let go of what kept her tethered to the past.

"Could we name him Buck?"

> With her attorney, Miss Burgemeister appeared immediately in the District Court and surrendered. She was weeping, but when the warrant of arrest was read by the Sheriff she quickly regained control of herself.
>
> *St. Louis Post-Dispatch — St. Louis, Missouri October 10, 1917*

# CHAPTER NINETEEN

EVER SINCE MEETING HIM at the empty pool, Mabel had imagined what it would be like to kiss Erik. She lay on her pillow imagining the feeling of his lips on hers only to recall the memory of Artie doing the same. Souring the dream of it.

When they'd been so close back at the brewery, Ernestina's interruption came as both welcome and unwelcome. But at the theater, with no threat of interruptions, she found her resistance losing ground to the desire to be loved and cherished. She'd been on her own too long. Not only in a romantic sense, but from nearly all human connection. Not even realizing how much she missed it until the possibility of it arose.

Erik held back, even as Mabel was certain of the magnet-like pull between them. She was convinced that he felt it, too. There was a look in his eyes. A linger in his touch as he'd helped her back into her coat after they put away the paints and prepared to leave.

She knew that he had his own hurts and maybe he was wise enough to be cautious, knowing that two wounded people should-n't take such risks. His strength said much for his character. But despite her hopes that the war would even out the disparities between men and women, she still longed for the man to make those kinds of overtures.

If Erik wanted to kiss her, she was ready to let him. But she would not be the first one to do so.

Making good on his promise to Helga, he got Mabel back to the Koehler mansion before supper, but declined the house-keeper's invitation to stay and eat. He said he had to return to check on the new temperature controls at Pearl.

Helga walked away from the front door before Mabel stepped in, a move that seemed to be intentional in its discretion. Perhaps she was more of an ally than she let on.

Mabel and Erik remained on the porch, its hearty marble arches casting misshapen shadows across the floor as the sun descended in the west. They'd been alone for hours in the theater, but this moment had all the trappings of a man walking a woman home after an evening out. She felt far more nervous here.

Then Mabel saw a curtain in the window next to them rustle and a little girl's face peeked out. One of the young cousins: Lotte, if she recalled correctly. Helga appeared, her reflection distorted by the panes, as she pulled the child away.

Mabel could tell that Erik had noticed, too. He smiled and looked down at his feet.

"Well, I need to get back," he said. "You have a good night."

"You, too."

He rocked back on his heels and she could hear the flutter in his voice. That told her as much as a kiss might have.

"See you soon?" he asked.

"I'd love that."

"Tomorrow?"

"Yes." It came out in a whisper.

She would never have guessed that so much could be con-veyed in so brief an exchange. But, as she'd learned from taking Mrs. Koehler's dictation, life had so many more shades than what could be expressed in mere words.

"Where did we leave off?" asked Mrs. Koehler, when they met in the parlor the next morning. The sun had returned and sent its rays through the prism glass, casting tiny rainbows on Mabel's notebook.

"You were returning home from Germany with the recipe and the yeast for Pearl."

"Ah, yes. Our new beginning. Life is full of beginnings, isn't it? They offer so much hope—at the start. Then comes the tarnish. But the beginnings are nice while they last."

*1898*

*I was so proud of my husband. With his acquisition of the Pearl recipe and my involvement with the German community in town, the brewery quickly grew to producing thirty thousand barrels a year. It became such a popular brew that all the other, official names of the company were forgotten: City Brewery, San Antonio Brewing Association. It was soon known just as "Pearl," fitting for something that became such a treasure to San Antonio. A pearl of great price.*

*That particular milestone happened much more quickly than any of us anticipated, and much more slowly than Otto wanted. I made him an apple cake in celebration, though our good cheer was dampened when my monthly blood flow occurred later that evening.*

*Otto Koehler could achieve anything he set out to do, but he could not give us a child.*

*To be fair, it might have been my own defect, but we didn't bicker over who was to blame. In typical Otto form, he threw himself into work and denied any disappointment on our childlessness. And all too quickly, I lost my husband to it again.*

*It was difficult to ignore the ache I felt to be a mother.*

*I felt another fissure grow between us and I longed for us to be united. We were such excellent partners when we didn't shut each other out or wallow independently. But we were each too stubborn to lean on the other in this sorrow.*

*Instead of children, flesh and blood, Otto drank his beer and mulled* over other investments. Railroads and mining ventures. I think he imagined himself to be the next Cornelius Vanderbilt. He seemed to grow bored by the process of beer making and began to spread himself into so many activities that he rarely saw sunshine. His skin again took on that pallor that concerned me, but nothing would entice him to slow down his maniacal pace.

I wasn't his yeast. I wasn't his lucky charm.

I wasn't his anything.

Otto next sought to have Pearl earn the XXX rating, a designation going back to medieval times and coveted among brewers. When European royalty traveled in the countryside, they would send a courier ahead to sample the local beers. If the taste was adequate, they marked the door with an X. A double XX would indicate that it was very good, and a XXX that it was exceptional. The designation stuck all these centuries later and it was Otto's newest obsession.

I would have thought he'd find some peace having finally reached this pinnacle. Instead, he had the idea to expand our tiny fortune into real estate.

I could hardly argue with him where the brewery was concerned. As the brand grew and the coffers swelled, he oversaw the expansion of the facilities. Bricks and iron to protect against fire, and the finest brewery architect in the country: August Martizen out of Chicago. We were not equipped to produce enough beer to fill half of it, but Otto was one to think ahead to the future. He was certain that someday Pearl would be big enough to need all the empty space he was enclosing. He even bought acres and acres of surrounding land with designs to grow beyond anyone's imagination.

The newspapers called him crazy.

I intercepted worried letters from investors, banks and private parties who'd financed Pearl now that it was seeing success. But they were upset about the rapidity of his expansion. I answered their concerns, withholding my own. My husband was many things, but he was not a fool when it came to business and he did not need voices of dissention to distract him. Not if it was going to work.

And he was right. Production increased to an astounding sixty thousand barrels a year in a short time with the ability to be able to store ten thousand more.

The newspapers called him a genius.

It only fed his lust for more.

Left alone again, I resorted to other means of getting my husband's attention, the only one that had, even for a short duration, brought him back to me. It wasn't for my sake alone that he needed to slow down. I was concerned for his health. His breaths were shallow at the slightest exertion and his eyes sagged where once they'd been bright.

I made him promise to come home early enough one evening so that I could make dinner for us, and to my surprise, he agreed. I visited a market and learned how to use lime juice and goat cheese and tomatoes to make a sauce to pour over beef, a nod to our adopted town. I slipped raspberries into white wine for a change from the beer.

Candles were lit, one in front of each of our chairs, their flickering glow landing on his empty seat as one hour and then two ticked beyond the appointed time.

At nearly three hours since the plates had been set, the key turned in the lock and a bedraggled Otto slumped in, dropping his coat to the floor. I looked down at our meal, long since grown cold even as I was determined not to.

I pursed my lips and held back the flow of angry words that wanted to escape. Challenging Otto only served to become a war of wills. One that I was quite sure of stalemating, for I could be as formidable as he if I cared to.

But if I wanted my husband to be pliant, to be restful, it called for a soft, conciliatory approach.

I rose from my chair and pulled him into my arms, forcing platitudes that I only half-meant.

"Oh, darling. You must have had such a long day."

He rubbed his eyes with fisted hands, unaware of my touch.

"The shipment of labels for the bottles came in. Two Xs. Two. Not three. It will be a week before they can send new ones and I'm not shipping

out our beer with an inferior designation."

"Isn't that something for Daniel to look after?" I asked, referencing the man who oversaw such things. "Is it so utterly necessary for you to be there to manage every little detail?"

He looked up at me at last, resentment poisoning his glance. "Yes, it's necessary. What if he hadn't caught the mistake? It would be telegraphing to the world that our beer is substandard and I'll not have that."

I knew Daniel to be excellent in his attention to the minutia of the brewery and had long been frustrated that Otto couldn't relinquish control to people who'd been extensively interviewed for their competency. Did he expect that it should all be on his shoulders? Or that mistakes never happened?

I didn't pursue the long-worn conversation. At least not with that tactic. If I had any hope of bringing my husband around to my thinking, I would need other measures.

And I'd prepared for that very thing. After settling him into a chair in front of the fireplace and bringing him a beer, I slipped into our bedroom and pulled a nightgown from my bureau. It was an indulgence and I was grateful that Otto knew nothing about women's garments or else he would be appalled at what I'd spent on something that he'd only see as serving a limited function. But we were making an enviable salary now and it was a worthy investment if it meant saving our marriage and bringing some sense of normalcy to Otto's life.

The peignoir was magnificent. Made of white bridal lace from France with silk chiffon so delicate and thin that it rendered the whole thing unnecessary, at least if modesty had been the aim. But it was the opposite of my aim. I needed to remind my husband of what we once had.

I shivered; the evening was cold and I was wearing so little. I pulled a magazine from under my pillow, a gift from Mrs. Terroba. It was a Victorian piece full of poems and illustrations that were, let's just say, far from what we imagine of the Victorians. I didn't even know if such things were legal, but she'd acquired it and given it to me much in the same vein as she'd taught me of the aphrodisiac natures of chocolate and chili. Though I hadn't worked for her in a year since her daughter had come from Mon-

terrey to live with her, we saw each other socially and she continued to share secrets that made me blush.

This was no different. I flipped through its pages—already quite familiar to me—and pressed it against my beating heart. Normally, I wore long flannel to bed and pulled my hair up into the tight bun befitting of a married woman. Would releasing my curls from their pins and wearing something that was almost nothing pique Otto's interest? Or disgust him?

The illustrations in the magazine were that of a fallen woman. Not of a wife.

But Mrs. Terroba assured me that it was the perfect combination: a wife who did more than lie on her back would keep her husband's attentions better than one who was too prudish to be inventive with him.

I hoped she was right.

She was right.

Otto would have had to be either ill or made of metal to have ignored so lavish an offering on my part, and I can say summarily that he was neither. Once again, he came home to me in the evenings and rekindled an enthusiasm for our partnership, both in the boardroom, and the bedroom.

A woman of today might scorn the notion of using these wiles to achieve what she wants, but there was so little on the side of women at the time that we had to make use of whatever we could—even the power of our own bodies—as we quietly strove to make advances where we could.

And so I did, and I felt no shame for it. He was my husband, after all. And it was for his own good, or so I hoped.

Otto's renewed vigor quickly inspired him to turn his sights toward building a home for us, focusing his excessive energies, at least, on something other than becoming the next captain of industry. I argued that a little cottage on Dolorosa or Zarzamora would provide more than enough room for our needs. After all, we had no children to fill it. But in true Otto form, he barged on ahead designing the very home we sit in now.

He believed he would not be respected in the community until we had a house befitting our newly minted status, and he told me that every businessman worth his salt either built his own mansion or renovated an important historic one. I quite liked the stately houses south of us in King

William and suggested as much, but Otto wanted to be close to Pearl, which limited our ability to move into something that already existed.

It was a tremendous endeavor, much of which fell on my shoulders. Otto was a man of big plans. I was the woman who made them happen. When he said he wanted a study with a turret, I sat with the architects and planned out every curve. When he said that we should have a large porch made of Texan stone, I did the research to source it from a quarry outside of Austin. Some of his contributions were odd, such as the cross on our door or the bare-chested carving on the fireplace, but I humored him with these and did not ask questions.

In the end, it cost us a hundred thirty-three thousand dollars to build, as expensive a home as I was aware of in San Antonio.

I thought that would be the end of it. The pinnacle. We would have Pearl. We would have the house. And we would have each other.

I should have known better.

Entrusting the house I didn't want to my care, he was now free to return to even more new pursuits: the Continental Mining Company and the Monarch Mining Company. The latter was in Idaho. You can only imagine the journey to get all the way up there from here and my nights were once again cold and alone. Now, in a house in which my lone voice echoed.

And that wasn't the end of it. He invested in the American Lignite and Briquette Company of Texas.

Coal.

At least his railroad investments made some kind of sense. He cut his teeth sinking money into Panuco Mountain and Monclova Railroad in Texas. And when he was satisfied that he'd mastered that industry, he came full circle to helping establish the Texas Transportation Company. And I say full circle because it was Otto's idea to have the San Antonio Brewing Association lay a track from Pearl to Sunset Station because horse drawn carriages were no longer sufficient to transport the amount of beer we were brewing. New supplies came in by railroad.

Word spread that Otto was unstoppable in his quest to always be growing. Even dear Adolphus wrote and pled with him to slow down.

*Though, I must say, tensions were still at a peak after Otto left them high and dry at Lone Star. I believe Adolphus wrote more out of concern for me than he did for my husband. I've committed his note to memory, for it addressed what I could not seem to say:*

"You take good care of the brewery and promote its interest to the fullest extent; this is a far better investment than dabbling in mines and all kinds of outside affairs which give nothing but worry and bring losses. Now you have no children and there is no early reason why you should burden yourself with all these responsibilities and cares; you ought to live like a king and enjoy life."

*Still, he was unstoppable. Seeing an opportunity to sell XXX Pearl in an even more lucrative way, he built saloons throughout San Antonio. That way he made money on the wholesale and the retail. One still remains. The Scholz Palm Garden downtown.*

*The only time I outwardly doubted Otto was when he insisted on buying the defunct Hot Wells Resort and Sanitarium. It had burned down twice and sent a previous owner into bankruptcy and I was certain that there was some kind of curse cast upon it. Even though I didn't believe in such things.*

*I pled with him not to purchase it, but he went ahead against my warnings.*

*And I believe I can trace every subsequent misfortune that befell us to that moment.*

OCTOBER **9**, Miss Burgemeister walked into the Thirty-Seventh District Courtroom and surrendered to District Attorney D.A. McAskill. She was re-arrested by Sheriff John W. Tobin. Her attorneys, Ex-Governor Tom M. Campbell, C.M. Chambers, and Dave Watson, immediately filed application for release on a write of habeas corpus. Judge Anderson declined to hear the application immediately, by agreement, the hearing was set for October 19. Miss Burgemeister was released, pending hearing, on a bond of $25,000.

*Pratt Daily Tribune – Pratt, Kansas*
*January 14, 1918*

# CHAPTER TWENTY

TO MABEL'S SURPRISE, Mrs. Koehler took a tissue from a bag attached to her wheelchair and dabbed it at her eyes. Though she'd known her for only a couple of weeks, she'd never seen the old woman be anything less than stoic.

Mabel shifted in her chair. Today she was on the Queen Anne and its back and seat were particularly uncomfortable. As if all the furniture in the room had been designed for the purpose of keeping visits to short intervals.

Mrs. Koehler crumpled the tissue in her hand and leaned over to place it back in the bag. But she leaned too far. Before Mabel could catch her, the old woman had fallen to the floor, clutching her chest. She hit her head on the wheel's metal casing and a gash cut across her head. Drops of blood began to spill onto the white carpet.

"Helga!" Mabel screamed for the housekeeper, then rushed to the floor. She lifted her up, noting that she weighed considerably less than Mabel would have thought.

She heard Helga's steps echo off the grand staircase and Frieda, too, rushed in from the kitchen. Together, they picked Mrs. Koehler up and laid her on the sofa. Her breathing was shallow and labored, but at least it was present.

"I'll call for a *krankenwagen*," said Frieda, turning back toward the foyer.

"No." Helga's German accent was forceful even in the small word. "I'll drive her to Green Memorial. I can get her there faster. Frieda, help me get her into the car and then stay with the house. Someone will need to be here to receive news. Miss Hartley, call Mr. Garrels at the brewery. He'll want to come be with her."

"I will."

Mabel left the parlor and hurried over to the study, where she knew the telephone to be. She'd never used one outside of Mr. Oliver's office, and rarely then. She picked up the black receiver, only to hear other voices on the line.

"Then, Iris told Melba that Irving wasn't going to make it back in time for Christmas after all, so it was a gas when he showed up and surprised her."

"Excuse me," Mabel cut in. Blasted party lines. The war had slowed the progress of such luxuries on the home front even for those with money, but they'd been told that an independent one would be installed any day.

"Excuse me," Mabel said with more urgency.

"What is it?" an irritated voice said on the other line.

"I need to use the telephone."

"Honey, I've been trying for two weeks to get a call through to my sister in Denver and you're costing me precious money. Hang up."

"But it's an emergency."

"That's what all you young kids say when you want to cut in. Hang up now or I'll report you to the phone company."

Mabel replaced the receiver. Helga and Frieda seemed to be managing Mrs. Koehler well enough, so without another option, she ran out the front door and headed toward Pearl.

The smokestacks of the brewery rose above the myriad of one-story homes and businesses and she had the passing thought that she should follow Mrs. Koehler's example and get to know the community by taking walks, street by street. She kept running now, though, filling her lungs with the cold air and breathing out its steam. Her hair came loose in the bobby pins she'd set in them and her stockings began to bunch around her ankles. But she didn't stop to fix anything. It didn't matter what she looked like when she saw Erik. It only mattered that she brought the news of his aunt.

As she approached Pearl, she could see that it was surrounded by an iron gate that was closed. She hadn't noticed it a few days ago, but then again, her head had been so filled with the notion of driving with Erik in that car, she hadn't paid attention to details.

There was no one about. She walked along its perimeter, hoping there might be a loose bar or some place wide enough that she could slip through, but it was in immaculate condition.

She ran back around to the gate, catching her blouse more than once on low-hanging branches. This time, she saw a couple of men walk out of the bottling building, pushing a cart full of heavy-looking boxes.

"Hello!" she shouted. They waved and began to walk on.

"I need your help," she pled. This time, they stopped, settled the cart and walked over.

"What can we help with, miss?" said that taller one with the thick beard.

"I need to get a message to Mr. Garrels right away."

"And who should we say is asking for him?"

"My name is Mabel. But that doesn't matter. Tell him that his Aunt Emma collapsed and is heading to the hospital."

The shorter one stepped forward and his face took on the appropriate alarm. "Mrs. Koehler? What happened?"

"I don't know. Helga is taking her to the hospital now. I tried to call, but I couldn't get through. I need to talk to Mr. Garrels. Now."

The men looked at each other, as if questioning whether it was wise to let this wild-looking woman onto the grounds. But at last, the tall one walked over to the gate and unlocked it.

"I think he's over in that office," he said, pointing to the gold-bricked one she'd seen before. "I'll walk over with you."

She felt like she could keep running, but slowed to his pace. He opened the door, and the warmth of the room welcomed her like a blast of heat, in contrast to what the weather was like outside. She half-feared that Ernestina would come out from the back rooms, looking elegant against her own disheveled state, but that wasn't what was important right now.

A receptionist sat at a typewriter. Her brass nameplate said *Miss. Sullivan.* An irony since that's what Mr. Oliver had called Mabel and every other secretary in the business. Mabel might have laughed otherwise, but was still too concerned about Mrs. Koehler to give more thought to it than that.

The man spoke, the pitch of his voice higher than what his size might have suggested.

"We need to talk to Mr. Garrels."

The receptionist looked up, hands on keys. "I believe he's on the telephone right now."

Mabel felt exasperated. No one seemed to be treating this with the urgency it deserved.

"Please. Tell Mr. Garrels that Mabel is here. There is an emergency with his aunt and I need to speak with him."

The woman looked her over, frowning, and at last, got up and walked through a swinging door.

The seconds plodded by, but the minute hand on the clock above the door had barely moved when Erik came rushing out ahead of the woman.

"Mabel! What happened?"

She caught him up with what little she knew.

"Helga's taking her to a place called Green Memorial," she finished.

"Let's go then." He took his coat from the hat rack and put it on. Only then did Mabel stop to realize how cold she was. She'd left her own jacket back at the Koehler Mansion, having given no thought to anything but getting here as quickly as she could. Instinctively, she wrapped her arms around herself and headed toward the door.

"Mabel, stop," he said. When she turned around, he'd taken off his coat and was already holding it out for her.

"But you'll need that," she protested.

"Nonsense. Take this. I can get another one."

He helped her into it and hurried back through the swinging door. He came out wearing a giant covering of some sort. Several sizes too big for him, and made from a rubbery-looking material. The Pearl logo was embroidered onto the right side of the chest and Mabel supposed it must be one of the jackets that workers wore in the coldest part of the brewery. Despite his height, he looked like some kind of pint-sized fisherman in it.

They headed out the door and over to the larger building.

"Lucky for us, I drove today" he said. "I have several appointments this afternoon around town, so I took the Ford to work. I'll have to cancel those, of course, but at least it came in handy."

"I can head back to the house now," she answered. "I only came to tell you. Your aunt will surely want you there."

"Come with me. If you want to, of course. It's not far."

"But shouldn't that just be for family?"

He opened her car door and continued speaking as he came around and slipped into his own seat. He started the ignition.

"Auntie Emma has always had a liberal definition of what family is. I have it on good authority that she received several hundred letters in response to her advertisement and *you*, Mabel Hartley, are the one she picked. So there is something about you that charmed her from the start. And in her book, that is family. What do you say?"

Mabel was relieved. She was desperate to know how Mrs. Koehler was doing. "I'll go with you."

It took only ten minutes to get to Green Memorial, and in

that time, Mabel learned from Erik that Mrs. Koehler, indeed, had little time to live. Hearing it from someone else's lips made it seem more real, and she found herself already grieving at the possibility of not having more time to get to know her. To learn the full story she was here to memorialize.

"Auntie Emma's not one given to hyperbole," Erik said. "She's outlived each of her siblings by decades. They all died rather young and it's long been considered that the Bentzens did not have the best constitutions. The fact that she's been kicking for as long as she has is a testament to her own brand of tenacity. And if she could challenge God himself to make her immortal, she'd dare to do so. But what is it they say? That all that is certain is death and taxes?"

Mabel smiled, her first of the day. "That's what I've heard."

"Well, Emma Koehler has certainly taken advantage of every tax break available over the years. But she's not going to escape the other one. The official diagnosis is *old age*. But the doctors have been concerned with her increasing senility. Have you noticed it?"

Mabel recalled several times when Mrs. Koehler's story veered off the topic at hand or where she repeated things she'd said moments before.

"Here and there. But I assumed, like you said, that it's part of old age."

"Scary to watch, isn't it? We all want to live a long life, but when you see what that actually looks like, it's not so romantic."

"She does it as well as anyone I've ever known." Mabel had encountered few people who'd lived into their mid-eighties. "Though she tires quickly. What I thought would be long hours at this job rarely lasts beyond two or three before she's ready to lie down."

"Which is exactly why I thought you'd enjoy working on the set over at the Little Theater. Nothing to do at Auntie Emma's unless you want to read one of those old leather bricks about

Greek philosophy."

"I do love a good book," she said, "but I have to say that those are beyond me."

"Me, too. I prefer fiction. I started *The Labyrinthine Ways* by Graeme Greene last night."

She appreciated the distraction he was offering, and the book title was a relief. If he were attached to the kinds of books that the Koehler study held, she would have felt the sinking inferiority that she did around some of Robert's friends. Always going on about Roman emperors and Greek wars with the same enthusiasm as some boys gave to sporting events. With more money, he could have been a scholar at Georgetown or Oxford or some other illustrious place. Now they would never know what he might have become. But she wasn't ready to share that part of her life with Erik yet.

"I've seen *The Labyrinthine* at the bookstores, but I haven't read it yet."

"I'll give you my copy when I'm done. It's a perfect winter read. Takes place in Mexico, where you can pretend it's warmer than it is."

"Has your aunt read all those books they have?"

"I dare say not. Can't recall Auntie Emma reading much at all come to think of it. She's always been a workhorse. She bought volumes and volumes for Uncle Otto over the years, from what I understand. It's likely that he valued them for their prestige more than their content. She did mention once that he was a fan of Machiavelli's works, though."

Erik turned into the parking lot of a five-story building. It was made of sharp, ninety-degree angles and made with a similar gold-toned brick as some of the Pearl buildings.

"Here we are," he said. Mabel knew that he would come around to open her door, and while she appreciated the chivalry, she was quite capable of doing so herself and they might have few seconds to spare.

He didn't seem offended when she did so.

They walked in long strides toward the columned entrance and were told upon inquiring that Emma Koehler was on the fifth floor.

"No doubt Auntie Emma was given a posh room with a good view." Erik walked swiftly toward the bank of elevators.

Given her wealth, that would be no surprise. At one time, Mabel might have felt resentment toward special treatment when so many were suffering, but by all accounts, Mrs. Koehler had such a philanthropic heart that if an additional comfort were afforded her in this dire time, she could only say that it was well-deserved.

He pushed the button for floor five as they stepped in.

"If so, I hope she's in a condition to appreciate it."

"Yeah," he sighed. He'd been hurrying to get here ever since he'd burst through those swinging doors, but now Mabel saw his features melt into one of concern. "She donated twenty thousand dollars to the building fund for this place. It was a year after Uncle Otto died. She always believed that if he had gotten better medical attention, he might have survived the gunshot wounds."

"Do you think that's true?" What a horrible thought. That something *could* have been done. She thought of her father and dismissed it just as quickly.

"No. He died at the scene. She knows that. But in the case of any tragedy, one looks back and wonders what more they could have done to prevent it. Auntie Emma is no different. There's a lot of tenderness underneath that shell of hers."

Mabel was moved at the thought that a wife so betrayed would still have had the heart to save him if it were within her ability to do so.

The elevator dinged and they arrived. The thought struck Mabel that she'd not been in a hospital since she was eleven. Mama had been admitted after the cancer caused an especially bad night of pain. They'd lost her only a week after that, but she'd passed, at least, in her own bed as she'd wished. The memory upset Mabel's stomach and she had to grip a nearby railing to steady herself. All the things she'd felt as a child in the sterile halls of the hospital in Baltimore returned to her. Worry, grief, fear.

"Are you alright, Mabel? You look flushed." Erik wrapped an arm around her waist, likely to support her, as she'd already felt her legs buckling.

She could not faint. It was not about the cold or their pace, but she wasn't ready to talk about what it *was*, and certainly not here when they were here over concern about Emma.

"It's nothing," she assured him. "I'll be all right."

He let go of her, but stayed so close that his arm brushed hers. As if he was ready to catch her at any moment. The feeling passed, but she was relieved to know that Erik was there if she needed him.

"There's Helga," she pointed down the hall, saving them the hassle of asking for the location of Emma Koehler's room.

They walked to the end, a corner room, which was flooded with a light softened by the whiteness of the winter sky. One bed sat near the windows, and a doctor hovered over Mrs. Koehler. Her eyes were closed, and clear tubes ran from her nose into a machine on a nearby table.

A thin waffle-weave blanket lay on top of her and its faint movement indicated that they'd made it in time.

CHOKED BY KOEHLER
WHEN SHE FIRED TO
**PROTECT HERSELF**

Attorneys representing
Miss Emma Hedda Burge-
meister, German nurse,
charged with the murder
of Otto Koehler, wealthy
brewer, have announced
their intention of basing
their fight on 'self
defense.' They will claim
Miss Burgemeister was
being choked by Koehler
when she fired to protect
herself.

*The Daily News – Lebanon,
Pennsylvania January 14, 1918*

# CHAPTER TWENTY-ONE

"I DON'T KNOW what you have all been fussing about, especially when we have so much work to do."

Mrs. Koehler awoke on her third day in the hospital. The room smelled like a greenhouse, the entirety of the space filled with every kind of flower imaginable. Even in January. Their yellows, oranges, reds, and greens contrasted to the stark whiteness of the room and the sky outside its windows. Mabel couldn't imagine what they must have all cost, but Mrs. Koehler had no shortage of well-wishers. Illustrious names adorned the cards.

Adolphus Busch II and Family

Gus B. Mauerman, Mayor of San Antonio (Not to mention the mayors of surrounding towns like Alamo Heights, Pflugerville, Floresville, New Braunfels, Selma, and San Marcos. Even the mayor of St. Louis had sent pink lilies.)

Coke R. Stevenson, Governor of Texas

Forrest C. Donnell, Governor of Missouri

Mabel even recognized the names of some movie stars among the cards.

"Those roses there are from Cecil B. DeMille."

Mabel's ears perked up. He'd directed *Reap the Wild Wind* last year with John Wayne, a favorite of her father's. She'd taken him

# CAMILLE DI MAIO

to see it on a rare day of sobriety. Strange that so far away from home, there were still reminders.

"He's a friend of yours?" she asked, impressed.

"Oh, my, yes. Going back to the days when Hot Wells was open. He came out regularly, especially when he had to travel between New York and California. His father died of typhoid fever and it spurred an interest in natural means of health."

Mabel pulled a notebook from her purse. It was smaller than the one she'd been using to take notes on Mrs. Koehler's story, but would do in a pinch. She hadn't expected to be here for anything other than a visit, but Emma seemed determined to continue. The nurses had already come in for their hourly check on her blood pressure and now they were alone for the moment. Mrs. Koehler was propped up on pillows and looked like she wanted to talk.

"Hot Wells was one of Mr. Koehler's other businesses?" began Mabel.

This was where they had left off in their last conversation before Mrs. Koehler fell ill. But the old woman did not seem to remember having told her that, so Mabel found it to be a good segue to continue.

Mrs. Koehler sighed. "Yes. One of many. I opposed it at first, but I knew that Otto would carry on regardless, so I gave in. And, though it was a disaster in so many ways, I can't deny that it was magical."

*1900*

*Otto woke early on Christmas morning, nudging me to come open the presents under the tree. I'd been suffering from a head cold and would have greatly preferred to stay in bed. But he'd already opened the curtains in our little bedroom and I knew I'd never get back to sleep.*

*And, I was curious.*

*Despite my penchant for practicality, I often got swept up in Otto's excitement. It was impossible not to.*

188

"Come on," he insisted, pulling on my hands until I sat up.

I fumbled for my slippers and felt for my eyeglasses atop my bureau. He was two steps ahead of me as I followed him into the next room. Our Christmas tree was a meager one, bought on a rare Sunday ride to a farm in Helotes. It was late in the season, and the best ones had been chosen weeks before.

Under the tree were small packages, covered in brown paper and twine. I'd put some thought into the ones I'd bought, drawing holly wreaths on them and adding sprigs of pine to the bows. Otto's were haphazardly wrapped, but I was moved, at least, that he had done it all himself and not pawned off the job to an employee. I daresay he purchased the gifts, too. If he was going to work as hard as he did for his money, he also liked to manage how it was all spent.

The small boxes were, no doubt jewelry. I had a few simple pieces, but he liked to add to this collection.

"Success breeds success," he'd say. And I knew that his choices had less to do with my tastes than they did the impressions they gave around town and what they could resell for. Already he'd sold a sapphire bracelet he'd bought me once the death of its maker had raised its value.

I'd thought today, from his enthusiasm, that he might have purchased something for the house, which still sat unfurnished. A chair, an antique mirror perhaps. But he only handed me a thick envelope.

"Merry Christmas, dearest Emma," he said.

"What is this?" I turned it over in my hand, but there were no markings.

"You have to open it, you ninny."

I tore at the seal and pulled out a pile of papers with small print.

It was a deed.

HOT WELLS SANITARIUM

My hands shook and rattled the paper. What had Otto done now?

"What do you think?" he asked with the anticipation of a spoiled child. "Our own hot springs resort. Can you imagine it?"

He looked up and waved his arm into the air, seeing some kind of picture that I had no vision for.

"*Swimming pools with steam rising from the ground. Greenhouses growing exotic flowers and plants. Movie stars shading themselves under umbrellas. Concerts. Lectures. And—and!*"

He actually leapt up when he said that.

"*And it has an octagonal-shaped room where we can restore the baths to their former glory.*"

I tried to smile. I curled my lips up despite their bitter protest, but it did not reach my eyes. I watched Otto's expression journey from exuberance to confusion to anger.

"*You don't like this. Why don't you ever support my ideas?*"

Sarcasm gathered in my throat and spread to my tongue, a retort waiting for me to open my mouth. Why did I never support his ideas? How could he ask this? I left my beloved family and my beloved state to follow him to Texas, only for him to leave the very company that had been so good to him and form one that was their biggest competitor. And yet I kept silent. Arranged for the loan from my brother. Researched the market for Pearl and got the word out. Indeed, I was in agreement with Adolphus that my husband had gotten in over his head with all the businesses he was starting, but for the most part, I'd kept my own council and given Otto no objections.

I was weary, though. Building a house—a palazzo—had been tiring enough, and I'd begun to take on responsibilities at the brewery. To start a venture as wild as the one he was proposing was simply beyond belief and the last of my tolerance had been spent just getting out of bed this very morning.

But still, I said nothing. There was no point. The paperwork said, "deed" and Otto's signature was at the bottom of each page, the ink almost glistening in its newness. It was done and an argument would do nothing but put us at odds when our current harmony had been so hard won.

I leaned into the chair nearest the fireplace. "*I'm sorry you don't think I support you, Otto. I'm certain I've demonstrated the opposite on every occasion possible.*"

I folded the contract and deed and put them back in the envelope, handing it back to him. "*So, tell me more about this.*"

*I could not feign enthusiasm.*

*Over the next year, barely a word was spoken between my husband and myself that didn't involve business, beer-making, furnishing the house, or restoring the Hot Wells resort. Otto had built separate bedrooms into our cavernous house against my wishes and he insisted on using the one he'd designated for himself. He said that it was to keep from waking me when he arose so early, but he knew I woke before dawn. Then, he told me that all of the fashionable people did it—look at the king of England. Did I really think that he shared a room with his wife?*

*That was a tangent that was patently absurd, but I didn't argue it. For I'd discovered that I quite liked my own space. I went ahead and selected a lace canopy over a four-poster bed, and angled it in the room to face the sun. I chose a pale pink coverlet and a white sable blanket to lay across its foot. I commissioned a desk made especially for the turret that faced the smokestacks of Pearl. And a cushioned vanity seat to fit into a table dedicated to my cosmetics. My bedroom became my sanctuary. My own little refuge when Otto's talk of new ideas grew scattered and his interests jumped from project to project.*

*Of all of them, it was only Pearl I cared about. I'd taken the time to meet each employee and knew most of them by name, and the names of their wives. Sometimes, the children. I knew the horse carriages' handlers: Jim Bacon's daughter had caught the whooping cough and Jim Tanke's wife was expecting a fourth child. I knew that the payroll clerk was named Janice Heff and that she'd taken over the job when her husband, Pete, died leaving the position vacant. It was a remarkable thing to see a woman working among all the men and I vowed that if I ever had a true say in it, there would be more of them.*

*Like I'd done with all the people I'd met in my years taking daily walks around San Antonio, I'd created a family out of the employees at Pearl. I would look after them with everything I had, even as my husband gave it less and less consideration.*

An hour had passed and a nurse came in to check on Mrs. Koehler again.

"How are you feeling? Are you ready for some lunch?"

"Not if it's the slop you gave me for breakfast. Do you have any more of those rolls from dinner last night? With some butter?"

The nurse's eyes widened, but she had the sense not to counter her. "I'll see what I can find for you, Mrs. Koehler."

Mabel had distinctly heard the doctor tell Emma that she was not to have butter under any circumstances. Nor salt. Nor cream. He'd even written it in the notes, which Mabel had seen the nurse read.

Well, she wouldn't be the one to keep Mrs. Koehler from having whatever pleased her. Why not give her some small joy? If she had to, Mabel would smuggle in anything she wanted.

When the nurse had closed the door behind her, Mrs. Koehler took Mabel's hand in hers. She held it perpendicular to her own, with the curves at the base of their thumbs resting in each other. It was such a small thing, but Mabel had to fight back tears at the gesture. This was how she used to hold Mama's hand.

"You poor thing. I promised to tell you about Hot Wells and I let my mind wander. I didn't mean to go on about my marital woes. You will find a young man for yourself someday and see soon enough that there is no marriage that is perfect. Each person arrives with his or her flaws, and Otto and I were no different. Do you intend to marry someday?"

Mabel set her pencil down with her free hand. "I supposed that's what every girl is supposed to want."

"Look at me, Miss Hartley."

It took some effort to do so. Mabel was quite comfortable taking dictation from Emma, but had not intended to share anything of herself in return. Yet here they were, reminding her of the precious time at her mother's bedside. She had to fight tears every time she walked into the hospital. The very smell of it took her back to those days.

"Yes?"

"I didn't get to be my age without learning a thing or two. And one thing I've learned is how to read intentions. Lots of people have wanted lots of things from me. But you're the opposite. You seem happy to sit in a horribly uncomfortable chair day in and day out and to do my bidding. But you're afraid of something. I don't have to know you well to see it. Whatever is holding you back from happiness has to be let go of. Life is going to throw some tomatoes at you. Your path will be determined by whether you let them mold over or whether you add them to soil and let something grow from them."

It was an unusual analogy, but it was not unlike the more traditional one that Mama always used to say: "When life hands you lemons, make lemonade."

Mrs. Koehler had suffered more than many and had earned the right to make such statements. Without her parents and brothers around to share their wisdom, Mabel knew she would be wise to take these words to heart.

The nurse returned and Mabel slipped her hand out of Mrs. Koehler's. But the feeling of it remained.

"The doctor prescribed chicken broth and cooked carrots for you, Mrs. Koehler. But—I did bring up a few rolls."

She pulled up the corner of a cloth napkin and revealed the forbidden pieces.

Mrs. Koehler's lips almost curved into a smile, but stopped short. She did manage a *thank you* and the nurse left.

"What about you?" she asked Mabel. "Are you going to eat something?"

"Erik—*Bernard*—is coming for me in an hour and he said we'll get something to eat on the way back to the house."

She stiffened at letting his more casual name slip. It implied a familiarity that she was still uncertain of, and one she was not yet ready to reveal to his aunt.

But Mrs. Koehler didn't miss it, and this time the smile reached her eyes. Did she read more into the lunch invitation than either Erik or Mabel might intend?

"He never did like his given name. He's been trying for years to get me to call him Erik as all his friends do. I'll give him the satisfaction at least once before I pass on."

Mabel was getting more comfortable with Mrs. Koehler's fateful pronouncements. It was practical, she had to admit. She'd watched her review funeral plans with Helga and confirm the readiness of her plot at Mission Burial Park, and there was a certain calm that overtook what people often looked upon as grim.

"Shall we continue with the Hot Wells discussion?" asked Mabel. The minutes were ticking by too slowly in her anticipation to see Erik again and she was desperate to distract herself from looking at her watch.

"Yes," replied Mrs. Koehler. She set aside the broth she'd never wanted and nibbled away at a dinner roll. She shifted her pillows to support her back and continued.

*To no one's surprise, Otto's vision for Hot Wells had exceeded anything he'd first spoken of. While he originally wanted to bring its bathing pools back to life, he soon calculated that if he also added lodging, it could become a destination with far-reaching acclaim. And, in Otto Koehler fashion, it succeeded.*

*Despite my inward doubts and protestations, it was remarkable by anyone's definition. One would be met at the entrance on South Presa by a grand horse carriage and taken on a jungle-like journey through fan-shaped palm trees and greeted with wildlife not normally found in Texas. Though they were safely behind discreet wire fences, visitors could see peacocks and ostriches roaming the grounds. A taste of the delights to be discovered later.*

*Upon arrival at the lodge, they would become enamored with the Victorian look of the building: white walls that reflected the sunlight, thanks to Otto's exacting demands that it be painted regularly. A red-shingled roof set at all kinds of angles. And in the back, an expansive green covering for* the baths that could be found on multiple levels. There were two public pools: one for the men and one for the ladies, their separation noted by large letters painted in black gloss on the brick walls.

Below sat forty-five private baths. Private being a relative term in that there was still a sense of openness, but they were not shared pools. They sat under a canopy and pillars that resembled an ancient cistern.

In the meantime, our large, half-furnished house allowed us to come and go without the other's knowledge, and although we rarely argued, we continued to grow apart.

Only where Pearl was concerned did I insist on interfering. To everything else, I left Otto to his empire.

Despite this, I did not shirk my social duties as a wife and I gave great credence to the important role we were beginning to play on the landscape of San Antonio. I made my appearance at the grand opening, cut the ribbon alongside my husband, and even chose a dress, white lace with red trim, to complement the design of the hotel. My hat was resplendent, if I do say so myself. I commissioned a milliner to make it especially for the occasion: white felt rising a full nine inches above my head, bedecked with three peacock feathers that rose another twenty.

My father would have been amused at such a concoction, but also would have applauded the success it took to purchase such a thing. I hoped, if there was such a place, that he was perched somewhere in a heaven that would allow him to look down on me and smile. I felt, at least, that the sunshine on that day—after a particularly long bout of thunderstorms— was his blessing.

Over the next decade, I made monthly appearances at the resort, greeted the employees, gave comments as to how things were running. I came more frequently when the movie stars started getting wind of this oasis in the middle of Texas. Many arrived in their own private rail cars and Otto petitioned the city for a track spur that could reach Hot Wells directly. He won, of course, and before we knew it, Hollywood could be in Texas in only two days.

For the locals, he arranged for a streetcar line to be built there as well. "If the hoi polloi want to come, their money is as good as anyone's," he would say. Though he did not mean it with the condescension one might take from his words. To Otto, a dollar was a dollar was a dollar, no matter who had it to spend.

Still, there was an extra energy about him when someone from the pictures came to visit. It would be difficult for even the most prosaic person to not be dazzled by the glamour that they brought. I played dominos with Cecil B. DeMille, tennis with Sarah Bernhardt, and sat at concerts next to Douglas Fairbanks.

But for both Otto and myself—in this, we continued to share a similar passion—it was all about business. The thrill of this elbow-rubbing meant nothing in comparison to what it meant to growing our presence in the business world. Otto secured the resort as the home of the Cincinnati Reds' training camp and he penned a contract for a movie about the Alamo to be filmed on its grounds. It was silent, of course. All pictures were back then.

It was fascinating to watch the actors moving about, wearing garish cosmetics, enhancing the melodrama for the cameras. And to later watch it in the theater—familiar and yet unfamiliar. So different from what we are accustomed to now. The pictures flickered, their mouths moved without sound, their speech was printed across the screen. Disembodied words that moved too quickly to convey anything more than the most simple of stories. Of course, we didn't know that then. It was all astounding to us—quite, quite new. The fact that photographs, when laced together, could give a sense of movement was an absolute wonder.

Otto brought home some abandoned filmstrips for me to see.

Well, at least, that's what he said. I found out that they weren't for me at all.

He must have thought I'd gone to sleep one particular evening. The one that changed everything. I became thirsty and the little bell on my nightstand could not be heard over a terrible thunderstorm that was brewing outside. I left my bedroom, moved downstairs out of necessity, and heard muffled laughter coming from the parlor.

In the glow of the fireplace, I could see my husband sitting on the couch, the one I'd had specially made with fabric ordered from St. Louis.

*He was holding a filmstrip up to the light.*

*And next to him was my nurse. Emma Dumpke.*

*You see, and we'll discuss this part another time, I'd just been in a terrible automobile accident while traveling abroad. Otto hired the woman to tend to me, as I'd been confined to a wheelchair.*

*The "other Emma," I heard people call her. She was everything I wasn't: petite and stunning, and possessing the kind of innocent confidence that is the unique characteristic of those who have not yet known hardship.*

*And my husband was in love with her.*

**JURORS** are being drawn today for the trial of the famous Burgemeister-Koehler murder case.

*Baxter Springs News –*
*Baxter Springs, Kansas*
*January 17, 1918*

# CHAPTER TWENTY-TWO

MABEL'S PEN RESTED on the notepad, its black ink pooling on the paper as she contemplated these words.

*And my husband was in love with her.*

Mrs. Koehler said it with the same flat tone that someone might have if they were reciting a market list, yet Mabel felt indignant on her behalf. Her father had loved her mother *fiercely*. It was his grief over her death that led him to smother the pain with alcohol. The idea that a man could love a woman besides his own wife would have been outrageous to him.

Mabel pulled a handkerchief from her pocket and dabbed her eyes. Oh, to go back to the days when her family was whole. Pops working as a fabric cutter for a garment factory. Bringing home scraps to Mama, who could make even the tiniest bits into something beautiful. Most she'd sell for extra money, but some she'd fashion into a treat for Mabel: a hair ribbon or colorful trim for her socks. And on Christmas, Mabel could always look forward to a new dress.

It was the little, daily moments that stung the most. Robert and Buck wrestling in the living room, careful not to knock over lamps, though not always succeeding. Mama calling everyone into the kitchen for supper. Listening to the *Ed Sullivan Show* on the radio.

All the baseball games, tickets bought on the day for half the price.

Mrs. Koehler might have been a pioneer in the business world, but she'd been robbed of having the kind of family that Mabel had been blessed with, even for too short a time. Robbed, too, of the devotion of a husband who was so very undeserving of her.

One might have all the money in the world, but without love, what was it worth?

Lost in these thoughts, she didn't hear Erik walk in and it seemed as if he just appeared in front of his aunt. He leaned over to kiss Emma on the forehead. Something about the gesture was so tender that it stripped away the last sense of safeguarding that Mabel kept around herself.

Erik was no Artie. Or better said, Artie was no Erik. If there was ever going to be room in her life to love again, she had to learn to trust. And she was pleased that she'd been working hard to do so. Erik made it almost easy.

He sat at Emma's bedside, stroking her hand until she'd drifted off to sleep again. He turned to Mabel.

"Hungry?"

"Famished."

"Good. I know exactly the place. Are you up for a short walk?"

She looked out the window at the stark white sky. It had been chilly on her way over when Helga dropped her off. But she thought again of Buck. Any small sacrifice made on behalf of the boys overseas might be one step closer to bringing them home. She could put up with a little cold if it means saving precious gasoline.

Erik helped her into her coat, a kindness she continued to appreciate. She slipped gloves out of her pocket and pulled a knit cap over her ears.

They continued straight down North San Saba, venturing further than Mabel had yet explored. Unlike the manicured neighborhood of Laurel Heights, this had a distinct feel and grit of a city. Erik stepped to Mabel's right side, keeping himself next to the street. No sooner had he moved, a car came hurrying past them, spraying a fan of dirty slush onto the sidewalk, barely missing the cuff of his pants.

"Oh, Erik, that almost got you!"

"Better me than you. I know that stockings are not easy to come by in wartime."

How perceptive. She'd torn a pair when helping Frieda in the kitchen, and the cook had generously offered one of her own. She'd insisted that she didn't have as much use for them as a younger girl like Mabel might.

"Thank you."

Erik took her arm and slipped it into the crook of his, patting her hand with his own.

"Where are you taking me?" she asked, trying to steady the nervousness she still felt by having him so near.

"I figured you'd had enough German food these past few weeks. Time for something more exciting."

They crossed West Commerce and entered a long, rectangular building with arches that lined the street.

The courtyard inside was noisy. It was a marketplace full of produce sellers and trucks serving hot food from their back doors. A cacophony of color against the white sky hovered above them: flags of pink, purple, green, and blue lined the arches. Women wore their dark hair in buns and their skirts were decorated with bold patterns.

"Ok," said Erik. He pulled her to the side, never letting go, and gave her the penny tour. "The farmers come in every day with produce. The summer months are more plentiful, as you can imagine, but south of here, they can still get some pretty good onion and beet and lettuce crops."

He turned to the left. "Its official name is the Municipal Truck Market, and you can well see why. But more commonly, you'll hear it called the Farmer's Market. It's only a few years old—built as part of the Works Progress Administration."

"I remember that. I think most of the roads in Maryland were built as part of the WPA."

"Anything to pull the people out of that depression."

"Did it hit San Antonio as hard as the rest of the country?"

"Unfortunately, yes. Have you seen that six-sided building downtown? The one with the green roof?"

She nodded. She'd seen it on the train ride in.

"That's the Smith-Young building," he said. "It has gargoyles perched all around it to ward off financial ruin. But it didn't work. The day after construction was complete, the stock market crashed."

Mabel had been only five years old when that black day had occurred. Too little to understand what the panic in the adults' voices meant. But as she'd grown up, she'd felt the difficulty of a country still recovering from that time. Only to be hit with a war that once again stole any sense of normalcy they'd had. It seemed that chaos had become the rule rather than the exception.

Would it ever end? Or were they to continually hold their breaths for the promise of a day that would never come?

"So sad," Mabel added, pulling herself away from her own thoughts. "Which is why it's all the more remarkable that your aunt kept the brewery afloat during such a difficult time."

He grinned. She loved his grin. Every time he did it, she had the feeling that everything would be all right in the end. For her. For the world. Was that what it felt like to be in love? That something as simple as a smile felt like it made everything right again? Revealed a hope long dormant?

"Has Auntie Emma told you that part of her story yet?"

"No. Before you arrived, she'd only gotten to the part about Emma Dumpke. She skipped over the car accident entirely. So, there is still a ways to go."

The grin disappeared, replaced by a shadow. "Poor Auntie Emma. The accident happened before I was even born, but the older relatives say that's when everything got worse."

Erik led her through a maze of produce stalls, rapid words flying past her ears in English and Spanish, negotiations over prices and squabbles over quality. It was a wonder, quite unlike anything she'd ever seen in Baltimore. She would have liked to stop and pick up something exotic for Frieda, but Erik seemed intent on heading to the other side of the arched adobe courtyard.

And with good reason. As they approached the end, a waft of something savory and delicious hit her nose. Indeed, all senses seemed to come alive in this marketplace—the scent, perhaps, being her favorite.

There were only three tables inside the hot room that Erik stepped into. The sign above read *Mi Tierra*.

She turned to him. "That means, *my land,*" doesn't it?"

Before he could answer, a small crowd pushed in from behind them, pressing them toward the front of the line. Offices must have released employees for lunch breaks, for nearly everyone behind her was in a business suit and had looks of urgency on their faces.

Her eyes hurried across the menu printed across the small room, most with words she had never heard.

*Costillas, Picadillo, Sesos.*

At least one was familiar: *Chili.* It sounded perfect.

"What are you having?" she asked Erik.

"The *chili con carne.* There is nothing like it."

"I'll have the same."

He ordered for both of them and Mabel slipped away to save them a place at the last of the three tables, engendering some disgruntled expressions from the businessmen.

Erik returned promptly with two heaping bowls. As he set one before her, the steam warmed her face. And the smell was nothing short of divine.

"As I said, it's not German food. After a few weeks, you must be wanting something a little different."

Mabel dipped her spoon in and blew on it before taking a bite. "I think before the war, I would have said so. But now ...."

There seemed to be no need to complete the thought. Even in the moments where life went about in its usual way, the war was a pervasive thief, grief stealing even simple pleasures like good food.

Erik looked down at his own bowl and sighed. He set his spoon down and slid his hand across the table to hers. It might have been the crowd in the tiny room or the heat of the chili, but she felt such warmth at his touch as to feel faint. His thumb found her palm and he rubbed it with tender circles, meeting her eyes with his own.

"Dearest Mabel," he said. "You say so little, but suggest so much."

Her lip trembled. It was all the invitation she needed, having promised herself that she needed to open up. If she lived only on the scraps of hope that she would see her father or brother again, her existence would be one of starvation. She took a quick bite of her food, knowing that it would burn her tongue, wanting to send the pain somewhere beside her heart.

The spiciness brought tears to her eyes, but maybe they'd already been there. She dabbed them with a napkin and took a breath.

"Cancer took my mother. Alcohol took my father. And the war took both of my brothers."

Those three little sentences had taken on a mythical size, enhanced by Artie's betrayal, and had served as a barrier all this time between her and any other human interaction. But it had taken only Erik's touch and patience to deconstruct it. Little by little, every time she'd seen him, a bit more sunshine was allowed to seep through until she could now feel the fullness of its power.

Her chili cooled as she poured out her story to him, taking small bites, finding each word easier than the last. Artie was the only part she remained silent about. Not because she cared any longer, but because spending even two words on him felt like giving him a power he no longer had over her.

She had to take back that power.

By the time she was finished, Erik was gripping her hand so tightly that it had turned red. But she didn't move it.

She understood now what people meant when they said that a weight had been lifted. Right now, she could fly.

"Dearest Mabel," he said again, and she thought those might be her favorite words in the world. "There is nothing I can say. Only that I'm sorry. But that sounds so inadequate that I'm embarrassed to even try. Is there anything I can do? Go with you to Baltimore to find your father? Write to the Department of War and demand information on Buck?"

She smiled. A real smile. Not the tepid one she'd put on like a mask when people asked how she was doing.

"I appreciate that. There's nothing that you can do that I haven't done."

He still didn't let go, and she never wanted him to. He'd begun eating with his left hand, which was clearly not his strongest one, because it dripped as he brought it to his mouth. The fact that he didn't even notice made her think, not for the first time, that she could fall in love with him.

"Erik," she laughed. "You spilled a bit on your shirt."

She pulled her hand from his and dipped a new napkin in her water glass, and leaned over to touch it to his collar.

"Oh!" he said, taking it from her and rubbing it. She sat back, feeling herself blush at this little intimacy.

His eyes lost the concern they'd held for the last twenty minutes and an amusement spread across them.

"Um, Mabel," he said.

"Yes?"

He pointed to her without saying anything. She looked down, and saw a teacup-sized brown stain on the belly of her sweater.

She hadn't even felt it when she'd reached out to him.

"We are a sight!"

"We are, aren't we?" he answered. He put the spoon in his right hand and hurriedly finished the last few bites.

"Let's get out of here before we can do any more damage to ourselves," he suggested.

"And stick to German food next time?"

"And stick to German food."

Erik took her hand as they left the market and when they spoke, their words turned to little clouds in the cold air. For the first time, Mabel envisioned it not as a scientific occurrence, but a spiritual one; as if a piece of our soul was carried in our speech and only in the winter did it take form.

"I told you that saying I'm sorry felt inadequate after telling me the story of your family," he started. "But I thought of something I can show you that might better convey what I'd like to say. Do you have to be anywhere the rest of this afternoon?"

It was a Tuesday. She assumed that he would be going back to the brewery, but perhaps his relation to Emma Koehler gave him some freedoms. "I only work for your aunt, and I don't think she'll need me the rest of the day."

He smiled. "Then I can't wait for you to see this."

They'd walked a few blocks when Erik turned a corner onto Houston Street. He took more rapid steps as they approached a marquee. Above it sat one word in lights: *Majestic*.

"What is this?" she asked.

"It's my favorite place in San Antonio."

Erik chose a side door, seeming to know that it would be unlocked even though the theater seemed to be closed.

Dim light lay subtly across mosaic tile floors and as Mabel's eyes grew accustomed to it, she was able to see the opulence of what was no more than a hallway. Carved chocolate-colored doors towered above her and the sound of their steps echoed through the empty space.

"It's beautiful," she said in a whisper that she could hear all the way down to the end.

"This is nothing. Wait and see."

"How were you able to get in?"

He turned to her and raised an eyebrow in an exaggerated way, even as he continued to lead her through it.

"I know people," he said in a flawless Italian accent.

Mabel smiled. It's the kind of thing someone would say in a gangster movie.

They arrived at another set of elaborate doors. Erik held it open for her and she stepped through into a pitch-dark space.

"Do you trust me?" Erik asked.

She nodded, though he wouldn't have been able to see it.

"Yes," she whispered.

"Ok. Wait here."

Erik let go and she could hear him fumbling around, brushing up against a wall. Only last week, he'd done the same thing at the Little Theater. He liked his surprises.

She waited. Then, a click. And with that, the room was flooded with light.

Mabel gasped at what lay before her.

It seemed as if they had stepped into an extravagant Spanish *palacio*. All around the sides were facades of buildings covered in scrollwork and niches for terracotta statues. The underside of the mezzanine contained friezes of turquoise, coral, and gold. Stained glass diamonds adorned the windows. Erik returned and took her hand, leading her down a side aisle. It was here that she could see the feathers of an albino peacock perched on one of the balconies, reigning over it all.

And the framework—had anything this beautiful ever existed

before it? It surrounded the enormous stage like an Egyptian crown. Cherubs adorned it on either side.

Erik pulled her in closer to him, wrapping his arms around her waist. She did the same and they stood there as if dancing, though they remained still. She felt flushed even as chills shot through her body. The smell of winter lingered on his wool coat, mixed with some kind of musky cologne. Together, they were an intoxicating scent. So thoroughly *Erik* that she would bottle it up and put a label on it if she could. Being wrapped in his arms felt like being *home*, even if she barely knew what that meant anymore.

Nearly a head taller, he looked down at her and her skin tingled with the anticipation of a kiss. She didn't dare close her eyes and distracted herself instead with studying his face. This close, she could see that he hadn't shaved this morning, and knew that he had spent the night at the bedside of his aunt. That alone made her begin to love him—yes, *love him*—in a way she'd never felt before. His consideration was written on his face, all the way up to soft eyes that watched her with tenderness.

"Look up," he said.

Mabel hadn't realized how much she'd been looking forward to his kiss until it didn't happen. But his nearness, the way his thumb was stroking her back in little circles, told her that he returned her feelings and she knew that all would happen as it should.

She followed his gaze and her eyes glanced up to the ceiling. How could she have missed this? It was the best part of it all.

The ceiling was painted cobalt blue, the color of the sky when dusk was over but nighttime was only beginning to emerge. Tiny lights became stars scattered over the orchestra. And wispy clouds skimmed it, moving across the room. If she hadn't known better, she would think that they were outside on a perfect summer evening.

"How did they do that?"

"There is probably a better name for it, but my friends have always called it the *cloud machine*. A projector casts them up there like a movie, the ceiling being the screen."

Mabel turned her neck, and knowing what she was looking for, saw a tiny camera-looking device pointing upward from the front of the mezzanine.

"It's magnificent." She turned back to him, their faces so close again. "Thank you for taking me here."

"Thank you for telling me about your family. I had already wanted to show this to you, which is why a buddy of mine left it unlocked for us. But when you shared that sadness, I wanted to do everything I could to take it away from you."

He took one hand and brushed it against her cheek, taking an errant strand of hair with it and tucking it behind her ear.

"Mabel," he whispered. "I wanted to remind you that even though there is so much ugliness in the world, there is also so much beauty."

Despite the opulence around them, the embellishment of every surface that had been touched with a creative hand, there was no beauty that compared to Erik's blue eyes as he said this.

She opened her lips to speak again, but his were suddenly pressed against hers. Sweet and delicious, overwhelming her to the point that she felt like she could collapse right onto the carpet in the aisle. Erik's body tensed, like a racehorse being restrained in its pen. But he didn't push for more even though she would have happily lost herself if he had.

"Mabel," he said again. She'd always thought her name to be a plain one, but carried on his breath, it sounded beautiful. "You've woken me up again."

He pulled away, leaving just enough space to speak.

"What do you mean?" she asked. Because she could have said the very same thing.

He ran his hand along the length of her hair, as if it were some rare artifact.

"Working at the Little Theater has been my only joy this year.

Until you came along."

That was difficult to believe. He was employed at one of the most successful businesses in Texas and glamorous women like Ernestina fell in love with him.

She hoped for him to explain, but he offered no more.

He pulled back. "We have already had enough sad stories for today, though. I want to show you one more thing before we head back."

Mabel followed him back up the aisle aware of the way she could feel her pulse on her lips. When they reached the main gallery, she saw a staircase, so equal in splendor to the rest of the theater that it nearly blended in. She would never have thought such a feast to the eyes would be possible, yet even one square foot of the Majestic proved it to be true.

Erik started up the steps, eager in his pace. On the second floor, he opened more doors and reentered the theater from the mezzanine. From here, the sky was even closer, though still towering above them.

"I've always wanted to do this," he said, not telling her what *this* was.

They took a few steps down, passing sections of seats likely reserved for wealthy patrons. It was probably the closest Mabel would ever get to such an arrangement, and she imagined what it would be like to come here in fine clothes and enjoy a night of carefree entertainment.

As they neared the edge, she felt her legs weaken again. This time, not from Erik or *that kiss*, but from the dizzying height. She felt silly; it was only one story above where they'd been, but the painted sky overhead added to her sense of vertigo.

She took a deep breath and gripped the back of a seat, hoping that Erik didn't notice.

He leaned over the balcony at what seemed to be a dangerous angle and let out a laugh.

"I think this will work!"

Her curiosity won. "What will work?"

He gestured to her to join him. "Come see."

Holding in a breath once again, she ignored the rapid beat of her heart and took one more step toward him.

"Watch this." He folded his hands together and repeated his stance. Only then did she understand what he was doing. He was standing behind the cloud machine that was projecting the images onto the ceiling. When he put his hands in front of it, it cast an enormous image of his fist onto the sky. It looked like a thundercloud. Then, he shifted his two pointer fingers and turned them upward.

"It's a rabbit," he grinned.

She could see it. His hands created a round body and his fingers became elongated ears. She nearly forgot how close to the edge they were standing.

"Wait, I can do it better than that," he decided. Erik unlocked his hands, trying different shapes, wrinkling the corner of his mouth as he tried to work it out. Mabel's heart swelled with affection at this childlike turn, happy that joy could indeed be found even among so much sorrow. She'd forgotten how to live, how to *play*, and it reminded her of what it was like to be in a family. Buck used to be great with shadow animals, as he called them. And though he'd spent hours entertaining his little sister, Mabel had never tried it for herself.

"Got it!" Erik had contorted his hands into two C-shapes, one backing up to the other, fingers crossed in impossible positions. But he was right: when she looked up, a more detailed rabbit took up the space of the theater. Paws, feet, and even a space for an eye as Erik left a gap at the bottom of his thumb to let the light shine through.

"I love it," squealed Mabel. "Make his ears wiggle!"

Erik obliged, and his two fingers did a little dance that was magnified across the arch of the proscenium. When they'd both exhausted their laughter, he stepped back.

"Do you want to try?"

"I'm not sure I could top that."

"You won't know until you're up here."

Her legs tingled with fear once again, but less so than before. The lure of long-withheld amusement was greater than such irrationality.

What was it that Buck had done? Some kind of billy goat, she recalled. Complete with a beard and parted lips that appeared to bleat when her brother made a guttural sound in his throat. She'd peal over at that.

But it was a complicated one and she wasn't sure she could replicate it.

Something simple then. With her right hand, she gripped the balcony, and she crouched down, placing her left hand in front of the projector. She straightened her fingers, extended her pinky down, and lifted her pointer finger up, bending it at the knuckle.

"What is that?" asked Erik. "It looks like some tadpole you'd find skimming a pond."

"It's a duck!" she answered. "Don't you see it? *Quack, quack, quack.*" She opened and closed her hand to mimic a bill.

"Well, now that you add the sound effects, I can imagine that it's duck-like."

"Duck-*like*?" She looked up at the ceiling and felt her cheeks blush. It did resemble a tadpole swimming across a blue that could be mistaken for water instead of an artificial sky.

She shifted her fingers, this time watching the image rather than her hands. And with a few changes, it became a proper mallard.

"That's better, I think," she said.

"Much. That's the best duck shadow in the history of duck shadows." Erik smiled again, the corner of his lips wrinkling, but in a different way than before.

"You've seen so many in your lifetime?"

"My dear, I have a veritable zoo up here." He pointed to his

head. "That's what comes from growing up in a war-ravaged country and having to find a way to pass the time and amuse yourself."

That's exactly what Buck had done, she realized. She'd been
too young to understand how little money they had. But her brothers, Robert and Buck both, had entertained her with all sorts of
antics. She had never appreciated that until now. What fun they'd
had.

But surprisingly, the memory of those times did not bring
the melancholy they might have just a few days ago. Instead, she
felt only the sweetness of a joyful time. Long gone, but not forgotten.

Mabel became disoriented by the height and stepped back,
dizzy. She pulled down the seat of one of the folded chairs and
sank into its velvety cushion. Erik did the same, the hinges of his
seat sending an ear-piercing sound through the space.

"You'd think for what these seats probably cost, they could
oil those," she commented. It was not an untrue observation, but
she made it only to fill the quiet seconds that passed. Having him
sit so close to her, sharing the moment of laughter, she found her
heart racing and feared that he would hear it. It seemed to echo
in her own ears.

"You would think," he repeated. But his words were hollow.
He was facing her again, as he had downstairs. And the jovial
nature of their last minutes faded as his eyes grew serious. "You're
beautiful, Mabel Hartley," he whispered.

She parted her lips to speak, but no words would come. She
didn't know how to answer a sentiment that filled her with emotions that could not be expressed in any language. There was only
one response that could come close to conveying all that she was
feeling toward him; love, gratitude, peace. She shifted her body
closer to his, realizing as she did that the armrest between them
could be elevated. She pushed it all the way up, moving even
closer until her leg touched his.

She was aware of every part of her body, inside and out, each beating to a different rhythm as her heart tried to keep up. She was terrified that she might let herself be bold enough to try things that she'd never dared before. And knew Erik to be too much of a gentleman to encourage it.

But they'd already *kissed*. That sweet but glorious kiss lingered and she ached for another. She held Erik's stare and leaned in, enjoying the look of surprise that came across his face as they both realized what she was about to do.

She moved one hand to his leg and lifted herself up to kiss him, fireworks shooting through her lips as they touched his. Erik's response was hesitant at first, but she could hear in the intake of his breath that he wanted this as much as she did. She didn't pull back and in no time, he was kissing her back. Not the delicate variety of before, but one more ignited. She forced her eyes to stay open at first, amazed at the look of pain that seemed to cross his face. A heartfelt pain that she could understand; one that wanted more than it could have. But once the spark was set, how was one supposed to extinguish it?

Erik's hands moved to her waist and she lifted herself up ever so slightly, responding to his touch. She had the wildest idea to swing her legs up over him, her body wanting to find every way possible to become closer. But the limitations of the seating acted as a much-needed chaperone, forcing her to give everything she had to this most exquisite kiss.

If this was anything like drunkenness, she could understand the need to have more. She thought of nothing in this moment but her love for Erik. Of how he erased the brokenness in her heart every time she saw him.

She felt his hands tighten their hold on her waist, even as his lips pulled at the bottom of hers.

A door closed down below.

"Erik?" The voice of a man carried through to them as if he were sitting in the next seat.

Erik pulled back and smoothed his hair, looking at Mabel with apology.

"Up here, Erwin."

"Erwin?" she mouthed.

"My buddy who works here," he whispered.

"What are you doing up there?" came the voice.

"Reupholstering the seats."

Erik stood and placed his hands on the balcony, looking down. Mabel could see the top of Erwin's head, capped with a black hat.

"Get the ones up on the balcony, then, too, will you?" the man laughed. "There are some shabby ones way in the back."

"Sure thing."

"You must be Mabel." She peeked over and waved, and Mabel could just make out his eyes, nearly hidden by a crop of disheveled bangs.

"He told me you were pretty, but he didn't say *how*."

Erik had talked about her to one of his friends? She'd thought nothing could be better than the moment they'd just shared, but she'd been wrong. It was one thing to express it in the darkness of the theater when it was only the two of them. But to breathe their names together into the larger world signified something even more.

"Thank you," she managed.

"Hey, I hate to break up the party, but we have a rehearsal starting in half an hour. I thought you'd want to know."

"We'll be right down."

Erik pressed a button on the cloud machine and the magic of the sky disappeared. But Mabel would never forget it.

As they walked back to the second-floor hallway, he pressed his hand at the small of her back, guiding her. Could he sense how unsteady he'd made her feel? When they reached the doorway, she paused and turned to him as he stepped into the frame. The space was tight, but he inched a little closer if that was possible, their bodies near enough to pass only a feather between them.

She looked up at him, hoping that he could read all that she wanted to say.

"Thank you for today, Mabel. You've given me a lot to hope for."

He turned, and took her hand as they headed down the stairs.

Hope. That's exactly what he'd given her, too.

Nervous, her voice now and then shaken by stifled sobs, Miss Emma Hedda Burgemeister, German nurse, Friday afternoon in simple words told the story of her life – a story of one of life's unfortunates; the story of the killing of the multimillionaire, Otto Koehler, president of the San Antonio Brewing Association.

Attired in a plain brown coat suit, a black hat, her face shaded by a dark veil, she sat in the witness box, her small figure almost swallowed up in its depths, her feet barely touching the floor.

And as she told her pitiful story, women, of whom there were many in the courtroom, wept unashamed, openly. When court reconvened at 2:30 o'clock Friday afternoon, Miss Burgemeister took the stand. As she walked to the witness box there was an outburst of clapping from the scores of men and women packed in the courtroom.

*The Houston Post – Houston, Texas January 19, 1918*

# CHAPTER TWENTY-THREE

MRS. KOEHLER RETURNED home three days later. The stay in the hospital had seemed to revive her spirits, though Erik said that the doctors continued to believe she had only months to live. She'd insisted that Mabel meet her in the parlor at ten o'clock, eager to continue their progress.

Mabel found her sitting on the sofa instead of her wheelchair, a blanket placed across her legs. She noticed, too, that the Queen Anne chair was missing. And in its place was a plush seat made of rose pink velvet, oversized and inviting.

"I hope the new arrangement is to your liking," said Mrs. Koehler. "I asked Erik to pick out a new chair for you over at Joske's."

Mabel remembered Joske's to be that large department store near the Alamo. She'd passed it on the train ride in, next door to the Menger Hotel, if memory served. She'd noted its location in case she had to buy anything while she was here, but had not yet had a reason to go.

"May I sit down in it?"

"You'll grow moss if you stand there and my money will have gone to waste. So, yes. Have a seat."

Several weeks in, Mabel had still not gotten used to Emma

Koehler's often caustic way of getting a point across, but she supposed that any recipe that led to a woman living as long as she had was one to make allowances for.

Then again, her actions belied that impression. The fact that Mrs. Koehler had considered Mabel's comfort to the point of purchasing what was obviously an expensive piece showed that she had a heart as soft as her words were harsh.

She sat down on the chair, which was even more comfortable than it looked. She imagined Erik visiting a department store and trying out the different options. Sitting in them, rubbing his hands along their fabric, thinking about what Mabel might like best.

"Don't get so comfortable as to fall asleep." Mrs. Koehler pulled her out of the daydream. Mabel opened her notebook and set it on her lap. She noticed that she'd used up more than half of its pages and wondered how many notebooks it would take to complete the story.

And when it was all done, would Mabel's time in San Antonio be finished as well? Suddenly, each page felt like a threat. As Mrs. Koehler began to speak, she wrote in smaller, neater letters, avoiding the end even as she knew that it had no bearing on what her employer had to say.

"Where did we leave off?" Mrs. Koehler asked.

Mabel swallowed, reluctant to remind the old woman of such a painful part of her history, but there was nowhere to go but through it.

Her voice faltered. "You'd been in a car accident. Mr. Koehler hired a nurse to tend to you. And then fell in love with her."

Mrs. Koehler closed her eyes and said nothing, and Mabel began to worry that she couldn't go on. But then she sat up straight and sighed a sigh that seemed to come from the deepest part of her soul.

"Emma Dumpke," she said. "Yes. I suppose we must talk about her."

*1910*

*The car accident was no one's fault, though a more emotional woman might have laid the blame squarely at Otto's feet. He had no part in the sudden rain that came upon us, nor in the poor quality of the tires on the automobile we'd borrowed for the day. And I might as well call it a con-traption rather than an automobile, because it was no more than an open pile of metal welded together to resemble a box on wheels. That's what they were like in those early days. Not even the luxury of windows. But there was no train that would take us to the rural brewery that Otto wanted to visit and though the car was rudimentary at best, Otto saw it as a great advance for humanity to not have to rely on horses.*

*If I blame Otto for anything, it is for cajoling me into accompanying him. I intended to stay in Bremen and do a bit of shopping for my family while he was away. By this time, we had buckets of money and I felt that we'd earned the right to enjoy more than a bit of it. I knew that if I visited the markets at a later date, Otto would join me and give his opinions— contrary ones, no doubt—on every purchase I made. I intended to bring back sheep wool slippers for each of my sisters and etched leather satchels for my brothers. Plus Christmas ornaments for all the nieces and nephews who were already starting to immigrate and pass through our house.*

*But Otto pled with me, saying that I was as much a part of Pearl as he was and the owner of the brewery would be most delighted to meet the "prettier half" of the San Antonio Brewing Association.*

*"Flattery gets you everywhere," my father used to say, and it's appar-ently an idiom my husband adopted as well. He'd given me so precious little attention since building that confounded Hot Wells Spring, that I was ready to agree to anything in appreciation of the compliment.*

*Starvation can lead people to do things they never would have done otherwise.*

*So, yes. Otto is to blame, but no more so than I am for my weakness and my desire to be needed by him. The rain, the car, those were the con-spirators, acting together to steer us off the road and change our lives forever.*

*I can't tell you much about the accident, truth be told. It rendered me* unconscious, and perhaps that is a gift. I woke days later in a rural hospital. Both legs were mangled, the right more so than the left, and my face was covered in unsightly bruises that looked worse than they felt.

My nurse was a petite blonde thing, young and beautiful. She waited on me as if I were her only patient. Beyond her regular duties, she took it upon herself to brush my hair, add rouge to my cheeks, and remind me that I was a woman underneath the casts and gauze. It was a hazy time for me, but I recall thinking that it was magnanimous for Otto to sit at my bedside every day.

How he must love me, I thought. Even if he doesn't say it.

Only in hindsight did I understand that it was part guilt, part infatuation—for my nurse—that kept him in the uncomfortable wooden chair in that room. Day and night, he stayed. I'd hear him say my name, "Emma," with a softness he hadn't spoken since we'd first married.

Weeks later, it was determined that I could be moved and was even ready for the arduous journey home. But I would need assistance. It was expected that I would be bound to a wheelchair indefinitely. And possibly forever. Otto offered a handsome sum to the nurse who had taken such good care of me and I was grateful for his seeming generosity.

She said yes, no doubt dazzled by the promise of America, and an escape from the country life when she was clearly made for more.

Our passage across the Atlantic was secured: Otto in a luxurious room, with one door connecting his suite to mine. And Emma Dumpke in one adjacent. I thought it quite extravagant of him, and very much out of character, to pay for such exalted lodgings for an employee when it was perfectly reasonable for her to ascend three sets of stairs to attend to me as needed. I was pleased—don't misunderstand. I thought she deserved it and began to believe that nearly losing me had rid Otto of his otherwise miserly ways.

Naiveté is a bewitching siren. Fooling us into dismissing what is right under our nose, even as truth pesters us. I was as guilty as anyone of succumbing to the lure of remaining ignorant to the growing affection between Otto and my nurse.

For his part, he certainly did his best to dissuade me from concern. On the passage, my husband was especially attentive. He consulted me on his notion to switch from wooden barrels to metal, and we discussed exactly which enzymes would need to be added to retain the beer's flavor if such a change were made. I suggested that certain ones might rid the brew of its cloudiness as well. Like old times, we calculated the cost of the new barrels, the amount of time it would take for them to pay for themselves, and set a course of action to proceed with the purchases upon our return home.

On the thirteenth night of our journey—an auspicious number by many accounts, though I don't ascribe to superstition—Otto burst into my chambers with a wild look of despair on his face. Emma Dumpke was assisting me at the time, helping me out of the ship cabin's claw foot bathtub. Otto had not seen my bare form in many months and all this time of convalescence had added unsightly pounds to my frame. He looked at me as if I were unknown to him, though if he was repulsed, he hid it well enough. To my nurse, his eyes softened and I saw an expression pass between them that left no doubt in my mind that he had already seen her bare form as well. She had a slender frame with curves in all the places a man prefers and I felt distinctly frightful in comparison.

I wanted to be sick. But I held it back. It would only make me look worse than I already did.

It was a moment of both death and birth for me. The final signal that my marriage was no longer all that I'd hoped for. Perhaps other women could overlook a husband's indiscretions and consider it part of the course of the union. But I knew my father to have been a devoted husband and my brothers to be the same. Not every man felt compelled to act upon his most base desires.

Otto motioned for Emma Dumpke to follow him out of the room. And I resolved, as their backs were turned against me in the most literal and figurative sense, that my marriage was over. Not in a public way. The scandal of a divorce would devastate Pearl and in turn, jeopardize the security our many employees enjoyed. But there would be no affections exchanged between us. It was too big a sin to forgive.

I waited to cry until they were gone. And I did. Heaving, breathless tears that constricted my lungs with their force and left them aching for hours after. I bent over and held a towel to my mouth so as to keep my anguish silent.

When I had spent them all, I knew that the only way to press on was to crawl out of the despair that encircled me like a menacing cloud.

From that pain arose an awaking; all the regard and time and energy I'd spent on serving Otto could now be redirected into Pearl and the workers whom I counted as family. Already, they had my devotion, but now they would have all of my attention.

Naturally, this would aid Otto as well—the scoundrel—but he was of insignificant concern to me now.

His next words tested my resolve, but I triumphed. When he returned to the bathroom, he handed me a towel and I covered myself even as Emma helped me into my wheelchair.

"It's terrible, my love," he said. The endearment either out of habit or pretense. "I've received word over the Marconi that there is a labor strike at the brewery."

"A strike? But whatever are they striking for?"

Conditions in a factory were never easy, but I was certain that Otto and I had made every provision for the comfort of our workers. There were rumors in other breweries that employees were beaten, either by foremen or when they came to fist-a-cuffs themselves. They were often placated by free beer, claiming that it was a staple of German life, but more likely a way to mollify them.

We had no such horrors at Pearl and the few foremen who had ever attempted to overstep our vision of decorum were promptly fired without references.

"It's the hours and the pay," he admitted. It was a sore point between us and the mention of it caused me to wince.

Otto had a wild look in his eyes. I knew it to be a familiar combination of anger and bewilderment, a duo that made its appearance whenever trouble arose. Otto was a man of significant intelligence and hard work. But it was my particular talent to remain calm during a crisis, as evidenced by my quick resolve to turn my shamble of a marriage into good for the brewery. I saw no sense in wasting time on emotions.

It was ridiculous to have this conversation with only a towel to cover me and a wheelchair as a makeshift boardroom seat.

"Wait in your bedroom, Otto. I'll meet you there shortly."

He nodded and slumped toward the door. When it had closed, my nurse wheeled me to my bedroom.

Oddly, I held little scorn for her. The girl, unwittingly, had done me a favor. I could not say that she had stolen affections when I had not possessed them in a long time. And now she'd freed me from my age-old preoccupation with keeping my husband happy.

"I'll wear the pink silk robe," I said. I had purchased it for myself years ago when the money that came from Pearl had truly started to multiply. Though it was an extravagance, we could easily afford it. Otto chastised me for such a purchase—even as he continued to build our ridiculous mansion—and insisted that I return it. Not only did I keep it, but I donned it every time I was angry with him. A nod to my independence and the perfect uniform for the auspicious nature of today. I didn't fool myself into thinking that Otto had any idea as to its significance for me, but that was no matter: I knew, and that was enough.

"You'll catch a chill," implored Miss Dumpke. "Mr. Koehler's room is quite drafty. He found a crack in the window."

I looked at her with sharp eyes, rather feeling like a cat with its prey.

"And how would you know about the conditions of Mr. Koehler's room? Have you suddenly become his nurse as well?"

Her eyes widened at the realization that her statement had revealed more than its simple words meant. "He—he," she stammered. "He told me so. Out of concern for you in the event that you should visit him there."

"I'm not the one visiting him, as you well know." My reprimand was well placed. The girl turned ashen and set to busying herself in my service.

"Mrs. Koehler. I don't know what to say."

"I'll have no words from you. You have a job to do. Do it."

Emma Dumpke's lower lip quivered, but she didn't press it. "Then let me at least set this blanket over your lap. And I can ring for some tea to keep you warm."

Good. Let the hussy squirm a bit. Why not have a little sport with the situation?

But really, I got far less enjoyment from the game than it sounds. I knew that she was eager to leave her tiny German town. What girl would not want to come to America when the offer was made? And what girl could refuse Otto's charms? When he chose to reveal them, they were quite irresistible. It's why he'd gotten along so well in business: people found it difficult to say no to him.

Away from home, away from family, away from all she'd ever known, the pitiful young woman was more pawn than prostitute. She might have genuinely fallen in love with my husband and he might even have a kind of affection for her. But though her body was lithe and willing, she could not know that his only mistress, his only love, his only wife was his blasted business folder. He'd been unfaithful to Pearl with the acquisition of so many other distractions. I was not the first who'd lost his attention. Merely the most recent. In time, no doubt, he would forget this simple girl in favor of something—or someone—else.

I almost felt sorry for her.

For no reason other than to amuse myself, I insisted on applying my cosmetics before she took me to Otto's chambers next door.

When I was finished, she took me over and I knocked. I did not wait for him to open the door; I turned the knob and dismissed Miss Dumpke. I rolled the wheelchair into his suite and closed the door behind me. My movements were becoming more graceful the longer I had to adjust to them.

Otto was sprawled across his bed, his hands running through his hair. The strike would indeed be devastating.

"What are we going to do, Emma? We have obligations to clients all across Texas, but only enough reserve to supply them for two weeks. Some of these labor disputes take months to resolve."

"You say it's their wages and hours that they are protesting?"

"Yes. Which is a pity. We pay the same as any other brewery in the country. Twenty cents an hour."

I took a deep breath, thankful for the opportune moment to bring up a point I'd wanted to address for some time.

"Dearest," I forced through my teeth. "I read the Wall Street Journal while you read the San Antonio Express News. The average wage across the country is twenty-two cents per hour. It's high time we matched that."

He shot up off the bed so quickly that the springs groaned in relief. "A raise of ten percent? Are you mad?"

"No, Otto. You are mad if you think that you can keep the status quo and expect that our employees will be mollified by the fact that you buy them warm jackets for the cold rooms."

"That's better than most."

"Don't try to justify it. That's like saying that it's enough to sprinkle a garden with a water hose when it's thirsty for a rainstorm."

"Your analogies are ridiculous."

"Your infidelity is ridiculous."

Zing. I felt a rush of electricity as I said it.

His voice quivered. I could play my husband like a violin.

"Emma—I—please ... I don't know what to say." He hung his head and fisted his hands together.

"I do know what to say, Otto. You've gone and stuck your prick into the first vulnerable woman who would have you and sacrificed countless years of our marriage for a dalliance."

He looked up, his eyes doing a poor job of concealing their panic. "That's not a ladylike thing to say. You surprise me."

"I've sharpened my edges, thanks to you." I was really feeling the momentum. Blood coursed through my body with more vigor than our love life had ever known in years. "You look at people as commodities, and I have learned that at your feet. You are no longer my husband, you are now my means to an end. And in the end, I want Pearl. You can have your railroads and your mines and your blasted, over-the-top resort. Give me control of Pearl and you will have my silence in exchange. Surely our upstanding clients would have second thoughts about purchasing their lagers from a philanderer."

"I can't give you Pearl. It's not mine to give. I'm only its president. You know there are other partners."

"Naturally. I don't mean it in the legal sense. But your eye has been wandering to more than other women. I want to start making some of the decisions for the brewery. I want a seat on the board and I want you to *vote the same way I do. And to champion my causes for it."*

*"You're insane." He stood up, hunched with rage and I saw his hand grasp the little pocketknife he had. But I was not afraid. And I would have none of it.*

*"No!" I shouted. "*You're *insane if you think that you have the upper hand here. With one word to the newspapers, I can whisper a kindling of a scandal that will turn into a wildfire. We're on the brink of a prohibition against our very industry and you need me more than you realize if we are not to lose it all."*

*"You wouldn't."*

*"Wouldn't I? I already see the headline:* Texan Brewer abandons crippled wife in favor of her nurse. *Can you see Adolphus Busch doing something as monstrous as that? I think not. He is* devoted *to Lilly. They've been married nearly fifty years and he looks at her still like he's the luckiest man in the room. You've never looked at me like that. Not in all this time."*

*"Oh come on, Emma. You and I were never sentimentalists. That's one of the things I loved about you."*

*Loved. Past tense. I wonder if he even realized that he'd said it.*

*But I didn't linger on the thought.*

*"Sit down, Otto." And he did.*

*"I may have more practicality in one strand of hair than most women have in a whole head, but that is* not *to suggest that I do not appreciate the tenderness that a man can show his wife. Your precious Hot Wells receives infinitely more of your regard than I do."*

*He couldn't answer. He knew I was right and that I'd backed him into a corner.*

*"What is it you want? A place on the board?"*

*I wasn't going to let him off that easy. "Not only that. I want twenty-two cents an hour for my employees." I paused. "No—twenty-three cents. Be magnanimous, Otto. Those people deserve it. They deserve better than average. And, on top of that, give them a week of paid vacation every year. And two weeks for those who've been with us for more than a decade."*

*His hands fisted again, but I knew I had him. "Vacation? Are they to think that they are some kind of royalty?"*

"*They are people, Otto. People with homes and children and worries and illnesses and dreams.*"

"*I know they're people,*" *he snorted.* "*You don't have to portray me as an unfeeling bastard.*"

"*You're the one who said it.*"

"*Be reasonable, Emma.*"

*I was not going to persuade him on the grounds of fairness. Otto had pulled himself up from his proverbial bootstraps and he didn't intend to pave a smooth path for anyone else when he'd never had one. I had to try a new angle if I hoped to win him over to my way of thinking.*

*I quieted my voice, but only as a tactic.* "*Look. A product is only as good as those who make it. Many of our workers have been with us for years and years. Long before it was Pearl. But some have started to leave. San Antonio is a growing city and there are many other choices. Wouldn't it be more economical to pay them a better wage and make them happy than to face retraining new employees who might also leave as soon as better opportunities arise? Why not make Pearl the opportunity? Pay them well and give them vacations so that the San Antonio Brewing Association gains a reputation for being a most desirable place to work. Then you will have your pick of quality workers. Innovative ones who will be motivated to bring fresh ideas to the forefront. In fact, I think we can even build some kind of advertising campaign around it. One that will put Pearl in such a good light in the community that beer drinkers will feel good about choosing Pearl among a growing variety of brews.*"

*He was silent, biting his lower lip in the way I knew to mean that he was thinking. Really thinking.*

"*You have a point.*"

"*I know.*"

"*I don't know how we'll get it past the board.*"

"*You're a clever one, Otto. You'll think of something.*"

*Flatter a man, and he will give you anything.*

# I KILLED HIM
## TO SAVE THE HONOR OF MY FRIEND

Early next week should decide the fate of the woman who has admitted she killed Koehler, but declared it was in 'self-defense.' Rigid cross-examination today failed to shake Miss Burgemeister's testimony, given without emotion. Other witnesses testified that when they found her with the body of Koehler in the little cottage here, the little house she said he gave her, that she cried out: 'I killed him to save the honor of my friend.' In direct testimony, the woman defendant had said Koehler told her he loved her; that he paid her expenses on a trip to Germany; that during 1913 and 1914 he was a frequent visitor at her house, and that 'he asked me to go away with him and leave Mrs. Koehler, but I refused.' Mrs. Koehler is an invalid and Miss Burgemeister was her nurse. Miss Burgemeister is of slight stature with doll-like blonde features. She has shown no trace of nervousness during the trial. The courtroom has been thronged.

*The Lincoln Star — Lincoln, Nebraska
January 20, 1918*

# CHAPTER TWENTY-FOUR

MRS. KOEHLER'S WORDS made Mabel think of Erik. She had not seen him since the Majestic, as work had taken him to Austin. She wondered if Ernestina had gone with him, but got her answer when the woman showed up to the weekly Sunday dinner while he was still away. She shouldn't let herself worry. Erik had made it clear that he had no affection for his former love.

The centerpiece at dinner was a beautiful display of yellow roses, placed there by Frieda after they'd arrived earlier that afternoon.

Mabel did not see the flowers until they all sat down to eat. The crowd was smaller than its usual size. Emma Koehler sat at the head, as was her custom. Helga led Ernestina to a seat in the middle of the table with Mabel across from her. Otto A. and Marcia sat near the other end, and eight relatives passing through filled in the remaining seats.

Mabel spoke as if from a secret script, unaware of the scheme that Helga and Frieda had thought up.

"What beautiful flowers," she commented. "Where did they come from?"

Helga stood at the doorway as Frieda ladled the soup into bowls. "Didn't I tell you, Miss Hartley? They came for you today. From Herr Garrels."

"Erik sent them?" She'd long stopped saying Bernard. Their mutual affection was not only known to Mrs. Koehler, but subtly encouraged. So the more familiar name revealed nothing that was not already brought to light.

"Yes," said Helga, exchanging a grin with Mrs. Koehler. "It came with a card."

Emma continued. "Why don't you read it out loud to us?"

Mabel was amazed at the extravagance of the flowers (there had to be fifty of them!), but was leery of making such a demonstration of it all.

"Oh, I couldn't," she tried.

"Don't be so shy. There's no one among us except for the children who have not had a bit of romance in their lives."

I looked up at Ernestina, and reached for the card.

*Yellow roses for a new Texas girl. One who has stolen my heart. Erik*

"I'd rather not," she said. She didn't care for Ernestina, but had no desire to humiliate her in public. Instead, she slipped the note into her shirt pocket. Close to her heart. She would read it again in the privacy of her bedroom.

"Very well," said Emma. Mabel realized that her employer had triumphed regardless. Ernestina didn't need to hear the words to be flustered. "I suppose some things between lovers are to be kept secret."

"We're not—" Mabel began. But Mrs. Koehler's attentions had shifted to praise for Frieda and the delicious accomplishment of the cabbage soup.

Mabel tried to catch Ernestina's eye in some kind of apology, but the woman would not look at her for the rest of the meal.

One day later, the flowers had bloomed even more fully, and Mabel took them to her bedroom while Helga was at the market. They were hers, anyway, and she far preferred to see them on the little round table in the turret. There, the light shone through different panes as the hours passed, illuminating the green of the stems and the veins of the petals as the day went on. She set the card near the bottom of the vase, face up so that she could read and read it again.

She'd never received flowers before and the number of them made up for every missed occasion. She decided then and there that yellow roses were her favorites; they were quite uncommon in Baltimore, to the point that she'd never even seen them.

"Miss Hartley?" Frieda's voiced sounded muffled behind the thick wooden door.

Mabel wrapped a silk robe around her shoulders, one of the many luxuries that appointed the room.

"Yes?"

Frieda's cheeks were red and her voice faltered.

"Telephone. For you. I hurried upstairs. A call from Los Angeles."

Los Angeles? She didn't know anyone in California.

"Who is it?"

"A man. It sounds urgent."

Mabel's heart tightened, but without any sort of idea as to what it meant, she couldn't begin to know how to worry.

"The hallway phone?" she asked.

"The kitchen."

Most households did not have one telephone yet, but Mrs. Koehler had four. The phone company had finally installed her independent line and they were all relieved to no longer have to share it with other parties.

Frieda stepped aside and Mabel hurried down the stairs two at a time.

Her hand shook as she pushed open the swinging door to the kitchen and picked up the receiver.

"Hello? Mabel Hartley here."

"This can't be Mabel Hartley. Why, she's a little girl. This sounds like I'm talking to a full-grown woman."

Her arms went numb and her head felt light.

"Buck? *Buck!*" Mabel collapsed onto the cold tile floor, dropping the receiver as she did so and buried her head in her arms. Her sobs echoed throughout the room.

"Sis? Can you hear me?"

The telephone! She stopped it from swinging on its cord and held it up to her ear, gripping it with both hands as if it were a life preserver.

"Yes! I hear you. Buck—is that really you?"

Her brother laughed. It was the best sound in the world. The most exquisite. The most beautiful. The most perfect.

"It's me. Most of me. I'm minus an arm and a Jap bullet took an earlobe off, too, but other than that, I'm all here."

Her heart tightened at the thought; how could he be so nonchalant about that? But for Buck's sake, she would keep to a chipper tone.

"I can't believe it. And yet I can. I knew I didn't lose you. I would have felt it."

"I could always count on you, little sister. You'd never give up on me. That one thought carried me through."

"But where have you been all this time?"

His voice muffled and then he returned to the receiver. "I've already passed up my time and there's a hundred guys who want to use the telephone. But I wanted to let you know that I'm alive and I'm coming home."

"Oh, Buck. Don't come to Baltimore. I've left."

"I'm not. Mrs. Molling told me that you're in Texas. That's how I got this number. What the hell are you doing in Texas anyway? Never mind. I can't take up any more time. But as soon as she told me, I put in a request to go to San Antonio instead."

"You're coming *here*?" It seemed almost impossible. Her brother was *alive* and he was coming to see her?

"Yep. I don't know when. There might be a quarantine and seats on cargo planes have a waiting list. So it could be days or weeks, but stay put and I'll get to you."

"Buck—I can't even tell you how much—"

But the line went dead. No matter. The whole world could shut down and she wouldn't care.

Her brother was alive.

In all her excitement, she'd nearly forgotten that tonight was a rehearsal for *Green Grow the Lilacs* and Erik was going to meet her at the house at five o'clock to walk over to the Little Theater. The set was nearly complete; in Erik's absence, other volunteers had painted most of what remained. Tonight would be what they called a *technical* rehearsal. They had to run through the play with all the lights to make sure that the actors hit their "marks," the bulbs were all working, and the layout of the fixtures were properly set.

Five minutes early, the doorbell rang, but Mabel was ready.

"I'll get it," she sang out to Helga. The housekeeper shook her head as she slipped back into the dining room, but Mabel could see the corners of her mouth upturned. Why did everyone in this household put on such a stoic exterior? As Mabel got to know them better, she could tell that they had soft hearts under all that stuffiness.

Erik seemed to have no trouble demonstrating his feelings, however.

She put her coat on and opened the door, seeing him as if for the first time. Because this *was* the first time that the newness of whatever they were together had been shared publicly: the yellow roses had, apparently, prompted quite the whispers among the Koehler family.

"Hi," she breathed.

"Hi." He smiled at her, looking down. The winter sun had nearly set. The porch lights illuminated him even as the yard behind him was dark.

Erik stepped forward and handed her a box wrapped in colorful foil. "I bought something for you on my way back from Austin."

A present! Mabel hadn't had a present since her birthday a couple of years ago when Ginger gave her a pair of silver-plated earrings. She'd learned to pass by Christmas-themed store windows and avert her eyes so as to avoid yet another season with no one to celebrate with. She pulled a tissue from her coat pocket and held it against her nose, hoping that he wouldn't see that she was trying to hold back tears.

"May I open it?" She spoke slowly so as to steady her voice.

"Of course! And—you have to share. But only with me."

She closed the door behind her. "It's almost too pretty to open."

He stood close to her and she could feel the warmth of his breath against her cheek. "If you don't, I will."

"You've convinced me." She pulled at the twine bow on top and carefully opened the foil, hoping to save it for a future use. A plain package sat within. She slipped a fingernail underneath the tape that held it together.

Inside were twelve chocolate balls. Such a rarity during wartime, but she had ceased to be surprised as to what the Koehler family could conjure.

"Thank you," she said, looking up at him.

"They're marzipan. An old woman in a little shop in New Braunfels makes them. She says it's a secret recipe. She grows almond trees on her property and trades the nuts for cocoa beans."

Perhaps the war touched Texas differently with all this land to grow your own food. Residents of downtown Baltimore did not have the space to grow their carrots and zucchini and let alone almond trees.

She offered one to him first, and then took one for herself.

They took a bite at the same time. The taste was perhaps the best thing she'd ever had, overwhelming her mouth with what could only be described as a cloud of flavor. If one could fall in love with food, then she was instantly smitten. Mixed into the soft paste of the marzipan were slivers of almonds, just large enough to add crunch. And the richness of the dark chocolate covered them both.

She watched Erik as he closed his eyes. He seemed to have a similar impression.

"I am never eating anything else in my life," she moaned, tilting her head back against the door frame.

"I told you. Isn't it sensational?"

"That's one word for it."

Erik took the hand that wasn't holding the box and swept it behind her back, pulling her closer to him. He leaned down and placed a delicate kiss on her lips.

"I'm never kissing another girl in my life," he whispered. "Just so you know."

Mabel felt her cheeks redden. The combination of the sweets, the kiss, and those words made her head swoon. She had no idea how to give an answer that could come close to saying all that she wanted to.

"Do you mind walking?" he said, pulling back and rescuing her from the impossibility of the moment. "It's a nice night out."

"Of course. Let's save the gas."

"Do with less so they'll have more," he said, quoting a popular war poster.

"Do with less so they'll have more," she repeated. Though as she put the lid on the marzipan box, a pang of guilt settled in her heart. Ever since last spring, she'd saved half of her sugar ration, one pound a month, to give away to a local church, as she had no one to bake for and had acquired a taste for black coffee. But maybe when these indulgences came her way, she should be grateful and not worry about it.

Maybe Mama sent little gifts from Heaven after all.

Erik held her hand as they walk toward the gate and Mabel

heard the quiet click of the door as Helga closed it behind them. "You have quite a bounce to your step tonight," he said. "I'd like to believe it's because of my excellent company, but you look like you have something to tell me."

She smiled. How astute that he could know this before she even spoke.

"Oh, Erik. I have the most wonderful news and I've been bursting to tell you all day. My brother Buck has been found alive and is already back in the United States."

He stopped and turned toward her, pulling her to him in a near-suffocating embrace. "That is the *best* news. The best! What are you thinking, going to the theater with me? For a *rehearsal*? You should go out to dinner and celebrate. If I hadn't already committed to this, I would join you."

She wiggled out, her body throbbing from how tightly he'd held her. But it delighted her to know that her news had been so genuinely welcome to him.

"I don't want to be alone. As much as I want to shout from the top of the Smith-Young building, I would far prefer to be around people tonight. I feel so jittery."

"I have a cure for the jitters."

"You do?"

He grinned and pulled her over to the iron gate, behind a hedge, where they couldn't be seen. He pressed her against the bars of the fence, but not so much that it hurt. This tiny space they'd slipped into acted as their own private cave, away from any eyes watching from the house or any headlights of cars on West Ashby.

Erik bent his fingers and brushed them against Mabel's cheeks. "You are so beautiful, my love." He bent down and placed his lips on hers, the faint taste of the dark chocolate still embedded on them. She gasped and he moved in closer, kissing her harder, even more so than when they'd been at the Majestic; for there, they'd been interrupted and here they were alone. He parted her lips with his and the most *exquisite* feeling raced through her all the way down to her toes. She arched her back, pressing her body into his, frustrated that two long winter coats separated them.

She thought of that empty pool over at San Pedro. How in the summer, she could wear a fashionable swimsuit and he could wear the trunks that most men sported and there would be very, very little between them. The very idea of it sent a groan from her throat, which only prompted Erik to kiss her more deeply.

He stopped, thankfully, not because she wanted him to but because she had no breath left. But as she sighed, he began to brush her neck, her cheeks, her *ears* with delicate strokes.

Oh, this was *far* more delicious than marzipan.

"Mabel," he said in hurried tones. "Mabel, Mabel, my darling. You make it so difficult to—"

He took a deep breath and stopped.

"Difficult to what?" she asked.

He put his forehead against hers and made the tiniest bit of space between them. "To be a good man."

"What do you mean? You *are* a good man, Erik. The best of them."

"You're a smart girl, Mabel. Surely you can see what you do to me. This is exactly why I've always called for you at Auntie Emma's house and never taken you to my apartment."

She wondered if Ernestina had ever been to his apartment and the thought sent a chill through her.

Had Erik wanted to be a *good man* with Ernestina?

She ached to know, but didn't want to ask him.

"What's wrong?" he asked. Again, it pleased her that he could read her so well.

"Nothing. Nothing. There's just so much to take in this evening."

He stood up straight. "Darling, I'm being terribly unfair to you. You've had some wonderful news today and you don't need me to muck that up."

She placed her hand on his arm to reassure him. "You were taking away my jitters."

"Did it work?"

She felt her cheeks warm. "It did."

They looked at each other for a moment, not speaking, letting the early moonlight find its way to them through the thick shrubbery and the iron slats.

It didn't matter what Ernestina might have had in the past. Erik had demonstrated his love for Mabel now and that's what mattered.

She tried to ignore the knot in her stomach. The fear that something would come crashing down.

## THE DEFENSE RESTED TODAY

Miss Emma Hedda Burgemeister, German nurse who came here from New York City two months ago demanding a trial on charges of murdering Otto Koehler, wealthy San Antonion brewer, November 12, 1914, believed tonight her case was practically won. Although the case had not yet reached the jury, Miss Burgemeister declared, 'I have never doubted that I would be acquitted.' The defense rested today.

*The Lincoln Star – Lincoln, Nebraska January 20, 1918*

# CHAPTER TWENTY-FIVE

"YOU'RE ALL ATWITTER this morning, Miss Hartley. Are you ill?" Mrs. Koehler's words were impatient. Mabel knew that her employer was agitated that they had not progressed more in the dictation. Mrs. Koehler did not lay the blame at Mabel's feet, but rather at her own, gnarled ones. It frustrated her that she drifted to sleep so easily and that she had only a few hours in a day when her mind was truly sharp. A recent attempt to begin the discussion on Otto's murder had been waylaid by a terrible bout of senility and paranoia in which she accused Mabel of trying to steal a silver punch bowl and Frieda of poisoning her with bad lemons.

Helga had called Doctor Weaver to hurry over and Mrs. Koehler finally allowed him to administer some medicine.

"That's how you know she's near the end," Helga whispered to Mabel as the doctor injected Mrs. Koehler with a calming serum. "She never accepts what she calls *chemicals*. Says all one needs to live a long life is unpasteurized ale."

That had been yesterday, and Mrs. Kohler had spent the rest of the day in bed. Today, however, she seemed to have lost ten years and was eager to get on with the work.

"Tell, me, Mabel, are you ill?"

Mabel shook off her thoughts. "Oh, yes. I mean no. I mean, I am quite well."

"You're fidgety this morning."

Erik had used the same word.

"I'm eager to get to work and I know you are, too."

Mrs. Koehler rolled her wheelchair over to Mabel's chair. She put her bony hands up to Mabel's chin and pinched it, turning it right and left. "Just as I thought. You're love struck."

"Emma!" She hadn't forgotten her employer's missive to call her by her given name, though it still felt unnatural on her tongue.

Mrs. Koehler sat back. "You're in love with my nephew, aren't you?"

Mabel felt flushed. "I—we—"

"Don't prance around things like an antelope, dear. Are you or aren't you? You must speak up. Women don't speak up enough. There's no question that he's gone and lost his head over you, so you might as well decide now if you're going to rise to the occasion or break his heart."

"We've only known each other a month." She'd only known Artie for a *night* before falling for him. But that was so different. Artie had not even pretended to be a *good man*.

Mrs. Koehler didn't buy it, either. "That's an excuse. You young people think you need to have all this *time* to get to know each other. As if you could know everything about a person before making a decision about them. Trust me. It takes decades. And you won't always like what you see. But what is it about Erik that makes you hesitate?"

"I'm not hesitating. I'm trying to be prudent." Mabel picked at her fingernails. It was uncomfortable to be having this discussion with his aunt. Still, Mrs. Koehler was a very wise woman and Mabel would do well to listen to her advice.

"Prudence makes old maids. Do you want to be an old maid?"

Mabel pursed her lips. "No."

Then she took a deep breath and continued. "But you wouldn't want me to be *imprudent* would you?"

Mrs. Koehler's mouth was firm, but her eyes sparkled. Mabel

got the impression that she enjoyed being challenged. People probably never questioned her. She was a formidable matriarch and an intimidating one if you weren't used to her.

"Don't assume in life that you have to be one thing or its opposite. Being reticent is as foolish as being reckless. Substitute those words with nearly any other and you will find the truth to be the same. It's all about finding the balance."

Like Erik's description of water, fire, and alcohol. Anything in excess was dangerous.

Mrs. Koehler sighed and continued. "My dear, my nephew does not have one questionable bone in his body. He is as fine a young man as there has ever been. I took Erik in when his father lost their home in Germany in a poker hand and his mother became destitute, forced to earn money by prostituting herself to soldiers. She died of a wretched illness she acquired because of it. If anything, Erik has been abundantly scrupulous in his behavior out of fear of becoming like either one of them. I half-thought that Ernestina's influence would give him just the right amount of tarnish, but even then he gave no leeway for her antics."

Mabel sat back, stone-faced. Erik had hinted at the troubles with his father and had never mentioned his mother at all. How similar their tragic paths were. Fathers lost to their addictions. Mothers lost to illness. And yet how stalwart Erik remained through that. Maybe because his aunt had rescued him. Maybe because it was in his nature to be optimistic in the face of challenges like that. Mabel felt duly chastised, but not by her employer. She again found herself guilty of wallowing. Of closing her eyes to the difficulties that other people were facing. She realized that adversity was not intended to rip one out of the fabric of life. It *was* the fabric of life. Strengthened in unity. She'd survived by hanging on to a single thread when she could have shared her sorrows with others and woven a rope of impenetrable thickness.

"Oh, Emma," she said. "I've wasted a lot of time."

Mrs. Koehler patted her hand. "That may be. But you are still young. My advice is this: don't waste any more from now on. Promise?"

Mabel nodded. "I promise." She felt a heaviness lifting from her. This is the counsel her mother might have given to her.

"Good. So, with that behind us, let's continue. We have much work to do."

A dark look came over her face. "My husband, you see, had few scruples."

*1911*

*I got everything I wanted for Pearl. A seat on the board. Otto's votes that supported mine. Though it was still a struggle more often than not.*

*My employees received their ten percent raise and I decided to postpone the hike to twenty-three cents until the following year rather than risk a rejection to the ground I had succeeded in gaining.*

*What I also received, which was a delightful surprise, was a sense of loyalty and camaraderie from the workers. It became known, though not from my mouth, that I was the one championing their causes. In return, they gave me smiles, tips of their hats, and little treats as they could afford them. Chocolates or grapefruits or bags of hand-shelled pecans from their yards. I would promptly tour the brewery and share the bounty, lest it ever be thought that my kindness demanded rewards. Or could be bought.*

*The result? I was one of them. I was one of the workers, even if I sat in a wheelchair in an office.*

*And more than ever before, I considered them my family.*

*I know for a fact that three infant girls over as many years were named Emma and I served as godmother to all of them.*

*Once the labor dispute was behind us, I set my attentions on more political matters. There was a groundswell of support to turn Texas into a dry state and I worked with the board to put considerable pressure on the governor to limit enforcement in dry counties. They could pass their laws, but if the police turned a blind eye, the laws were ineffective. I had our best Pearl lager delivered to officials in counties across the state.*

*It was a tiny effort in a tidal wave of change. Soon after, the Anti-*

Saloon League nationalized their support and petitioned congress for a federal amendment to the Constitution that would ban alcohol. Temperance advocates insisted that intoxication gave rise to crime and other immoralities in the population. I argued that those who were inclined to indulge in poor behavior would find their mischief with or without the assistance of ale and that to deny it to the wider citizenship for the sake of a few bad apples was woefully unfair.

From the throne of my wheelchair, I organized rallies with the local bar owners I'd befriended years ago and I personally subsidized the cost of certain Pearl products to entice the support of the public.

One of my victories was convincing the Texas Brewer's Association to pledge twenty-cents per barrel to support wet legislation and in a short time, we gained ground. So much so that the governor, Oscar Branch, earned the nickname "Budweiser Branch." I would have far preferred the name to be some derivative of Pearl, but alliteration won the day. And besides, the Busch family was essential in aiding us for the collective good, so I could concede the nod to their own product.

We were all in it together.

Those efforts began to work swimmingly, even as my legs did not. Emma Dumpke remained my nurse because I had no time to hire another. And I no longer cared where Otto chose to relieve his manly impulses. Whatever they did together, it didn't happen under my roof. Otto had bought her a little cottage on Hunstock Avenue. She came to the mansion during the daylight hours and served me. In the nighttime, I presumed, she served my husband.

Soon enough, the need for me to have more care arose. I was diverting all my time into my business and none into my health and it began to show. The irony that I'd turned into what I'd loathed about Otto early on was not lost on me. But I was too consumed with the work to care.

Emma Dumpke was skilled, I have to admit, at helping me in and out of my bath, in and out of my clothes, and assisting me like the invalid I still was. But I didn't want to be that way forever. The doctors in Germany had given me some hope that I could walk again, but I would need to address it with the same effort that I gave to Pearl.

Though San Antonio was coming into its own, its medical community was still rather provincial. So when Emma Dumpke mentioned that she had a friend in Germany who was skilled in the kind of therapy I needed, I decided that I had nothing to lose by accepting her offer to write to her. The girl was eager to please me for reasons that should be obvious, so I had no doubt that her recommendation could be trusted.

Two months later, Emma Burgemeister arrived, following the same arduous path that we had had to take. The train to Hamburg, the passage over the North Sea to Southampton, the journey across the Atlantic to New York, the train across thousands of miles.

So it was no surprise that when she arrived ragged and tired, I was not able to see beneath the weariness and realize the astounding beauty she was. Only days later when she emerged from the turret room upstairs— the poor woman had gotten quite ill on the voyage—did I discover that she was Emma Dumpke's opposite in every way. Tall. Strong jawline. Big-boned. Her brown-red hair had enviable curls that were natural and wild. She did little to tame them.

Once she'd been suitably restored by my cook's excellent chicken soup, Emma Burgemeister wasted no time getting down to work. While Emma Dumpke treated me with delicacy, as if I were some fragile flower petal, Emma B., as I came to call her, acted as if I were a rock in need of chiseling. And she let it be known that she was in charge, even though I was the one paying her.

I quite liked her brash style.

"Mrs. Koehler," she would say in a stern, husky voice. "We are not here to play. We are here for you to walk again. Now, stand up!"

I hadn't stood up in months. But I did not tolerate disobedience. I had not felt like such a child since the days I used to ride on my father's back as we walked along the Mississippi River.

I gripped the edges of my wheelchair, embarrassed that my attentiveness to Pearl had eclipsed all regard for my own care and that I had allowed Emma Dumpke to coddle me. My arms were strong enough, but they were not built to support me. As I tried to stand, my legs felt like gelatin: soft and easily pliable.

*They began to collapse and I nearly tumbled onto the floor.*

*"I'm sorry," I heard myself saying to my taskmaster.*

*"There are no 'sorries.' Only successes," came the retort. And so I tried again.*

*And again.*

*And again.*

*By the third day of nothing but attempts to stand, I was able to do so for a full five seconds and it felt like the biggest accomplishment of my life. Emma B. did not applaud me, however. She told me that we had to strive for ten.*

*And when I met ten, then twenty.*

*Twenty became a minute.*

*In between these tortures, she would allow me to sit and to press my feet against her folded hands. She would push and I would push back and she said that it was intended to strengthen the muscles that had atrophied for so long.*

*So exhausted was I by the end of a day that I rarely made it to the dinner table. The cook would bring my dinner to my room. I encouraged Emma B., however, to join whoever would be over any given night.*

*What I did not realize is that Otto had begun returning home in time for the meal. It was quite unlike him, as he usually took dinner in town with clients or partners in his various enterprises.*

*Weeks passed. I continued to grow stronger and could now walk the length of the long hallway. Emma B. never seemed pleased with my efforts, however. At each milestone, she rewarded me by setting a new and more difficult goal.*

*At long last, the efforts didn't tire me and I felt ready to return not only to Pearl on occasion, but to dinner in my own home.*

*And it was there that I noticed it.*

*Oh, it might have been indistinguishable to anyone but myself. A look between Otto and Emma B. A brush of his hand against her shoulder as he would get up from the table. And my thoughts were confirmed one evening when I heard disturbing sounds coming from the kitchen and found them both half-dressed and leaning over the countertop.*

*The betrayal! Did my husband have some sort of fetish for women named* Emma? *For I'd never suspected him of having affairs before Dumpke and Burgemeister came into the picture.*

*What made it worse—and, yes, it got worse—was that he had not ended things with Emma Dumpke. Quite the opposite. On another occasion, an afternoon in which I came home early from a visit to Pearl, I was surprised to see Otto's car in the driveway. He never came home for lunch.*

*But what I saw between the crack of the doors to my parlor suggested that Otto—well, I won't draw that ghastly picture. Needless to say, the blond nurse was with him on the sofa.*

*I didn't confront him then. I wasn't heartbroken: I'd long since not had even the tiniest romantic notion toward my husband. What I did mind was how brazenly they carried on in our own home. It was the height of disrespect for me. His wife, who had followed him to Texas. His wife, who had secured family money for his vital purchase. His wife, who had acquiesced to every new business whim. His wife, who almost single-handedly oversaw Pearl. Who took in his many relatives. And who had never once betrayed him in return.*

*The next day, I had the sofa removed from the house and replaced it with one that was much more to my liking anyway. It had a stiff back, firm cushions, was narrow in stature. Decidedly not one suited for lovemaking, though even that word seemed tainted.*

*Neither Emma dined with us that night and astonishingly, we were housing no relatives at the time. So Otto found himself alone with me.*

*We didn't speak at all through the soup course. Or the salad course. Or the meat course. Or the dessert course. It was not until the cook brought out a port for him and a lager for me that he spoke.*

*"What is bothering you, Emma?"*

*"Why do you think I am bothered?"*

*"You usually have plenty to say."*

*"I do have plenty to say. Just not to you."*

*"What do you mean by that?"*

*"Ask my nurses."*

*"I don't understand."*

"I think you do. Seems that they've been meeting your needs as well as mine."

He put his glass down. I expected an apology. Even one for the sake of decorum, but he gave none.

"A man has to be a man, Emma. And I haven't wanted to come to you with that burden since your accident."

I scooted my chair back and stood up. It seems like such a little thing to be able to stand until you've had the ability taken from you. But this gesture of indignation meant so much more to be because of how hard I'd worked to do this seemingly little thing.

"No, Otto. Our bed had grown cold long before the accident. You've been taking me for granted since the very beginning of our marriage. I've been there for you through everything. And this is what you do in return. You are despicable."

He slammed his hands on the table. If I'd hoped for contrition, I would have been disappointed. "Dammit, Emma, what do you want from me?"

"I want you to stop doing these vile things in my home."

"It's my home, too."

"Yes. This absurd mansion that I never wanted anyway. If it weren't for the gossip that would come from it, I'd be perfectly happy to move into a little cottage much like the one you bought for Emma Dumpke. In fact, it would be more than fine with me if you turned this into the den of iniquity you're clearly set on, and I'd happily live an hour's carriage ride away and leave you all to each other. But I will not abandon Pearl and all the people there. I will continue to live here and watch Pearl from this hill and soon enough, I'll be able to walk there once again."

His jaw was tight. "I'm not firing the Emmas."

I laughed. "I don't expect you to. Because even if they left, you'd waste no time in finding a fourth Emma and a fifth to satisfy this bizarre little fantasy that you've begun. But I do want Burgemeister out of here. Send her to live with the blond one for all I care. But neither will live under this roof anymore."

"Fine." Otto crossed his arms, but I could tell that I'd defeated him. It gave me no joy. Even with all that had happened, if I could turn back the calendar many years to the brief time that we had blissful happiness together, I would do so. But I didn't pine for it. I mourned over what was. What could have been.

Otto, on this point, was true to his word. Emma B. moved in with Emma D. and how that all worked out I neither knew nor cared. After sufficient time had passed and a string of far less qualified women had come to try to assist me, I at last relented and let them continue to do what they'd originally been hired to do. It was an unusual situation, to say the least. Receiving aid from the two women who warmed my husband's bed. They did not speak of it. Nor did I. We got to work and my health began to improve.

Life passed in this curious way. Until Emma Dumpke up and got married.

# THE VERDICT

Miss Emma Burgemeister, a German nurse charged with the murder of Otto Koehler… three years ago, was found not guilty this afternoon by a jury which had been out since 6 o'clock last night. Miss Burgemeister smiled when she heard the verdict and personally thanked each of the jurors.

*The St. Louis Star and Times – St. Louis, Missouri January 23, 1918*

# CHAPTER TWENTY-SIX

MRS. KOEHLER REGAINED her strength over the next few days. Helga said that she'd rallied, but Doctor Weaver cautioned that it would be short-lived. Some people who'd reached her age experienced a brief surge of adrenalin shortly before they died. A way to complete anything that was left undone. He compared it to an expectant mother: around the fifth or sixth month, she would become almost manic in her drive to prepare the house for the arrival of a child.

It was not the first time that Mabel had made the comparison between birth and death. She'd had a front-row seat to it with Mama. The woman who used to bathe her, feed her, coddle her, had needed those very things in her final days, and Mabel had been all too willing to serve her in that way. As heartbreaking as it had been to watch her mother wither into near-nothingness, the opportunity to play that role for her had given peace to Mabel. Maybe that's why Robert's death and Papa's drunken disappearances were especially grievous. Robert was just *gone*. He was there, and then he wasn't, his death heralded only by a typewritten form on yellow paper, delivered by a young man in uniform who had never even seen combat.

What was worse is that Robert hadn't died on a battlefield;

they'd lost him in a training accident shortly after arriving at the European theater. An inglorious end to a glorious young man.

And Papa. Mabel would have gladly nursed him back to health if only he would have chosen to come home. There was not a day that she didn't worry about him, especially as it was now mid-February and the weather reports out of Baltimore were grim.

But she would have Buck back any day now. He hadn't called her again, but she knew that he would do everything he could to make his way here as soon as he could.

Mrs. Koehler dismissed Mabel for the morning. Her lawyer was coming over to review her will. And she'd decided to write personal letters to each of her nieces and nephews, which were a considerable number. Especially since she even gave cousins like Erik those monikers. The family tree was vague, to say the least. If you shared blood, you were family, and that's the only name to which Mrs. Koehler ultimately subscribed.

The day was a beautiful one and locals said that February was always the first time spring hinted that it would arrive soon. Canadian geese began to arrive from the south, finding a temporary home in Texas before an eventual flight back north. Mabel had seen them from her windows, pecking at the bits of grass on the lawn.

She put a cardigan around her shoulders and decided to go for a walk. She knew Erik was at work, but even if he hadn't been, she would have wanted to take this walk alone. She was delighted to have love in her life again. One that was proving to be much more real than the sham she'd experienced before. But she'd learned from Mrs. Koehler that there was another kind of love that had previously eluded Mabel: the love a woman could have for herself. Finding her own way, forging her own path.

Emma Koehler had come to San Antonio as a bride, but set upon something that was uniquely hers by walking the streets of her new town and making it her own.

Mabel had no idea how long her employment with Mrs.

Koehler would last—until the woman died? Surely no longer than that. But now that she was here, she didn't want to return to Baltimore. There was the very real possibility of a future with Erik, but more than that, she felt like San Antonio was the place of a fresh start. Baltimore carried the sad memories of her old life.

Whatever it took, she would stay. She'd find a job in a shop or become a teacher or anything else that came along. She felt the electricity of *possibility* run through her veins. It was a new day for women.

Mabel walked past the parlor and heard Mrs. Koehler discussing things with her attorney. So she stepped out of the house. She hadn't ventured down North Main Street yet, and as she started down that way, she felt ashamed that she had been here so long and explored so little. But as Emma had said, not one more minute should be wasted. And that included time spent dwelling on regrets.

The scenery was not particularly exciting, at least for the first mile. The Koehler Mansion and Pearl sat well outside the boundaries of downtown. There were still patches of farmland and the occasional barber or gas station. But it was easy to see where growth had begun. Half-finished construction sites dotted the landscape, likely waiting for the end of this war. As drummed home by every poster created, all resources needed to go to the efforts overseas. It was difficult to make a case for needing steel to build a new hat shop when it could go toward reinforcing the sides of a naval vessel.

But the road took a livelier turn further down when she reached the boundaries of the downtown area. Here, green areas were deliberate, the first of which was Crockett Park. A stone slab stated its name and indicated that it had been established in 1875.

As she continued, there was far more bustle. Cars were driven by women or by old men: the young men were serving Uncle Sam. Fruit sellers had more variety than they'd had just weeks ago, though not as much as she imagined the summer would bring.

She came upon another open area, but it was more of a plaza. On the western side lay a stone cathedral, the seat, she knew, of the Catholic population of the city. Before Mama got sick, the family used to attend an Episcopal church on the occasional Sunday, but after she died, Papa never took them again. Mabel didn't remember much, but she did recall a feeling of serenity when they would go. Something about being a small piece of a large past. It assured her that everything would work out in the end.

She ascended the steps and was happy to find the enormous wooden doors unlocked. Inside, the notes of an organ wafted through the bell tower and the hallways, and the voice of a soprano carried its melody. They stopped and started; it must have been some kind of rehearsal, but Mabel appreciated the sounds. She marveled at the cream-colored stone and the octagonal window that sat above the altar. At the very back, an ornate gold structure held statues of unfamiliar saints.

Mabel walked the perimeter, which was made up of tiny chapels. One caught her eyes. It was a painting of a woman with dark hair, draped in a turquoise mantle, standing above a crescent moon, and being held up by angels. A plaque to the right said *Virgen de Guadalupe*. Mabel recognized it to be Mary, revered, as she recalled, by Catholics and Episcopalians alike.

A shiver passed through. Mama's name had been Marie, a variation. Perhaps Mabel was looking for signs where there were none, but it felt like a gift from her mother. To be here, in front of her namesake.

Before the painting was an iron stand full of candles. Only two were unlit. She picked up a long matchstick and borrowed the flame from a nearby candle to light the remaining ones.

"One for Papa, one for Buck," she whispered. She didn't know if Mama could hear her or if the brief prayer would do any good, but she left the church with a sense of peace.

She arrived back at the Koehler mansion feeling unusually plucky after such a long walk. She'd done it! Ventured out far past the Laurel Heights area, and without Erik or anyone else as a guide. Now she understood the sense of belonging that Mrs. Koehler had described about her own early years here. San Antonio was *hers*. And life was hers for the taking.

"Is that you, Mabel?" Emma's voice came from the parlor. She was stacking paperwork and her attorney looked like he was getting ready to leave.

"Yes. I'm back from a walk."

"Come on in here. I'll ask Frieda to make us some sandwiches and we can get to work."

Mabel went upstairs to freshen up and when she came down, the parlor looked as if the busyness of the morning had never happened. The attorney was gone, as was all the paperwork, and Frieda had set out a display of tea and sandwiches that the Queen of England would envy.

She was eager to tell Mrs. Koehler about her morning, and how she'd inspired her to venture into the community, but the old woman was all business.

"The time has come," she said. "We're going to talk about that dreadful day when Otto was murdered."

Mabel took out her notebook and began writing.

*1914*

*Otto seemed to lose his mind when Emma Dumpke got married. It all happened rather quickly. The girl went home to Germany for a month and came back saying that she'd met a young man on the passage over and the ship's captain officiated their nuptials. I had the occasion to meet her husband, Mr. Daschiel, when she came to the house to say goodbye. He was spiriting her off to New York.*

*Though I use the word "spiriting" loosely. If there was ever a more dull man born than Joseph Daschiel, I've never met him. He was not particularly well off, though he had a steady enough job at an insurance firm in Brooklyn. He'd been excused from the war due to one leg being longer than the other.*

*I can't say that I noticed any affection on Emma D.'s part. (Isn't it funny that she could still be Emma D. even with her new married name? How convenient.) Mr. Daschiel, however, looked irreparably smitten. She was a beauty; I did not have to use my imagination to see what attracted my husband to her. And she'd been a fine nurse to me, all things considered.*

*I suspected, then, that the marriage was rushed for the purpose of helping her escape the impossible position of being one of two lovers of an older, married man. Inexplicably, the friendship of the two Emmas remained strong, but the unusual situation must have worn on them.*

*So, good for Emma D.! We'd rescued her from the back roads of Germany. And Mr. Daschiel was taking her to New York. I'd say things were looking up for her.*

*Only Emma Burgemeister remained then, and she picked up some of the duties that had belonged to the other. Aside from working me to exhaustion with exercises meant to strengthen me, she ran errands, took me to appointments, and filled in for anything needed. I implored Otto to give her a raise. For reasons he would never explain, he'd paid Emma Dumpke three times what he paid this one. I could only surmise that Emma B. intimidated him and having control over her salary was his one way to exert dominance. Oh, Freud would have a field day with that one. I may have been way off the mark, but it was the only explanation I could come up with.*

*I learned later that he'd promised her the deed to the cottage. Money. Land. But he never delivered.*

*I made sure, then, to send her home with little treats whenever possible. An extra cake from the cook, leftover pocket change kept in a jar until it accumulated into a reasonable sum. She had really helped me when I needed her and I wanted to show my appreciation.*

*Her biggest favor, though she didn't realize it, was keeping Otto out of my hair. I'd begun to play a larger and larger role in the running of Pearl and the more occupied Otto was with his other businesses and his remaining lover, the more I was free to handle the board myself and steer the company into the direction I wanted. Already we'd seen an increase in production* since I first joined in an official capacity. Though the credit was given to Otto. He was, after all, still the president. And a man.

About a year after Emma Dumpke left us, I sensed a growing tension between Otto and Emma B. I heard from Helga, who had just come on to assist with the household duties, that Otto had proposed to his mistress. Emma Dumpke's departure had terrified him, leaving him to think that he might lose Emma B. as well. She'd refused.

And refused. And refused.

I confronted Otto about it during a trip we made to St. Louis, though I did not let on everything I knew. The threat of Prohibition was casting an increasingly alarming shadow over our industry. Some were expecting to close their doors, but Otto and I continued to share a similar mind when it came to the business of running Pearl: the only way we could save her if the worst happened was to diversify. Our correspondence with Adolphus indicated that he shared our concerns, and our solutions. His health was failing and he was unable to make the trip to Texas, much as he'd wanted to visit his Lone Star Brewery. So he invited us to Missouri, a trip I was most excited to take. And my health and mobility had improved tremendously so I was finally able to do so.

But the journey was tinged with sadness.

Even at that time, I'd already lost so many of my siblings; Dorothy and Herman had died long before we moved to Texas. But others, Anna, Johanna, and Helen had all passed after I'd left. It had crushed me not to be with the family at those difficult times, but Otto always insisted that he couldn't leave town and would worry about me going alone.

So only John and Catherine remained. Along with their spouses and children. The reunion was joyous even as we all mourned the many losses.

Though one of John's many qualities was his sharp mind, a dimwit could have seen that Otto and I were not in harmony. My brother didn't like that Otto came back to St. Louis once there was a business purpose to do so, but never on personal accounts.

"What about his family?" he asked me. "Has he never wanted to see them? Bad enough that he kept you from us, but you'd think he'd want to see them."

"Otto Koehler's family consists of mining camps, railroads, quarries, and Pearl. In that order. He feels like opening up our home in San Antonio was enough. He never wanted the inconvenience of returning to St. Louis unless it was necessary."

"I have never told you this, Emma, but I've not liked Otto from the beginning."

"Then why did you invest so much money in him?" Without John's early trust, Pearl might not exist.

"It was for you. Whatever my feelings, you chose him. And I chose to help you."

Our trip was a success by any other standard. Together with Adolphus, we hatched any number of plans about how we could transform our breweries and stay afloat if the Grim Reaper of Prohibition turned his bony hand onto the production of alcohol. Otto and I both hoped that it would never come to that, even as we were certain that it would.

Our marriage came to a head once again on the train ride back. Perhaps the stress of all that lay before us caught up, but Otto and I bickered terribly at every turn. At last, he told me what was bothering him.

"I've asked Emma Burgemeister to marry me." I already knew this, but didn't let on.

We were in the dining car. I'm certain he selected this time and place because he was afraid I would make a scene.

"You're married to me, Otto."

"I love her, Emma. God help me, I love her."

"You loved me once. And then Emma Dumpke. Are you really that fickle?"

"Please. You don't need to give me a history lesson."

I pressed a white linen napkin against my mouth and set it on my lap. "You should know that I will refuse to sign divorce papers."

I'd had much time to consider my response.

"Why? You can have anything you want. But I can't do this without you." His face wrinkled in fear; did he really think that I would give no resistance?

"I'm beginning to think that you can't do anything without me," I told him.

"That's not fair."

"Maybe it is, maybe it isn't. You wrestle with your conscience tonight and let me know what you come up with. But I will not release you from this marriage, dead as it is. That would be devastating to Pearl. And I will not allow that for my employees."

"Our employees."

"Oh, now you are taking some responsibility for them? Come now. Let's not have that same old conversation."

Otto removed his eyeglasses and rubbed his face. "The two of you must be in cahoots. She refused me, too."

"Emma B. turned down your proposal? Why?"

"Because she said that she felt bad enough about our arrangement and couldn't do that to you."

"I knew I liked her, despite it all."

"She's even ended our relationship." He took his glasses off and rubbed his eyes. "I am a lost man. Emma refuses to have me in her bed. She refuses to marry me. And you refuse to divorce me."

"I feel so terribly sorry for you." I did not try to conceal my sarcasm. Had anyone been dining near us, what on earth would they have thought of our bizarre conversation?

"Am I to be alone all my life?"

I almost relented. I saw in his pain the young man I had married. Eager to make his mark on the world, but wounded by an impoverished past. He'd had no compunction leaving his parents and his homeland when opportunity arose across the Atlantic. He'd left Lone Star Brewery and betrayed the trust of the Anheuser and Busch families by starting the San Antonio Brewing Association. He asked me to leave my family and all that I loved so that he could have a fresh start in Texas.

Perhaps I should have seen the pattern earlier. People were expendable if they stood in the way of his ambitions.

But he was not a young man anymore. He'd achieved the status of being one of the wealthiest men in America. And yet, he remained poor when it came to relations. Friends, wife, and lovers—all had been casualties. And now he was paying the price.

So my lapse toward mercy was brief. He'd never learn if people kept smoothing the path and forgiving when there was no real contrition.

Good for the other Emmas. They'd had better backbones than I.

"Are you listening?" he asked, like a repetitive child.

"I'm listening, Otto. I'm just not capitulating."

Two months later, he was dead.

The jury had been out more than seventeen hours. This closes one of the most sensational murder cases in the southwest in recent years.

The Arkansas City Daily *News – Arkansas City, Kansas January 23, 1918*

# CHAPTER TWENTY-SEVEN

MABEL WAS MOST EAGER to hear the next part of the story, even if she already knew its details. Frieda had wrangled up some old newspaper clippings from Mrs. Koehler's attic and Mabel had already spent several late night hours pouring over them. It felt a bit like reading the last page of a book just to find out how it will end. And yet, Otto's death had not been the end. It had been the *beginning* where Emma Koehler was concerned.

"Shall we continue or are you feeling tired?" she asked Emma.

"Doctor Weaver must have given me miracle pills. I feel twenty years old. Let's continue."

Then, the doorbell rang. It escaped Mabel's attention save for an acute awareness of it. Letters were always arriving and family was always stopping in, especially as Mrs. Koehler's days waned. And Mabel had no doubt that her meeting with the attorney would prompt more of them to stop over in the hopes of being remembered in her will.

Mabel picked up her pen and turned her notebook to a new page. But then, she heard a voice—a *particular voice*—and they both fell to the floor as she rushed to her feet.

"Buck!" she cried. She ran into the foyer and saw the tall but gaunt figure of her brother standing at the threshold, where Helga had just opened the door.

That knot in her stomach that she'd been feeling left as she took him in. She'd been afraid that she'd dreamed his phone call or that something would happen to him before he could get to Texas. But here he was. All six feet of him.

She noticed how the left arm of his coat was folded and pinned to the shoulder. But she'd spent so much time picturing it that the shock of this loss was somewhat diminished.

"As I live and breathe, my little sister has gotten even prettier." Buck swept her toward him with his right arm, picking her up as if she were a toothpick and swinging her around without regard to the large furniture pieces that decorated the room. She was mindful of her feet and didn't hit anything.

Helga closed the door and slipped into the parlor to wheel Mrs. Koehler out, but Mabel stopped them.

Holding Buck's hand, her petite one disappearing into his calloused one, she introduced him. "Mrs. Koehler, this is my brother. Thomas Hartley. But we call him Buck."

She nodded. "Mr. Hartley, it's good to meet you. Thank you for your service. Our Mabel has been quite worried about you."

*Our Mabel.* A slight thing, perhaps, but to Mabel it was an endearment as much as a treasure. Mrs. Koehler, sharp tongue and all, had grown a place in her heart like a substitute mother.

Buck took off his hat, leaned over, and gave her a kiss on her cheek. Mabel could see the surprise in Emma's eyes, but then a blush rose on her skin. "I wouldn't let the Japs keep me away. We lost too many good men over there, though."

"I read the newspapers," she said. "Dreadful times. Dreadful times."

She turned her head to Mabel. "I imagine you will both have a lot of catching up to do. We can pick up again tomorrow. Helga can make up a room for him upstairs and Frieda can scrounge something up in the kitchen."

Mabel had never expected Mrs. Koehler to extend such generosity to her brother, but, expressing her gratitude, she helped him get situated in the bedroom opposite hers. After he'd eaten—Frieda could whip up anything, even on short notice and with rationing limits—Buck said that he'd like to get some fresh air.

Mabel slipped a sweater on and they headed east. She hadn't intended to walk toward the towering smokestacks of the Pearl Brewery, but she realized later that it must have been some kind of homing instinct inside her. The lore of Pearl had become a part of her heartbeat.

She took Buck's arm and leaned her head against it as they walked. She was afraid to ever let go.

"You know about Robert?" she asked tentatively.

He sighed. "Yes. I received a letter from Pops before we took off on the *Yorktown*. Bad business. Killed in a training accident in Northern Ireland. Before things even heated up over there. Maybe it's for the best, though. If you're going to die in the war, better to go before you've even seen combat rather than to suffer the ravages. It's brutal out there, Mabel. I wouldn't wish that on my worst enemy, let alone Robert."

She hadn't thought of it that way. By avoiding combat, he'd missed the torment of its brutality. Even if the ending was the same.

"He was such a dear soul," she said. "He should have been in a university, surrounded with stacks and stacks of ancient books. Not in a U-boat on the other side of the Atlantic."

"No one should be anywhere near this. But there is evil in the world and sometimes the battle requires more than words."

"I know. I think every soul on earth has been touched in some way or another by this war. I was too wrapped up in my own worries to look up and realize it."

She stopped and turned to him. "It was so much for me. *Too* much. First Mama. I know that was many years ago, but you never really get over a loss like that. But then Robert left and then you. And we got the news about him and worried constantly once we'd heard that you were missing. Pops didn't take it well, Buck. And he wasn't in a good place to begin with."

His voice quieted. "I heard. When I called Mrs. Molling, I asked for Pops and she told me. You've had no word from him at all?"

She shook her head. "He doesn't even know I'm in Texas. I was sure that he'd come back to the apartment at some point and Mrs. Molling would ring me up. But we've heard nothing."

Mabel felt the sting on her face of tears that had gathered. She let them fall, gasping at first, and then a full cry that hurt all the way down to her chest. Buck pulled her into his chest and stroked her hair. When they were children, he used to tug at her braids as any brother would do. But now he was all grown up, a man before he should have had to be, taking his turn at caring for her.

"It's not your fault," he said several times. She wasn't sure if she could believe that, but it sounded good coming from him.

"Was I wrong to come here? To leave him back in Baltimore?" Her voice was muffled as she spoke against his wool sweater. It scratched her cheeks, but she didn't pull back.

He lifted her chin with his hand. "No. No—don't believe that for one second. Pops always had one way to deal with problems: the bottle. Ever since Mama died. And this was two more big blows right at once."

"Why wasn't I enough, Buck?" Mabel found herself saying the words that she'd felt all along but couldn't bring herself to acknowledge.

"What do you mean?"

She looked up, seeing his tear-stained eyes matching hers. "Why wasn't I enough to keep him from drinking? He hadn't lost *everything*. I was still there."

Buck took a deep breath. "Do not think that. You are *more* than enough. You are the one who became the little homemaker after we lost Mama. You learned her recipes and even improved on them. You did all the market shopping and all the mending. And you still managed to go to school and earn good grades. God, when I think back to that, I think about how selfish Robert and I both were, letting you take on all those roles with so little help. So, Mabel, you *were* everything. But Pops' brain was pretty well pickled even before Robert and I left. Maybe it was all more than he could take."

So many things made sense, just talking them through with Buck. It's no wonder she'd been swept up in Artie's pursuit of her. She'd been so desperate to be *wanted* by someone that she hadn't stopped to consider the intentions of the one she got involved with.

That's why everything was so different with Erik. He made her feel like she was truly *valued*. Not merely *desired*.

Buck's words, added to Mrs. Koehler's commission to not waste any more minutes in the past, put some balm on the wounds in her heart. She had to trust that Pops would make his way back from wherever he was. And if he didn't, at least her brother was here to bear that with her.

She slipped her arm in his again and they continued walking.

"I haven't asked about what happened to *you* yet." She wondered if he was right that a boy as sweet and sensitive as Robert might have been better off being lost so early. He might not have survived whatever duration Buck had had to endure.

A dark look crossed his eyes. "I flew my plane off the *USS York-town*. We'd received intelligence that there was a Jap destroyer in the Coral Sea. We followed orders to sink it. And we did. But they'd shot at my gas tank and I went down. I clung to a piece of the wreckage and swam to a tiny island off the coast of Australia. My arm had been badly injured. The village doctor tried to save it, but there was no use. It had become badly infected and he warned that it would spread and kill me if he didn't remove it."

What a ghastly thought! Silence passed between them before he continued. "And when I'd rested and regained my strength, I made it further to a town called Conway. Thank God Australia picked the right side of this fight."

"So you weren't in enemy hands?" She shuddered at some of the horrors she'd worried over. Accounts of terrible tortures made their way to this side of the Pacific.

"Only the enemies of starvation and weather. But once I made it to the shore, I was well taken care of by locals."

"Then why did it take so long for us to hear from you?"

"It was a primitive area. No telephones. Spotty mail service. And it was many weeks before Australian troops came by and I could hitch a ride in a transport vehicle to somewhere that had communication with American forces."

"I'm so relieved."

"It wasn't a cakewalk, Mabel. Or a vacation."

She hadn't meant it that way. Just that it could have been worse.

"I know that." Words, once spoken, couldn't be taken back. If only we could reclaim our breath and start over.

"I found out later that the ship we sank, the *Shōhō*, wasn't a destroyer at all. It was a light air carrier vessel. So it was all for nothing."

"Wasn't it a military ship, though?"

"Yes. With three small aircraft on it. And yet we pounded it. Waste of torpedoes. And Devastators. We lost three attack planes in that skirmish. And it took me out of the rest of the fighting."

He said that with agitation. Mabel supposed she'd never understand. She was glad that her brother was alive, but maybe there was more to it for him. She remembered Erik's disappointment that he wasn't able to go and fight. A woman might be relieved to have the opportunity to stay on safe ground and contribute here. But a man seemed to hear the call of war like a siren. A primal need to go to battle. Or, more likely, a desire to defend their country.

Their walk had taken them closer to Pearl. Mabel changed the touchy subject and hoped to bring her brother's attention to things of the present. She told him all about her past few months, from answering Mrs. Koehler's advertisement, to the trip to Texas, to the fascinating story of the brewery's matriarch.

She did not tell him about Erik. Buck hadn't been around for the Artie saga, but he wouldn't have liked it. Older brothers were historically defensive of younger sisters and Buck would surely be no different.

"But you don't even like beer," he said when she told him about the brief tour she'd taken of Pearl.

"It's not the taste, or what I imagine it to be. It's my silly fear that I'll turn into Pops if I try it."

He stopped and turned her toward him.

"You're not Pops, Mabel. You're your own person. I wouldn't let that stop you from trying it, not if you otherwise want to. Robert and I—" he stopped, probably realizing that speaking of him in the present tense was no longer possible. "Robert and I used to throw many pints back. And we never turned into our father. It depends on why you do it, I guess. He did it to escape pain."

"You're probably right," she agreed. "I know it doesn't make any sense. But I did learn about something called near-bear. They call it *La Perla*. All the taste and none of the effects."

"Sounds dreadful."

"Why?"

"Because half the fun of it *is* the effect. As long as you don't lose your head about it."

"I'll leave that to you boys, then." She realized that the reference was intended to include Robert. How easy it was to slip back into old habits with Buck around.

"Frieda taught me something neat, though." She was anxious to turn the conversation. "She told me that if you soak your hair in beer for two hours and then wash it, it will come out looking more clean than any shampoo would do."

He looked at her with a funny crook in his eyebrow. The same one that always preceded a laugh.

"Don't tell me you tried that," he chuckled. "I can't quite picture you with your head over a basin seeing if she's right."

"I haven't *yet*." In fact, she'd planned to try it in the morning. Opening night for *Green Grow the Lilacs* was tomorrow night and she wanted to look her best. Frieda wouldn't steer her wrong.

"My sister, the living stein."

She tried to think up some retort, but just then, a light blue convertible drove by.

Erik.

He pulled over and honked the horn. She worried what might be going through his mind, seeing her walking with a tall and handsome stranger in uniform.

She waved and smiled, gestures he returned in kind.

"Hey, darling. I was on my way to see you." He stopped the car and hopped out. He looked Buck up and down, but his expression was one more curious than jealous.

"Hello!" She pulled away from her brother and lifted up on her toes to give Erik a quick kiss on the cheek. She wondered what Buck might think; he'd never known her to have a beau. But Erik had become too important to her to slight.

She took his arm. "This is my brother."

Erik's mouth broke into a wide smile and he put out his hand. Buck took it, looking at Mabel with questions in his eyes.

"Buck Hartley," he said.

"Yes. Mabel has told us all about you. We've been so anxious for your arrival."

Mabel had to pinch her lips together to keep from grinning. Erik's welcome was more heartfelt than she could have even hoped.

"I've been anxious to get here. I thought my little sister might need some looking after, but I may have been wrong." He looked back and forth between the two of them.

"Mabel looks after herself quite well. It's no small thing to travel across the country on your own and start over."

The men hadn't let go of each other's grips. Mabel watched her brother's jaw tighten. She really wanted them to like each other, and though Erik seemed willing, Buck would not be so easily won over.

In time, she assured herself. In time.

"Gentlemen," she said, forcing a smile. She pulled away from Erik and stood between them. "What a lucky girl I am to have the two of you in my life. Buck, this is Erik Garrels. He is Mrs. Koehler's nephew. Well, really, her cousin. But she calls all family by the more familiar name. Erik works at the brewery and moonlights as a stage hand at a local theater."

"Does he moonlight at anything else?" Buck released Erik's hand and put his own into his pocket.

Mabel appreciated his concern, but there was no excuse for rudeness. She would have preferred to tell Buck privately about this, but here it was. It was up to her to set the example for how things would proceed from here.

"Yes," she answered her brother, moving back to stand by Erik. Her heart felt like it stopped as she prepared her words. "You might say that. Erik is my beau."

Buck opened his mouth to speak, but she laid a hand on his arm. "And before you say anything about it, I expect that you will trust my judgment. I've had to grow up a lot in the last year. I'm not the little girl you left behind in Baltimore."

She watched a thousand thoughts race through his mind, but at last, he took a deep breath.

"You're right. Old habits, I guess. I'll probably never think anyone is good enough for my sister."

Erik spoke again. "One can never have too many people who hold them in such high regard. I assure you, Mr. Hartley, that I have excellent intentions toward your sister and I know that I will prove that to you if you give me the chance."

"Buck. You can call me Buck."

It came out in such a staccato pace, but Mabel knew that he

wouldn't have corrected Erik if he weren't willing to concede some familiarity. It was a start.

Erik continued, looking at Mabel. "I was about to swing by Auntie Emma's house to tell you that I'd reserved some seats in the front row for us for opening night tomorrow." He turned to her brother. "But now that you're here, I'd be happy to set one aside for you as well."

"Theater?" Buck looked skeptical. He was all baseball and wrestling. Not acting and dancing, despite his talent with a paintbrush. But she shot him a look that told him she wanted him to come.

"Sure," he said at last. "Thank you."

"Well, then," Erik said, putting his arm around Mabel and giving her a light squeeze. "You two must have lots to catch up on and I will only get in the way. I don't need to come to Auntie Emma's after all, then. Give her my love and tell her that if she changes her mind about tomorrow, I'll save a seat for her, too."

"I will." She smiled. He'd been so patient through this exchange. "See you tomorrow."

"Buck?" He put his hand out again and her brother took it more readily. "If there's anything I can do for you, say the word. I'm happy to set you up with a job at Pearl should you need it and my car is at your disposal. And don't hesitate to ask Emma for anything. She's like an apple pie. Crusty on the outside, but all soft when you get to know her. And there isn't anything she wouldn't do for family."

Apple pie. Mabel smiled at the metaphor. Not a turtle, not a porcupine. Apple pie was just right.

Erik stepped back into his car and waved as he drove off. Mabel missed the goodbye kiss—not even a peck on a cheek. But she had to respect that Erik would naturally take things slow in front of her brother.

She turned to Buck. "Oh, isn't that wonderful? You could stay here in San Antonio and walk right into a job. Pearl is one of the best employers in the city."

That dark look passed across his face again.

"What is it?" she pressed.

"I'm not staying."

The knot in her stomach returned. "What do you mean?"

"I'm only on leave. I'm going back to the Pacific in a week."

Emma Hedda Burgemeister marries
James M. Turley
February 11, 1919
New Orleans, Louisiana

*Source: New Orleans, Louisiana Marriage
Records Index*

# CHAPTER TWENTY-EIGHT

BUCK'S WORDS HAD SET a cloud over Mabel for the rest of the day and all of the next. Of course he couldn't be here forever. What had she been thinking? The joy that he had returned mostly unscathed turned to bitterness when she realized that his soundness of mind meant that the Army Air Corps owned him for the duration of the war.

Or until he was hurt again.

Or worse.

She'd asked him about that, why the loss of an arm wasn't enough to disqualify him from service. And he admitted that it had been offered to him. But he'd argued for at least a position in an encampment away from the front lines; he was convinced there was still much service left in him.

She was determined not to sink again into that pit that she'd wallowed in for too long. Buck was alive. A hero, even. And at least he'd be assigned out of combat's way. She had reason to hope.

As much as she would have liked to spend every minute of his leave together, his hourglass was not the only one dripping time by all too quickly. Mrs. Koehler had taken a turn for the worse last night after rallying for the past few days. Doctor Weaver made a call to the mansion in the middle of the night, and this time Emma had put up no protests.

After breakfast, she called Mabel into her bedroom.

Mabel had not yet ventured into this place. It had never been said that she couldn't see Mrs. Koehler's private chambers, but it was simply not done. Even at her age, she liked to emerge in the late morning with her rouge and lipstick on, her hair set, her attire pressed. But today was an exception.

Helga showed her into the room, oddly shaped with angled walls. It had never been intended to be a bedroom, but a secondary parlor. Less formal than the one in front of the house. The sunlight was good and Mabel could see why Mrs. Koehler had chosen this spot. It had been her room for years now, as the effort to climb the stairs became too much even after her recovery.

Mrs. Koehler's face was colorless, lacking in cosmetics and the natural rosiness to which Mabel had grown accustom. Her white hair lay unkempt against the pillow and her nightdress was unbuttoned enough that Mabel could see the canvas of wrinkles that lay across her neck. The room was a combination of stale air with a hint of rosewater. Not unpleasant. Not like it could have been in the room of an elderly person. Helga wore the hat of nursemaid as well as housekeeper and did her job well.

Mrs. Koehler beckoned with a frail finger and gestured for Mabel to sit in the high-backed chair at the side of the bed. As she drew closer, she thought for the first time that despite a month of Mrs. Koehler's dire words, this was the first time in which death really looked like it was drawing near. Her lips were cracked and her skin was translucent in its paleness.

Mrs. Koehler took her hand in a gesture that was becoming more frequent between them. Mabel found herself stroking the older, spotted skin with deep affection. "Your brother," the old woman said in a forced whisper. "He has settled in?"

"Yes. He's in the room across the hall from me. Frieda made him an elaborate breakfast. And he even agreed to take a tour of

Pearl today with Erik."

That last bit had felt rather like a miracle. But they'd gotten along remarkably well at the play and Erik rang last night with the offer. Buck actually accepted. Mabel wished she could be a gnat, flying alongside them unnoticed, to hear what they would talk about.

"I know you would much rather be with him today," Mrs. Koehler said. "But I'm afraid that we still have so much to cover and so little time in which to do it. I hope you'll indulge an old lady and spend the day with me."

"Of course. Of course I'm here, Emma. We can work as much or as little as you are up to."

"Doctor Weaver is coming by a little later with another shot for me. He's not a bad sort after all, is he?"

"He just wants to make you comfortable."

Mrs. Koehler nodded with effort. "Yes, yes. I've been too stubborn. Maybe if I'd let him give me his medicines years ago I'd have more time."

She took a deep, wheezy breath before continuing. "But, as I've said. No looking back. We have only the time ahead of us and I will use it well. Let's begin."

*1914*

*The accounts of Otto's murder are well documented and to learn the facts of it, there are many clippings in Helga's care. Including the transcript of Emma B's trial. There is no need to spend precious time here going over it, except for the most basic facts. Emma Burgemeister began to get plagued with migraines. With family so far away in Germany, she forged a letter in the name of a neighbor named Henry Cordt and wrote to Emma Dumpke, now Daschiel, begging her to come to San Antonio to take care of her old friend. She knew that her own plea would likely fall on deaf ears. Their relationship seemed to have suffered damage after all. Emma D. came reluctantly, likely burdened with the guilt of all that had happened.*

*Otto had been having fits lately. I knew that the coming Prohibition* terrified him and he lashed out over nothings. It angered him to learn that I had purchased a new wheelchair with the help of my nurse. He was furious, too, that I was in one at all after having made so much progress. But I had my setbacks, and he'd returned home during a particularly painful time.

He set out for Emma's cottage in some kind of rage. I reminded him as he left that the senator was coming over for dinner and he shouldn't be late.

When Sheriff Tobin came to the house that afternoon and told me in a pitiful tone that Otto had been shot three times and lay dead in the cottage, my first thought was of Pearl. So cold had our marriage grown that any sense of mourning for him was a secondary thought, quite distant after my concerns for the brewery. If that seems hard-hearted, I would understand, but I will not sugarcoat the facts and make myself out to be some beleaguered damsel. It was the death of one versus the survival of many.

Otto's death meant that I would have to fight the board for a more powerful position now that I had lost him as an ally, albeit a reluctant one.

When I learned that Emma Burgemeister had been the assailant, I was not surprised. The young woman had chutzpa, as my neighbors at the synagogue would call it. They'd found her on the floor, inconsolable, cradling Otto's body. She continued to be hysterical and clutched her forearm as they took her away. She'd been knifed, though it was unclear at the time if it was self-inflicted or if Otto had attacked her. Her only words were, "I killed him. I had to do it."

She was in too poor a condition to be brought to prison. Instead, they took her all the way to Baylor Hospital. Emma Daschiel was held for five nights on account of conspiracy for murder, but her husband hurried over from New York and paid her five hundred-dollar bail. We never saw her again and I think she was happy to be rid of us.

Otto's funeral took place on the same day that Burgemeister was released from the hospital and brought to the Bexar County Jail. I only learned that after the fact. I was inundated with letters and flowers from all over the country. Three thousand people came to mourn him. I used the excuse of being bereft to decline the opportunity to eulogize him. What role was I supposed to play in the public arena? The heartbroken wife? The ardent business partner? The jilted woman?

I've never been a skilled actress.

I chose to keep silent, mumbling a brief thank you to the many well-wishers who stopped by the pew to shake my hand and offer their condolences. I let them cast me in the part as they saw fit and newspaper reports around the country described me in whichever way they imagined me to be. The Beethoven Maennerchor sang. The robust voices of the men reminded me of the concerts my father used to take me to. Melodies of the old country that were more nostalgic than funereal. I dabbed my eyes and probably mollified anyone who'd suspected my indifference. But my tears were not for Otto. I cried, instead for the memory of my father.

I sat in my wheelchair as the pallbearers picked up his casket. All of them members of the San Antonio Brewing Association. All whom, at one time or another, had shared in the triumphs and tribulations of our industry. I let them think me to be a poor widow, weakened with grief.

You always have more power over your adversaries when they underestimate you.

Justice of Peace loses; Emma Burgemeister Turley gets judgment against R. Neil Campbell: Judgment for the plaintiff was rendered by Judge J.T. Sluder in the trial in the 73rd District Court of the suit brought by Emma Burgemeister Turley against Bessie and R. Neil Campbell for the setting aside of a deed to two lots in the city. The plaintiff alleged in her suit, which was filed before her marriage to J.M. Turley, that lots 58 and 59 in the South Park Hunstock Addition, which had been transferred in January 1915 was for no consideration and was to have been held in trust. Consideration was cited, she claimed, though none had been actually paid.

*San Antonio Express News – San Antonio, Texas December 1, 1920*

# CHAPTER TWENTY-NINE

MRS. KOEHLER'S VOICE began to give out.

Mabel stood up. "May I arrange your pillows for you?"

She shook her head. "Water. Just some water. We have to continue."

"Emma, you look exhausted. We can take a break."

She shook her head again and attempted to sit up. She groaned at the effort "No. There's more to say. Fetch the water and let's keep going."

"All right."

Mabel left the bedroom and entered the kitchen, where Frieda was kneading dough for tomorrow night's family dinner.

"How is she?" the cook asked.

"Not good. But still determined."

"That could be the title of her biography."

Mabel leaned against the counter. "Is that what I'm doing? Writing her biography? She's never really said, yet I've filled three notebooks and then three more as I translated the shorthand." She hadn't given up on the idea of turning it into something that would inspire young women in a world that was barely beginning to welcome them. She hoped she would have Emma's blessing to do so.

Frieda handed her the glass of water she hadn't even asked for. "Whatever becomes of it, the story was only one part of her plan."

Mabel set the glass down. "What do you mean?"

"She was looking for a wife for Erik."

Mabel's throat tightened and she gripped the counter top to keep her hands from shaking. "She *what?*"

Frieda pulled a chair from the table and sat down. She patted the one next to her and Mabel slid into it.

"She never said that. Not specifically. But I've been here for many years and I listen to the comings and goings. She was delighted when Ernestina and Erik showed an interest in each other. Erik had come over from Germany devastated after things fell apart with his parents. He was only twelve years old and as her only relative on her mother's side, she felt especially devoted to him. He became the son she never had."

"But what does that have to do with putting the advertisement in the paper?"

"After Ernestina broke his heart, he threw himself into work both at the brewery and at the theater. But he was so unhappy. And she wanted to see him settled before she died."

"Such lengths, though. And how would she know it would work?" This conversation was so unusual. She felt like she was listening to a story, forgetting that she was an unwitting character in it.

"I think she just wanted to try. Remember, her whole life has been about finding a way to do something when no other options seem possible. Mrs. Koehler didn't get to be where she was by pursuing things through ordinary means. Or waiting for things to happen."

She had a point. It explained much: why she wanted a photograph included with the application.

"Why such a scheme, though? Surely there are plenty of nice young women right here in San Antonio."

"When has Emma Koehler ever done things by conventional means?"

"Not in the brief time I've known her."

"I suppose this way she could cast the net wide. And, test the mettle a bit."

"How would she do that?"

"Well, someone who would answer would have to be adventurous enough to come out here, not otherwise attached, hungry to better her life."

Mabel opened her mouth to counter this, but realized how right it was. Then, the question that burned in her mind.

"Does Erik know?"

Frieda shook her head. "No. I don't think he has any idea. He's nothing like his aunt in that way. He's as much a pawn in her well-meaning plan as you are."

It relieved her. Much could be forgiven of an elderly woman, desperate to put things in order with the remaining time she had. Less so a man who would have played a part in something that seemed at once conniving and brilliant.

The cook continued. "I think she wanted something else that she couldn't admit. Or at least, she found something in you that she hadn't bargained for."

"What do you mean?"

"I've seen how she interacts with you. Our Emma has grown quite fond of your time together. I think she even sees you as the daughter she never had."

Mabel's throat tightened. One of Mama's gifts: sending a motherless girl to a childless woman. Neither could fully fill the voids that had been left, but there was an undeniable affection between them that had made the void somewhat less painful.

Could Mrs. Koehler have foreseen that? Or was it a happy coincidence that the old woman picked the girl who needed her most?

Either way, Frieda's observation was eye-opening.

"So is all this dictation for naught? Have I really only been here as some kind of audition for her nephew?"

Frieda shook her head. "No. Mrs. Koehler doesn't do anything without purpose. She always liked the phrase *kill two birds with one stone.* No doubt she wanted these memories recorded. She hates how the story of Pearl has always been shaped by reporters, by the men on the board, by her husband. Regardless of what you choose to do with this work—and she has entrusted that decision to you—she'll go out knowing that she did everything she could do."

She stood up and poured a second glass of water. She handed it to Mabel. "There's not much time left. I'd say that forgiveness is in order, and remember that neither of us know what it's like to be an old woman at the end of her life. And things seemed to have turned out pretty well, haven't they? Am I wrong or are you and Mr. Garrels as taken with each other as she might have hoped?"

Mabel's cheeked warmed with embarrassment. "Yes. It looks that way."

"Then is any harm done? It worked, then, even if it was contrived."

"I suppose you're right." Mabel took the glass from her. "She'll be ready for this."

"Mabel? There is one more thing to consider."

"Yes?" She stopped and looked at Frieda's saddened face.

"You've seen that she's losing her mind. Slowly. The senility. My mother went the same way. But it wasn't only the forgetfulness. It was the paranoia. The compulsion of rash decisions. Mrs. Koehler's sharp and has only experienced these mildly, but I've seen how they ravish a mind. She may not be entirely to blame for her actions."

Mabel shrugged her shoulders. "I know. Don't worry. I forgive her. It's just a lot to think about."

She left the kitchen, feeling heavier. She was rather proud of her work for Mrs. Koehler, aimless as it had started out. It had such potential and when Mrs. Koehler passed, Mabel would get to work organizing it into something that could really make a difference to women. She'd not forgotten her epiphany in the Walgreen's cosmetics aisle.

But Frieda was right. No matter how she'd gotten here, the feelings between Erik and her were genuine. They'd even met on their own, at the empty San Pedro pool, hours before Mrs. Koehler's Sunday dinner.

As if it was meant to be, regardless.

She wondered what would have happened if she hadn't met Erik that afternoon at the park. If she'd taken a right instead of a left on her walk. Met him at dinner and been introduced to him as *Bernard*. Would their story have played out in the same way? Would they have felt the confines of something set in motion by design? Or would the natural attraction they felt have been evident and put them in this exact place: on the edge of being in love.

It shouldn't matter. They were together. Happy. That's what mattered.

She knocked and reentered Mrs. Koehler's bedroom. Her breathing was light and rhythmic, but she awoke as Mabel set the water on the nightstand.

"Ah, thank you," she said with a feeble voice. "I'm parched."

Mabel took a new look at her employer. Mrs. Koehler was so thin, so old. Her white skin and white nightgown against the white sheets contributed to the anemic look. It was impossible to feel anything but compassion as she lay there. Was there really anything so wrong in trying to secure the happiness of someone she loved as much as she loved her nephew? And wasn't Erik deserving of finding love after so much tragedy in his life?

Wasn't Mabel?

She took her seat again. She placed her hand on Mrs. Koehler's. "Tell me about what happened next," she said. "Tell me about Pearl."

I might have known that my position at Pearl would be challenged upon Otto's death. I'd been tolerated by the other board members as long as he was alive. My pact with my husband had allowed us to hold many cards. I kept silent about his romantic affairs. He voted my way on the board. But without his vote, my position was tenuous.

It meant I had to work harder. Twice as hard as any of the men. I came to work before they arrived. I stayed after they left. I made rounds at the brewery, even from my wheelchair on days when my legs betrayed me. I asked questions about the latest shipment of hops, challenging my managers to always be looking for better, less expensive sources without compromising the quality.

On every floor, I tasked them with two charges: tell me one way we could improve in their area, and tell me one way they could diversify their equipment should the worse happen.

And the worse did happen. Two years after Otto died, enough dry men had been elected to the United States Congress to give real teeth to the eighteenth amendment. The men in the boardroom would argue about what to do. Envoys were sent to Austin and Washington to plead our cases. But where they believed this would be won politically, I believed we would survive on ingenuity.

Adolphus Busch II agreed with me. After his father's death, he'd taken over the brewery headquartered in St. Louis. We encouraged each other to look for alternate means of keeping our industry afloat.

So while the men were occupied with their high-stakes lunches and conversations over golf games, I set out to create a malt extract syrup that would be the beginning of our salvation. It provided a condensed taste of Pearl beer. The plan was to market it as an ingredient in bread. It could be sold legally on the shelves of grocers and bought by any housewife. They could substitute one half tablespoon of our product for the sugar in the recipe.

Now, this sounds like so little a quantity. And it was. One bottle could last a household an entire year. But we made it known that the extract had another use. A recipe for converting a whole bottle into several gallons of beer was made widely known. It went like this:

*Heat two gallons of water.*
*Add a bottle of malt extract.*
*Add four to six cups of sugar.*
*Slow boil for fifteen minutes.*
*Transfer it to a six-gallon container in a bath of ice water.*
*Fill to the top with water.*
*Add activated yeast*
*Put on a lid and keep it in a warm room for two weeks.*
*Pour into smaller containers with half a teaspoon of corn sugar in each.*
*Place caps on bottles and store in a cool room for two weeks.*

*If that sounds laborious, it was. But the scheme proved brilliant. With the stroke of the pen ratifying Prohibition on January 16, 1920, our malt extracts were already on trucks waiting to be shipped out. The board had finally agreed with this move. Later than I would have liked, but with hard work and long hours, we were able to make the switch in time for a strong introduction into the market.*

*It was challenged in court, of course. Housewives could now make their own brew at home with what was being sold as a baking product. But since the extract itself contained no alcohol—it was the fermenting process with the yeast that did this—it was ruled that it could be distributed legally.*

*The taste depended on so many things. Though the extract was consistent in every bottle, much depended on what the wives did at home. The kind of yeast they used. The source of their water. The brand of their sugar. I was invited into many homes in Texas and had the opportunity to taste it. I wanted to wretch in more cases than not. These were not seasoned brewers who had developed an acute taste for its nuances as I had. But it pleased the people. They had their beer, I had my business.*

*Pearl was not the only brewer to evaporate their wort and sell it as a syrup. But we had it on shelves the day Prohibition was signed into law, establishing ourselves as the premier, trusted brand.*

*This was not enough to get us through such tumultuous years, however. Not every housewife wanted to go through that effort. Not every husband wanted to risk having even that made illegal. Many became dry by law and by fear, if not by taste.*

*So we had to do more. We turned our coldest rooms into icehouses and ice cream kitchens. I used my own funds to purchase laundering equipment and we set up shop to clean clothes. I directed my brewery mechanics to learn the anatomy of an automobile so that they could work on cars on our grounds. We even had a small division that made advertising signs, making use of the employees who had artistic gifts.*

*We also used our bottling facilities to manufacture root beer and other soft drinks.*

*On this point, I was insistent: we removed the xXx label from our bottles. It was not there to be an advertising ploy. To me, and I know Otto would have agreed, it was the designation of the finest of beers, the finest of brewers. And although it had become a recognizable symbol of our products, I felt like it would cheapen its meaning to slap it on root beer or near beer labels. Other brewers chose the opposite route. And though I disagreed, I understood that in these difficult times, we all had to survive however we could.*

*The difference is that they saw survival as the goal. I saw it in another way. If this was merely about scavenging our factories to convert them into something else, was that to be our new existence? Was that to be our new occupation? I'd become a brewer at heart. This malarkey about changing everything was temporary. I had great hopes that the stupidity of Prohibition and the misguidance of teetotalers would wane. I wanted to think ahead to what would happen after, after, after. I was convinced it would be repealed and this was merely about biding time. Not about survival.*

*Mercifully, the board members began to see things my way. I'd like to say that I stood my ground for all of womankind, but all that came later. My only hope was to see my Pearl get through this dark time and emerge on the other side stronger. I advocated for more equipment even as other companies were pulling back.*

*The men on the board thought I was crazy! Buying more equipment to make beer when it was illegal to make beer. But I argued that the price would never be better. Those who made the machines were hit as well. If we kept ordering, but demanded lower prices, we could increase our capacity at minimal cost.*

*They went along with it. We bought enough to double our production from what we'd output at the time of Otto's presidency. In exchange, I acquiesced on one point: we changed the name legally from San Antonio Brewing Association to Alamo Industries. I have to admit that it was in better alignment with our current mission, but I received verbal assurances that the name would revert to the original as soon as Prohibition ended.*

*A name change came about sooner than I expected and not as I would have liked. When one tries to be many things, they are good at nothing. And Pearl suffered from my enthusiasm. Within a year, the non-consumable divisions were failing. The dry cleaning, the auto repair, the advertising signs. Instead of closing them down, I sold them off to companies already in those lines of work. We made a small profit and I held my place on the board by a thread.*

*If I hadn't been the voice of diversification, we would have lost Pearl altogether. So there were some failures. But there were more successes.*

*Leaving the non-consumable ventures behind, the board voted to call our enterprise Alamo Food Industries.*

*Ghastly, if you ask me. Unimaginative at best. But necessary.*

*In the end, though, it wasn't the name or the product that mattered. What mattered is that we were the only brewery in Texas to keep every single person employed. And that was the victory I cared about most.*

"Any questions?" Mrs. Koehler's words were followed by a steady cough that could not be subdued easily with a glass of water.

Mabel waited until it had stopped before answering her.

"So what happened? At the end of Prohibition? Did it all happen as you expected it to?""

Mrs. Koehler smiled, perhaps the widest Mabel had ever seen on her.

"Oh, yes. At midnight on the morning that the Blaine Act ended that wretched amendment, we were ready. It was September 15, 1933. And in those dark, early hours, we rolled out one hundred trucks and twenty-five box cars, full to the brim of delicious xXx Pearl Beer."

Woman sues for $7,500 bond:
Mrs. Emma Hedda Burgemeister
Turley, who was acquitted of
the charge of murder of Otto
Koehler, San Antonio brewer,
brought suit in the 57th District
Court Tuesday against the
County of Bexar and John W.
Tobin, former sheriff, to recover
a cash bond of $7,500 which had
been posted and forfeited.

She asks that $6000 of the
money which Tobin is alleged to
have turned over to the county
treasury be paid into court to
await a decision, and that she
have judgment against the
county for the remainder.

Mrs. Turley stood trial in
1918 and was acquitted and
claims the bond now serves no
useful purpose and the money
should be returned to her. (She)
has been told it had been transferred from one account to
another and used for bridge and
road work, making it no longer
available.

*San Antonio Light – San Antonio,
Texas June 9, 1926*

# CHAPTER THIRTY

MABEL KNOCKED ON Buck's door minutes before Erik was due to pick them up for the theater. They all wanted to see the play again. In her eagerness to hear about how his time with Erik had gone, she'd all but forgotten about Mrs. Koehler's plan to play match-maker for her favorite relative. As Frieda had suggested, what did it matter anyway?

"Come in."

She opened the door to see Buck looking dapper in a pair of pants with a long crease down the front of the leg, a sweater over a dress shirt, and a dinner jacket over his shoulders. She'd grown accustomed to the emptiness on his left side.

He was straightening his tie in the mirror, but with some difficulty.

"What are you wearing?" she asked. She adjusted the knot at his neck and smoothed the length of the tie. "Even before you had an Army uniform, you didn't dress this swell."

"It's all thanks to Erik. I'd mentioned how I only had the one uniform and he opened up his closet for me for the duration of my stay."

*How chummy*, she thought, pleased. Wisely, she decided not to press the point. But they must have gotten along well for that to occur.

"What did you think of Pearl?"

He lit up. It was so so good to have Buck here. So, so good to see him excited about something. She put the thought out of her mind that he had only six days left.

"It's a wonder! You've seen it, so you know. What a place. Erik took me through just about every room. We even meet up with Otto A. The head honcho himself. In fact, by the end, Otto A. offered me a job, should I ever want it."

Mabel clapped her hands, remembering that Erik had made the same offer. How could her brother refuse? "Oh, Buck. How wonderful! Would you ever do that?"

He tucked the tie under the sweater, an easier feat with one hand. "You know, I think I would. I don't think I'm made for the university the way Robert would have been. Otto A. showed me some of the things they're already changing because of the war. They're experimenting with cans that use less metal. And creating inexpensive brews that can be sent to the troops. Fascinating stuff. And he has so many plans for after this war is over. I want to be a part of that. What is there for me in Baltimore? You're here and you look like you want to stay. And Lord knows that Erik fellow wants you to stay. I've never seen a boy quite as mad about a girl as that one is."

He said it so endearingly. The thought of Buck and Erik getting along was more than she could have hoped for.

"You've never seen a girl quite as mad about a boy as this one is." She nearly whispered it, testing his reaction.

"Well, you're both fools, if you ask me. But I'm happy to see you two fools together."

"There's nothing foolish about love."

He turned around to face her and pulled a comb from his pocket, running it through his hair. "After all that I've seen, and all that I have yet to see, I'm glad to witness that love is still alive. Makes me think of Mama and Pops before she got sick."

She hung her head and nodded. "They were beautiful together."

He agreed. "That's why he turned to the bottle. I don't think he wanted to continue a life that didn't include her."

"Do you—do you think we'll ever find him?" she asked.

He lowered his head and thought for a moment. "I don't know. Before the war, I might have tried to promise you hope. But life doesn't always work that way. It has an ugly side. I want to, of course. But maybe that's selfish. Maybe seeing us would remind him of her and it would be more than he could bear. Maybe drinking keeps him warm even as the weather is cold. Maybe he's already gone. Passed on to the next life where they're frolicking in a field of lavender for all I know. But I promise you this: don't let your days be full of worry. Live them *in spite* of the rest. Don't let your happiness depend on someone else's decisions."

The doorbell rang.

"That will be your man, Sis. Check the mirror. You've got a smudge on your lipstick and you haven't even kissed him yet today."

What a sport! No matter what happened, she would treasure this conversation with Buck. Adult to adult. He no longer seemed like a big brother to her. Not when she'd lived as much life as she had. But he was a friend now. The very best friend.

She flew down the stairs, straight into Erik's arms as he stood in the open threshold.

The applause began as a roar as the cast took their final bows. Mabel was among the first to hop to her feet. This performance had been even better than the first. And their seats had been amazing once again. She could nearly see the pores on the faces of the actors and actresses. The reflection of the lights on their sweat-kissed skin. She could see the details of the painting she and Erik had done: every streak in the tail of the horse. She'd begun to understand why Erik loved theater so much. It was a chance to create another world. To be encompassed by it. To forget what lay on the outside of these walls, if only for a few hours.

Encouraged by the story about the new statehood of Oklahoma, Mabel began to believe in new beginnings. Erik sat to her left, Buck to her right. She'd had nothing for so long and now she had nearly everything.

Erik wanted to linger after to visit with some of his friends, and asked Mabel if she could stay so that he could introduce her to those she hadn't met yet. He tossed his keys to Buck. "Take her for a spin," he said. "We'll meet you back at the house."

Buck was all too eager. He'd agreed with Mabel that Robert would have loved it. Flashing, unassuming Robert had always longed for a great car. His one nod to adventure. Buck and Mabel would have to live that one out for him.

The hellos and goodbyes didn't take long. The members of the cast had plans to move the party to a nearby dance hall. Some of the girls particularly pled with Erik to join them, but he held onto Mabel's hand even tighter and insisted that he was looking forward to a private evening. But they would find four cases of Pearl Beer in the green room to assist in their celebrations. He left them all to their merriment.

With Buck away in the car, Erik and Mabel strolled the few blocks, taking far longer than it should have. The night was beautiful. A late February evening could almost have been springtime. The stars were out in abundance, seeming like they were hung just for them.

Erik put his arm around her as they walked. "What are you thinking, love?"

She stretched out her arms and lay her head against his chest. "I'm content. Is that an odd word to use? I don't know. But I don't know how else to say it. I'm so very content."

"Just that? Not happy?"

She thought about that word before answering. "It's better than that. Happy is a temporary feeling. You can't know happiness without knowing sadness. So to have one, you know the other is coming again. Content is different. It says that I know there will be ups and downs in the road, but I am going to stay grounded either way. It says that I'm very grateful to be right here in this place."

"I like that. Then I'm content, too."

Their steps plodded along, one slow foot in front of the other.

Mabel spoke up. "Your aunt told me about your parents. I'm sorry about what happened to them. Has your father ever tried to see you again?"

She tried to watch his face in the moonlight, but its shadows were too pronounced to make out his expression. His voice, however, was unflustered.

"He's written a few times. And three times, Auntie Emma has sent him funds for a passage to come over here. But with each one, he gambled them away, certain that he could make money on them and come over here a wealthy man instead of an indebted relative."

Mabel's heart broke for him. "It's funny, isn't it, how sometimes our best lessons are learned by *not* emulating some people. Learning from their mistakes, I suppose. We can be thankful to them for that at least."

He pulled her in a little tighter. "I told you that I want to be a good man. It's because of my father. He *is* a good man. He loved my mother so much. And I will always know how to care for a woman because of that. But I also learned from him the importance of avoiding vices. Because gambling stripped him of everything. And in the end if you *truly* love someone, you'll put their needs above your own weakness. That's how I want to love. And I learned that from what he didn't do."

"My brother likes you," she said. "And he's always been a good judge of character."

"I like him, too. You're lucky to have each other. I don't have any siblings. Only the menagerie of Auntie Emma's relatives."

He stopped and turned toward her. They were standing at the intersection. Few cars were on the road at this late hour and the dome of the synagogue cast an ominous shadow over them.

"Mabel," he said slowly, "I wanted to finish that thought. About how I want to love. I've always thought of that as an ideal, but you put flesh to it. I want to love *you* that way. I know that it's early. We haven't known each other long. But maybe I've seen enough plays to have a romantic piece of me that believes two souls know when they've found each other."

"I love you, too," she whispered. And she did.

"I'm not asking for you to make any promises right now," he said. "But I couldn't let another day pass without letting you know how I feel."

"Your aunt will be so happy," Mabel laughed.

He pulled back. "How did you know?"

"Know?"

"Yes. About her little matchmaking endeavor. That's what you were referring to, right?"

She folded her arms. "Yes. But how did *you* know? Were you in on it?" This felt close to being maneuvered again, and despite where they'd ended up, she didn't want to believe that they'd begun so artificially.

He laughed. "No, no, no. *Please* don't think that. I only got wind of it when she was looking through the applicants. I was at the house one afternoon when Helga retrieved the mail. And there were way more letters than usual. So I pressed her about it and she told me that Auntie Emma wanted to hire a girl to write down her life story. I thought it was a fine idea, but I watched as Helga opened the envelopes and there were photographs in there. Now who requires a photograph with a job application?"

"That's what I thought, too."

"See?" he said. "So I suspected that she was up to something else, and knowing her as I do, it wasn't difficult to figure out. I could never get Helga to confirm it, mind you, but watching the two of them talk about the letters and pictures, I was fairly certain. So I made a point of being at the house as often as I could for a few days. Sneaking a look at the letters that came in. Tossing a few of them before they could get to Auntie Emma. But not so many that she'd notice."

"So you saw my letter and my photograph? Then you already knew who I was when we met at the pool."

He pulled her toward him, but she wasn't quite ready to share the embrace. She didn't know what to think.

"No, darling. I had no idea. I hadn't come across *your* envelope. To this day, I have never seen it. When we met at the pool, all I knew is that I was due to have dinner at the house and that Auntie Emma had told me that there was someone special she wanted me to meet. After meeting you, I was conflicted. I liked you so much. Immediately. But I wanted to be fair to Auntie Emma. She'd gone to great lengths on my behalf. That's why I was late to dinner. I had been at the brewery, but I really lingered. I didn't want to meet this girl she'd picked out for me. I'd already met the only one I wanted to know."

Such romantic words. She felt ashamed for having doubted him.

"Oh, Erik. That was unfair of me to think otherwise. I'm sorry." She put her arms around his waist and enjoyed the feeling of him kissing the top of her head.

"Imagine my surprise, love, when I walked in the door and there you were. It was perfect. Auntie Emma has always known me so well, and here was the girl who *both* of us liked."

"So you see what I mean. She'll be so happy."

"She will. I'm glad we can give her that."

They walked the final block to the Koehler house, arm in arm.

As they approached, the knotty feeling returned. "Look, Erik. That's Doctor Weaver's car."

Erik quickened his pace. "It is. He wasn't due to come until tomorrow. She must have taken a turn for the worse."

She matched his steps and they arrived at the porch in time to see Helga running out to meet them. "Oh, there you are. I was going to come looking for you. Mrs. Koehler is quite ill."

Emma Hedda Burgemeister died in 1942 from an overdose of sleeping pills. She was preceded in death by her husband, Jim.

# CHAPTER THIRTY-ONE

EMMA KOEHLER'S SENILITY came on like a storm. Her recognition of everyone faded, frustrating and frightening her. Doctor Weaver administered strong sedatives in response.

"I wouldn't give this to someone younger," he told the worried bunch. "But at this point, it can only help her. Or at least keep her settled."

What began as an episode became a vigil. Mrs. Koehler's consciousness returned only sporadically, and most of that was fitful. Buck's visit was eclipsed by what was quickly becoming a death-watch. Erik and Mabel took him to the bus station and he promised to return as soon as the war was over. He and Erik stepped out to talk privately, but Erik was evasive to her questions about what they'd discussed.

She slipped into the kitchen to help an exhausted Frieda after a night of preparing food for the never-ending stream of well-wishers and relatives. Otto A. and Marcia had assumed the roles of host and hostess, reigning in the house that would be theirs as soon as Emma passed away. Something about Marcia being the heir-apparent to this household unsettled Mabel, but it wasn't any of her business.

"I never got to hear the end of the story," she lamented to the cook.

"Well, I wasn't there, but I've heard enough about it that I can probably help. What do you still want to know?"

"I didn't want to prod, but whatever happened to Emma Burgemeister? Did she get convicted for Otto's murder?"

"Oh, that is going back a bit. But I do know that she paid a five thousand dollar bail and then escaped to Europe. She became a distinguished nurse in the Great War. But she returned to the United States two years after and hid out in New York City."

"With Emma Daschiel?"

"I don't know. But the Bexar County district attorney caught up with her eventually and brought her back to stand trial. She charmed the all-male jury, from what I understand, goading them into buying a self-defense plea."

"Wow. So she never served time in prison?"

"Only the time during the trial. It made national news. Trial of the century stuff, they called it. Her attorney was a former governor. A dry politician. And the prosecuting attorney had the last name of Onion. He was one of Mr. Koehler's pallbearers. He voted wet."

"Do you suppose it was really so divided back then? Down the lines about how one felt about alcohol?"

"To hear Mrs. Koehler talk, I would say so. Helga says there was a time when she called everyone by Dry or Wet, almost as if it were a title. Dry Thomas Smith. Or Wet William Harper."

"I think I would be Dry Mabel Hartley, then. But she didn't seem to hold against me the fact that I don't drink beer."

"Did you try it in your hair like I told you?"

Mabel stroked her hair, still marveling at its softness. "I did. Soaked it, then two hours in a towel, then I shampooed it out. It's like magic."

"Then maybe you're not so dry after all. You're wet on the head."

Mabel laughed. "I suppose. I hope she would have been happy with that."

"She liked you," Frieda said. "Goodness. I'm already speaking about her as if she's deceased."

"She's been planning on being deceased for the whole time I've known her!" Mrs. Koehler always insisted that the end was very near.

"Anything else you wanted to know?"

"Only about the Great Depression. We stopped the story at the end of Prohibition, but the Depression came about during the latter part of it. How did she get through that?"

"Much the same, I've heard. She defied the board and held on to all the equipment they'd used when they diversified. So when that terrible time hit and few people could afford to buy beer, she was perfectly poised to revert back to ice production and other things that people still needed. By the end of that, the board was approving nearly anything she came up with, and even voted to make her president. She retired just as this war was starting, but most of their success right now is due to her vision for how to carry through what she saw coming."

"She was quite a woman," Mabel said, realizing that she, too, was talking about her in the past tense.

"She was. Have you thought about what you're going to do with all those notebooks?"

Mabel had, in fact, given it much thought.

"I have. First, I want to talk to other people who knew her and flesh out the story some more. Then, I want to have copies typed and bound for each family member so that they have an accounting of her life. And after that, I'd like to send it to a publisher. I hope to encourage women to get into business and to forge their own path in a man's world."

"Well, well. We may have a writer on our hands after all."

"Maybe. I certainly have a lot of ideas."

"Everyone has ideas, Miss Hartley. Only the brave make them happen."

CAMILLE DI MAIO

A stream of family, friends, and notable people made the rounds through the mansion as word of Emma's failing health spread throughout the city. Mabel kept busy helping Frieda keep them all fed. But sometimes, she would slip a notebook out of her apron pocket and hover near the umbrella stand, listening to the stories passing between the visitors. After a couple of weeks, she'd amassed a wealth of details to add to her project.

She wished she could have known Emma Koehler for more than these scant months and felt the acute responsibility to memorialize her to those who'd never known her at all.

The parade eventually thinned and Mabel slipped into Emma's room on a rare quiet evening. A small candle flickered atop the nightstand, as it would at the vigil of a saint. She pulled a chair over to the bedside, careful not to drag its feet across the floor and wake Emma.

She took the aged, speckled hand into her own and rested her cheek against Emma's arm.

"I don't know if you can hear me," she said into the dimness. "The nurses said that you might. And so I want you to know—"

The words stopped in her throat, choked with inadequacy. What could she say to someone who had come to mean so much in so little a time?

"I want to say thank you. For picking my letter. For bringing me here. For giving me Erik. For all you've done in your life that inspires me to push forward even when I want to shutter myself away in darkness. But mostly—"

She lifted her head to wipe away the tears that had spilled onto Emma's paper-thin skin.

"But mostly, thank you for making me a part of your family. It's been so long since I felt like I belonged anywhere—or to anyone. Because of you, I have love and hope and all those things that I'd despaired of finding."

Mabel paused. There was still so much she wanted to say. She laid her head down once more, gathering her thoughts. She felt a

302

gentle pull to the end of her hair and turned just enough to see that Emma was stroking her loose strands with the gentleness and care that a mother might. She looked up at Emma's face. Her eyes were closed, but her lips were upturned in a smile.

She stayed there until the wax in the candle had turned to liquid. Emma's breathing was faint but steady, and her hand had stilled. Mabel stood up and leaned over her friend. She kissed her forehead.

"My Mama will be waiting for you," she whispered. "Give her a hug from me and tell her about the happiness you've given her daughter."

# EPILOGUE

April 1943

*SPLASH*. "Got you! Right in the neck."

"Don't be so cocky, Erik Garrels. You've got it coming to you."

Mabel put both hands in the water, cupping them for maximum capacity, and sent a small tidal wave toward him.

"Bull's-eye," she said, as he wiped his face.

"Truce. Truce," he laughed. He waded over to her, wrapping his hands around her waist and lifting her up to the side of the pool. Mabel was excited to wear her new swimsuit today. It had a golden yellow bodice that flared into a short skirt, trimmed with thin blue gingham.

"It's a lot nicer when there's water in it, don't you think?" He stayed in the pool, placing his arms on her lap and looking up at her.

"It is. Such a break from the heat. But I liked it when it was winter, too. Empty. It's where I met you."

"But you were all bundled in a coat and gloves and scarf. I like this outfit *way* better."

*Splash!* She got him again. "Watch it, there." But she loved to hear the compliment from him. Wearing a swimsuit felt both scandalous and scintillating, as she'd never had a chance to have one as a city girl. All afternoon, Erik's hands had wandered a little further than before. Not far enough to be considered indecorous—especially in this public place—but enough to send her imagination wandering. He still hadn't brought her back to his apartment.

He let go of her and pulled himself up to the edge. He stood up and held a hand out. "Let's head over to the tree there."

They each wrapped large towels around themselves. She dried off enough to put on a terrycloth robe and then joined him on a picnic blanket underneath a blooming pink crepe myrtle. Behind them blossomed a field of bluebonnets, which Erik said only showed up in April.

April, so far, had been her most beautiful month in Texas.

Erik opened the basket she'd brought and set some sandwiches on a plate. "Have you heard anything from Buck?"

She nodded. "Not in the last week, but he's been very regular about it. Some of what he says is redacted. But it's enough to let me know that he's alive and well. And mostly out of danger. I know he wants to get back into combat, but they're moving him to training staff. Teaching other pilots. It frustrates him, but I'm happy to say that there's a better chance of him coming home because of it."

"Home," Erik repeated. "So does San Antonio feel like home yet?"

"It does." She leaned over and gave him a kiss on the nose. Baltimore was firmly behind her now. Mrs. Molling had called a month ago and said that Pops had been found in a hospital in Gaithersburg. Pneumonia had taken him, and the doctor said he went quickly. The landlady sounded like she might be preparing for a flood of tears from Mabel, but they hadn't come. She felt strangely at peace. It was a sad end, to be true. But at least he was no longer in pain. No longer wandering the streets. And she knew that he was with Mama and Robert. Mama had sent her a gift. The morning after Mrs. Molling called, three cardinals perched on the branch outside her turret window. One might have been a coincidence. Even two. But three was just too perfect, too planned to be anything but a message from Mama saying that they were together.

"Yes," she repeated. "San Antonio is home."

Mrs. Koehler had passed on as well, leaving them a few days ago. But they'd had six weeks to say their goodbyes as she lay in her bed with little communication. Mabel treasured the last moment she'd shared with her.

Relatives had once again descended on the house en masse, prompting Erik and Mabel to get away to San Pedro Park. Emma would have wanted them to go out and enjoy the sunshine she loved so much.

"Frieda gave me something for you," he said. "It's a little package that Auntie Emma asked her to put together. She said you'd understand what it was."

He pulled out a wrapped box from his bag. The paper was a glossy gold foil with a silver bow, almost too pretty to open. Mabel pulled at the ribbon and carefully slipped the box from the paper. She opened the package. It was a black mortar and pestle. Inside its bowl lay four dried chili peppers, four vanilla beans, and a small block of chocolate.

She grinned.

"What are those for?" he asked.

"For cooking something up," she answered. Mrs. Koehler had taught her that the kitchen was not the only place to raise the heat.

"I have something else for you. This one is from me."

He took another box from his bag. A small one.. Mabel's heart beat faster. She knew what it was without opening it. Her hand shook as she took it from him. He didn't drop to one knee as was the conventional way of doing things, and she was glad for it. Instead, he sat right next to her on the blanket, shaded and hidden by the branches.

"I spoke to your brother before he got on the bus. I asked

him, that if you would have me, could we have his blessing to get married."

"Yes," she said, nodding and crying.

"I haven't asked you anything, silly."

"Yes anyway!" She threw her arms around his neck.

"Don't you want to see what's in the box? Aren't girls supposed to go right for the jewelry?"

"I have a lot of things to teach you about women, I guess." But she opened it anyway. Inside was a thick band made of gold, with little leaf shapes imprinted around it.

"It was my mother's," he whispered. "I can get you something fancier. But I've always imagined giving this to the woman I would marry."

"It's perfect. I only want this. I only want you."

Erik pulled her toward him and kissed her. A long, lingering kiss that promised more to come. She slid her hand down to the blanket, placing it over the chilies and chocolate and vanilla beans.

She would start this marriage off right. Mrs. Koehler had made sure of it.

San Antonio Pioneer Dies: Mrs. Koehler, 85, prominent San Antonio pioneer and widow of the later Otto Koehler, founder of the San Antonio Brewing Assn., died at her home today.

*The Monitor – McAllen, Texas April 26, 1943*

ABOVE PHOTO ©Rio Perla Properties, LP. Emma Koehler in 1936.
PHOTO ON RIGHT ©UTSA Special Collections. Pearl Brewery circa 1910.

# Author's note

I FIRST LEARNED OF Emma Koehler while living in San Antonio. For decades, I would pass the beautiful but dilapidated structure that was once Pearl Brewery and thought that it was magnificent, even in its poor condition. Several years ago, developers started to recognize the potential in its stunning architecture and turned it into a lively part of town that features a farmer's market, bakery, boutiques, and much more. The main brewery itself was turned into Hotel Emma. For months, the structure hid behind its façade, and on the exterior, we could only see the black and white letters painted onto the beige bricks. Little did we know what a wonder was being created inside. Shortly after its opening, it was named one of the top new hotels in the world by Conde Nast.

So, who was the "Emma" of Hotel Emma? She had to have been quite a lady to have such a place named for her.

What I learned was captivating. She'd been the wife of a German-born brewer. Her husband had two mistresses, also named Emma. And one of the mistresses murdered him. Emma the wife then took over the brewery, just as Prohibition began to devastate the beer industry. Taking advice from friends at Anheuser Busch, Emma Koehler kept *all* of her employees working by changing the nature of what they made. From ice cream to dry cleaning,

Pearl was one of the only brewing companies in the country not to go out of business.

Additionally, she had to steer her company through the Great Depression.

She emerged from that and put out production numbers that were twice what the brewery had manufactured under her husband's presidency.

While I found this all so intriguing, I grew frustrated that it was nearly *all* I learned about her. Not that I didn't try. Ancestry.com at least informed me of her parentage, birthplace, and siblings. But, as was so common to the era, almost everything there was to know was about her *husband*. His accomplishments, his triumphs. Next to nothing about her early life. Or how she ran the business for decades after his death. And with greater success.

Other investigative tactics proved challenging. With no descendants, there were not any children or grandchildren to talk to. Though they had many nieces and nephews, efforts to track them down had many dead ends and the few leads that had merit went unanswered. I was delighted when I was granted an opportunity to visit with the hotel's historian—and then astonished that he and even the hotel's archivist possessed little information beyond what I had already gathered. Attempts to get information from the college that now owns the Koehler mansion were fruitless; I was twice told that they didn't have anything to share with me.

A friend proposed a theory for the shocking lack of journals or documents, and it is based on this truth: in 1964, Otto A's wife, Marcia, committed their son, also named Otto, to a mental institution in Colorado Springs that was notorious for admitting perfectly well people and warehousing them so that their more wealthy family members could get them out of the way. (Wouldn't that make its own good story?)

Might such a person also have disposed of anything belonging

to Emma Koehler that did not have monetary value? It's just spec-
ulation, but with a surprising lack of first-source materials, I
couldn't help but imagine why that might be. Without any actual
documents available, I set out to create an imaginary one through
the character of Mabel Hartley writing down Emma's dictation.

This is the beauty of writing historical *fiction*: there is a wide
berth to create within the holes of a story. It is my hope that the
publication of this book will illuminate connections with people
I couldn't find during the research stage and if I learn anything
new, I'll be sure to update readers with blog posts. But, as it stands,
this is the story I fashioned from what I know now.

I also received gracious research help from a source outside
Hotel Emma. I met with the fantastic staff at the Virginia Anheuser
Busch facility, who took me on a tour and discussed the historic
methods of beer-making. I even attended a beer-making class at
Colonial Williamsburg, though the eighteenth-century research
had little bearing on my twentieth-century book. Of additional
help was staff at the St. Louis Anheuser-Busch headquarters, who
provided me with more historical documents about the process
and about some of the characters like Adolphus Busch, who figures
into this book in a minor way.

But this became my conundrum: how should I write a whole
novel that honors what had to have been a remarkable woman
when there are nearly no historical records of her? And yet what
we *do* know is so intriguing? My initial idea to write a book solely
about Emma had to go to the wayside unless I wanted to almost
*entirely* fictionalize her and I didn't want to do her that disservice.
So instead, I invented a companion character: Mabel. A timid girl
who was Emma's opposite: the daughter of an alcoholic, a young
woman whose heart had been broken both in love and in war.
She would arrive in Texas in the hopes of a fresh start, just as
Emma's life was ending. And together, Emma's story would not
only emerge, but would inspire Mabel to take risks, think bigger,
and leave the past behind.

We all need a dose of that and that's why I wanted to bring what I *did* know of Emma's story to light.

Along the way, I did find some additional facts that made their way into the story. Indeed, Emma Koehler was injured in a car accident and confined to a wheelchair. (Though the details, including the year, the location, and the duration, are at odds when you look at different reports.) She never married after Otto's death. She did continue to take in many nieces and nephews and help them get their start in the United States. She did hire a cook named Frieda (though the details of that character are all from my imagination.) She did live in a magnificent mansion on West Ashby Street, which still stands today and is owned by San Antonio College. Details of the mansion are true.

I learned, too, that Emma obtained a substantial loan from her brother so that they could go to Germany and purchase the recipe and mother yeast from Pearl and bring it to the United States. (Though I've heard differing accounts about his business: some saying that he had a gardening empire and others that he was a brewer as well.) It is also true that Otto had bought a cottage for his two mistresses on Hunstock Avenue. And that Emma's death certificate cited senility.

I included newspaper quotes about the trial of Emma Burgemeister throughout the book for several reasons: it was considered the Trial of the Century at the time, as evidenced by the international coverage. And it allowed me to touch on the part of the story that involved the mistresses without distracting from the Emma/Mabel narrative.

Besides those and a few other things I wove into the story, I was left with making educated guesses about some items, choosing between conflicting details, different spellings of names, and I fabricated other parts for the sake of story. (For example, I don't know how Emma actually felt about Otto after his affairs, but I can imagine what I would feel, and so I made that choice for her. I don't know if they chose not to have children or if they had infertility issues, but given the time period and culture, I chose the latter route.)

I always weave a romance into my books, but I did not want to give Emma a romance as a widow because there is no evidence of that. So Mabel and Erik (who is a fictional nephew, though he has the real last name of Emma's birth mother), get to have the love story to offset the lack of it in Emma's tale.

Thank you, dear reader, for taking this journey with me, one that was quite unlike my other books as far as research goes. It was my first attempt at taking a real historic person and making her the central figure of the story, stymied by there being almost no documents, books, or records from which to draw key points. My goal, instead, became to take inspiration from her life, explore the feelings of a women in such unique situations, and honor what she accomplished as a business-running woman in a man-centered world and industry. I hope you enjoyed the *essence* of her life and draw some inspiration for yourself.

PHOTO ©Alamo Colleges Foundation. Emma Koehler in about 1910.

# ACKNOWLEDGMENTS

EVERY BOOK HAS its own path and this one definitely had some surprises in store for me. But I had excellent companions along the way.

First, to my fellow founders over at My Book Tribe on Facebook: Tess Thompson, Kay Bratt, Christine Nolfi, Denise Grover Swank, Amanda Prowse, Julianne MacLean, Karen McQuestion, Susan Jones Boyer, Grace Greene, and Kate Danley. And to MaryAnn Schaefer and Cody Bauchman for all of your assistance! I marvel at the work and work ethic of all of you. Book friends—come find this group on Facebook if you want to be a part of an amazing online community!

To Nancy Cleary, editor at Wyatt-MacKenzie, for your immediate enthusiasm for the Emma book! So glad to be on this adventure with you.

To Tonni Callan and Kristy Barrett for being beta readers and for giving me a boost of encouragement EXACTLY when I needed it.

To Sarah Weaver for joining me on our odyssey to Hotel Emma and learning more about Emma Koehler.

To Jeff Fetzer at Hotel Emma for all your help and information about her.

To Gary Dronen and Tracy Lauer at Anheuser-Busch (Williamsburg and St. Louis, respectively) for wonderful assistance on the history of beer.

To Chanel Cleeton: I got most of my writing and editing done while we were hanging out. The best kind of peer pressure is someone sitting across from you being productive.

To Carolyn Taylor, with whom I discussed the Emma story very early on and who was so engaged in the possibility of it. And to Jim Peterson, who brought me the idea about the Koehlers—not knowing that I'd already written the book!

To my agent, Jill Marsal and to my developmental editor, Tiffany Yates Martin for advice and support that always light my way. (Crediting Tiffany, too, with the title. My first one was awful!) I am one thousand percent where I am because of the two of you.

To the Bookstagrammers, as numerous as the stars, who support my books, all books, and the bookish culture in general. Instagram is my happy place because of you all!

To my family: Rob, Claire, Gina, Teresa, and Vincent, I can't do what I do without you. And you are all why I do it.

And in thanksgiving to God for ... everything.

CPSIA information can be obtained
at www.ICGtesting.com
Printed in the USA
LVHW051735271020
669964LV00005B/1040